STORIES
FOR THE INNER EAR

by Cliff Durfee

LIVE
LOVE
LAUGH®

Also by Cliff Durfee

Feel Alive with Love, Have a Heart Talk
(*Book 1, 1979* - Couples & Family Communication)

More Teachable Moments
(*Book 2, 1983* - Listening Skills, Feelings, & Goals)

Editing - *Tim Griffen, Lianne Stevens, Lasca Terhorst, and Kim Yalda*
Front Cover Artwork - *Ken Joudrey* - www.kenjoudrey.com
Chapter Graphics - *Tina Laurin* - www.claurin.com
Graphic Design Consulting - *Becky Alvarado*
Cover & Book Layout Design - *Cliff Durfee*
More Info - see final pages of book.
www.StoriesForTheInnerEar.com

Printed in the United States of America
Current Printing (last digit)
10 9 8 7 6 5 4 3 2 1

Library of Congress Control Number: 2011917800
ISBN 978-0-935936-02-5

"I love the stories within the story. It becomes a compelling read, with a natural rhythm between the present and the truths beyond time that feel both ancient and eternal." ~ *Dana L. Terrell, LCSW, AC*

"This wonderful book took me to a forgotten garden of my own imagination and secret knowing... it's a lovely gift to the Self." ~ *Cathryne Bruce-Johnson*

"Fantastic book, perfect for those who like to read. I wish I had a grandfather who told me stories like that. Amazing!" ~ *Isabel Pichler, ten years old*

"This book should be made into a movie! I was thrilled to read it and couldn't put it down. It even helped bring back wonderful memories, which is a blessing at my age." ~ *Kitty Cameron, eighty-nine years old*

"*Stories for the Inner Ear* is an inspiring collage of short stories that are about transforming travel... traveling to places within... places that are familiar to us, mystically resonant. This book raises us up to the harmonious vibrations of our innermost Self and quells the seeming dissonance in our outermost world of self. I love what this book says and what it does." ~ *Tom Zender, Author of the book, "God Goes to Work"*

"Superbly written, very powerful... it captures your imagination with short stories intricately woven into the major plot. Brilliant! This is destined to become a classic. You will want to read the short stories over and over again." ~ *Edwin Robinson*

"These magical stories delight the heart and nourish the hungry soul... a joy for all ages." ~ *Lasca Terhorst*

"There have been so many times when one or another of these eleven short stories, as well as Shawn's story, have come to mind as it relates to something going on in my life. I love re-reading the gentle yet powerful messages and am moved and inspired all over again."
~ *Rev. Kim Yalda*

"These stories joyfully whisper to hearts that awaken and dance when reminded that dreams are not only possible, but are in process of becoming right now." ~ *Debbie Devine, MFTI*

"What a joy it is to read a book that entertains, inspires, and gives us the ability to answer so many of life's challenging questions. This book is like a comforting friend that speaks to you with love at every visit." ~ *Nancy Bright*

"Taking time to enjoy this book has been a gift to my heart. Thanks for the stories and the heartfelt adventures." ~ *Jane Cremer, M.A., MFT*

"Great books like this are with you forever. I love the way I can re-read any one of the 11 short stories and be enchanted each time with a new insight. Thus, they become useful tools in helping me overcome life's challenges." ~ *Tim Griffen*

"I am really amazed how each and every story feels like it is talking to me personally. Through subtle and playful ways, the stories clear my vision to see my best next steps to where I want to go." ~ *Denise Harmon*

"This book is highly entertaining with a message. I was pleasantly pulled through the book as the stories revealed timeless truths in unusual ways. A fun read that will help you answer life questions that seem so puzzling." ~ *Don Cramer*

"These stories hold timeless wisdom the readers can take with them long after the book has been put down. After reading my favorite story, *Mirrors*, I was reminded of the power that our personal perceptions and beliefs play in our experience of the world. The lessons learned by Myra in the story are lessons I will take with me." ~ *Holly Lecours*

"There is no limit to the imagination of Cliff Durfee, who brings the intrinsic wisdom of our world to life through charming parables of eagles afraid to fly, talking daisies, angels, and others who demonstrate spiritual principles in action. This book is an allegory, a support group, and a novel all rolled into one great resource for learning and inspired living." ~ *Alice Bandy*

"This book is a treat to oneself. It is a respite from the activities of life, allowing sweet silence to color your world. I found myself nodding my head in acknowledgment with every new insight." ~ *Barbara King*

"I was excited about the real insights I received about my life. This book is definitely thought provoking on many levels, and I think I'll be re-reading the stories many times." ~ *Donna Hern*

"Brilliant! Cliff Durfee has brought us magical, wonderful stories on how to align to our true selves within a story of reality. I love reading it to my daughter and discussing the lessons and meaning for life. A true gift." ~ *Kristin Pichler*

"Made me wish that the whole world was that wonderful. I received much excitement and enlightenment while reading. You get absorbed and feel you're part of the stories. This is a book I could read over and over." ~ *Carolyne Burkett*

ACKNOWLEGMENTS

I am so grateful and want thank everyone listed here, and anyone I may have missed. Please give extra attention to the following seven delightful beings who were extraordinarily valuable. They often rolled up their sleeves and did whatever it took from editing, providing financing, and giving inspiring encouragement, to running errands. Most of these people were supporting this book for more than two decades! My heart fills with love whenever I see the full list of names, and overflows with eternal gratitude for my seven special angels: my loving sister *Nancy Bright, Cathryne Bruce-Johnson, Debbie Devine, Tim Griffen, Holly Lecours, Lasca Terhorst, and Kim Yalda.*

Others joined in during recent years and have been amazingly supportive. Each and every person deserves special thanks and a standing ovation. I am so blessed to know such wonderful people, and am so happy they stood in support of *Stories for the Inner Ear.* Thank you: *Melissa Akers, Kay Allgire, Becky Alvarado, Karen Amato, Karl Anthony, Brian Atkins, Alice Bandy, Carolyne Burkett, Kitty Cameron, Alex Carpenter, Don & Whitney Cramer, Jane Cremer, Steven Durfee, Bob Feuge, Andrew Greb, Christine Green, Denise Harmon, Donna Hern, Day Joudrey, Ken Joudrey, Barbara King, Tina Laurin, Maria Lofkvist, Karen Lohof, Lisa Longworth, Tania Marie, Phyllis Mertin, Reva Moore, Isabel Pichler, Kristin Pichler, Edwin Robinson, Christian Sorensen, Lianne Stevens, Herb Tanzer, Dana Terrell, and Tom Zender.*

Certain people were essential in the actual production tasks. Heartfelt thanks goes to *Tina Laurin* for providing wonderful chapter graphics and back-cover graphics. I'm also thrilled and grateful that an artist I've admired for over a decade, *Ken Joudrey*, provided the amazingly beautiful front-cover art. Thanks to my long time friend and illustrator, *Becky Alvarado,* for graphic design consulting. And, I have so much appreciation for the detailed text editing by *Tim Griffen, Lianne Stevens, Lasca Terhorst, and Kim Yalda.*

FOREWORD BY JACK CANFIELD

Jack Canfield is cocreator of the "Chicken Soup for the Soul®" series, and the coauthor of "The Success Principles."

It was about 1980 when I walked by a table and picked up a little red velvet heart. Upon asking the person behind the table what it was all about, Cliff Durfee told me it was used in a process that aids communication, and that one of its eight agreements reduced interruptions. He said that whoever holds the heart, talks, and everyone else must only listen. I was intrigued. Little did I know that I would go on to use this powerful and supportive process called a *"Heart Talk"* in countless workshops I would lead throughout the years. In fact, I devoted an entire chapter to it in my book *The Success Principles* in 2005, where I describe Cliff's first book entitled, *Feel Alive with Love, Have a Heart Talk*.

In 1983, Cliff published his second book, which is a curriculum for teachers entitled *More Teachable Moments*. Once again, I chose to endorse this book as did the world renowned psychologist and author, Dr. Carl R. Rogers. This book contains experiential classroom lessons that develop listening skills, the expression of feelings and mutual support for each others' goals.

I have given this background to illustrate that I've seen tremendous value in Cliff's previous work, and now this book is another wonderful contribution to readers—yet in a much different way. His first two books were non-fiction, helped heal relationships, and taught powerful techniques. This book, on the other hand, is a novel containing very unique short stories. One might conclude this latest book is only for entertainment, yet in its own subtle way, it is also very transformational.

As varied as these three books are, there is a common theme—a focus on "listening." However, a contrast exists in that his first two books were on listening to other people, whereas this book shines light on the wonderful world of listening within.

Over many years, I've led countless workshops filled with people seeking answers in their lives. Throughout a weekend or a week, we would do various interactive activities that would stir up thoughts, concerns, and emotions, followed by time devoted to sharing and learning from the experiences. However, one of the most important and integral parts of the workshops, which always led to successful outcomes, were the periods of silence. These were special times to go within and discover answers already there and awaiting discovery. One of my greatest joys is helping participants learn to give up excessive dependency on outside factors for their guidance, and develop a relationship with their own higher self and intuition. Participating in connecting them to their own inner compass was, and is, a particular joy of mine.

I have often thought it would be incredible if there were a way to package this special experience of connecting with that inner voice. Could this book do it for people? Though nothing can quite compare to an experiential workshop with a hundred or more other supportive people, I believe *Stories for the Inner Ear* can lead one to a profound discovery of how to get in touch with that voice within. Somehow, Cliff has been able to capture the delicate essence of what causes the mind to dive to greater depths in the inner world. Through the eleven stories and fable-like storytelling, you experience reading a story while your inner voice whispers how it relates to your life. Even after you finish a story and some time has passed, a scene out of one of the stories may come to mind and you will have a delayed epiphany.

Though I have expressed much enthusiasm about the eleven stories, I also want to say the novel portion of the book is more than entertaining; it helps enhance the experience of each story. As various people interact and share about the stories, much like participants do in my workshops, vicarious learning abounds.

The totality of the experience of *Stories for the Inner Ear* is something far beyond where most books can take you. I found that this book can take you on a journey to meet someone very special—you.

Enjoy the ride.

Introduction By The Author

It is with great joy that I can finally share these eleven stories for the "inner ear" with you. They have touched and inspired me; helped resolve dilemmas; and expanded my inner guidance, imagination, and intuition. To me, sharing these stories is like soaring above the clouds, and I invite you to come fly with me on an adventure that is entertaining and uplifting.

It is especially rewarding if the stories contribute to your listening to that deep inner voice more often. That voice is always there, gently whispering great insights but only after gaining your attention. It's been said that our greatest gift is hidden within: so close, yet it is secure from casual discovery since our focus is generally outward.

Oprah Winfrey is a famous example of a believer in one's inner voice and shares that divine inspiration, not strategic planning, is the key to her company's success. She is quoted as saying, "You always know the truth for yourself . . . When you get still, you know."

Steve Jobs of Apple said, "Don't let the noise of others' opinions drown out your own inner voice. And most important, have the courage to follow your heart and intuition. They somehow already know what you truly want to become. Everything else is secondary."

The eleven stories act as portals to the soul and help you in many life situations through fable-like allegories. Over and over they reveal ways to listen with your "inner ear" and hear your inner voice. They are like insightful comforting friends always supporting your highest good.

By reading a story within the context of something currently happening in your life, you can arrive at remarkable realizations and gain clarity about life-changing decisions.

To those ready to start reading now:

There's only one thing to know before you start your adventure. You have a choice to read individual short stories that are conveniently located at the beginning of each of the chapters 2 through 12, or, read the book as a novel. If you are a fan of short stories, feel free to read them in any order. However, if you want an ongoing adventure that weaves the stories together, start at Chapter 1 and enjoy *The Orion Connection* that continues its intriguing plot after each short story completes.

That's it. After all, if you just rented an exciting new video and the popcorn is hot, you probably wouldn't delay the excitement by watching clips of how the movie was made. So, if you like, just start reading now and get on with the fun. You can always return here later if you're curious.

To those wanting to know more before reading:

Though first impressions may remind you of stories for children, they are more than that. Part of their adult fascination, and the reason they are reread for years, is because they keep introducing you to different parts of yourself. Since you keep changing in relationships, goals, careers, desires, health, fears, loves, cherished dreams, and so forth, the stories renew as you do.

After gaining insights from reading between the lines, you can easily recognize the thought-provoking content of the stories wrapped in innocent-looking clothing. The book is great for adults, but as preteens and teenagers become more self-aware, they too are drawn to read it due to their pressing quests of 'Who am I?' and 'Where am I going?' Young children eight years old or younger may not have the attention span for a story like *Angels*, but *Turtles* could be appealing. This book truly offers something for people of all ages.

Each story for the "inner ear" made its appearance by actually demonstrating to me the power of going within and listening. As I practiced being in silence while listening within and writing the stories, I found myself taking notes and being continually surprised with each new page. These stories came thundering through in virtual downpours of words spaced by months of complete silence. Also, there is something you might find remarkable about this unique writing process that took place. All of the eleven short stories remain almost unchanged from when the words landed on paper except for spelling, grammar, and punctuation.

The eleven stories were written in only a few hours per story even though months would pass between each story's appearance. That is why I referred to them as "inspired." However, the connecting overall story took years off and on, and I finally resorted to conventional methods of writing. I was greatly aided and influenced by Maren Elwood's book, *Characters Make Your Story*. I began to live with the characters as though they were my closest friends.

The first character, who appeared to me in *The Orion Connection*, was Shawn: a middle-aged man with a tremendous dilemma. The second character was his grandfather: a wise, old man living in the mountains who believed strongly in each person's ability to discover answers from within. Other unique characters joined in, and I'm pleased to say they came to life within my mind. I will admit, *The Orion Connection* came mostly from my mind, whereas the eleven inspired stories came directly from my inner voice once I could hear it with my "inner ear."

Shawn has become so real to me that I can almost hear him asking to help describe this book to you. Since I've had the privilege of introducing some of this book to you, I will now turn it over to Shawn to introduce topics near and dear to him.

A word from Shawn

My role in this introduction might seem unusual to some, you see I am the main character in *The Orion Connection*. I'm writing to you from within this book to share from the inside out, so to speak.

This story threads all the other stories together by telling what happened during my incredible weekend while seeking an answer to a life-changing question. I traveled to see my grandfather because he generally tells me an enlightening story. I so needed it to help solve my dilemma.

During the weekend I saw many people react to the stories. It's always fascinating because each person receives different insights from hearing the same words. I know it's true for me just hearing the same story over again. By the way, I discovered how much people like to talk about their insights from a story after reading it in a group. It sure did spark some discussions that weekend.

My grandfather's name is Art, and though I'm middle aged, I still call him Grampa. He lives in a cabin with my grandmother in the southern California mountains—Idyllwild to be exact. Friends and family all come to Grampa, especially when they have problems. That may seem odd in a way, since he never gives advice to anyone. He just listens intently without talking about the problem. Then he simply says, "That reminds me of a story; do you want to hear it?" If the person listens with the "inner ear," the answers appear from within.

I wish you could visit Grampa when you encounter decisions in your life, since he is so good at selecting the most appropriate story to be of help to you. I asked him about this and here's what he said: "If you know the stories and have a challenge, you'll be guided to the proper story to reread."

If you could visit Grampa Art, imagine the thrill of driving up to the mountains and pine trees to sit by the fireplace sipping tea with him. You would then sense the quiet comforting living room with only the sounds of a crackling fire and Grampa's deep resonate voice. You might also feel at ease knowing he won't give you advice or tell you what to do, yet, through his stories, he'll lead you to that sacred place within where you joyfully say, "aha, I know."

In the process of seeking a solution to a crisis, I discovered that there is much more about my Grampa Art than I could have imagined possible. I discovered how he's able to tell all the stories the same each time—word-for-word. That always puzzled me. And though I can't reveal it now, it will be clear why the novel portion of the book is referred to as *The Orion Connection.*

Just a final note: do not underestimate the power of the stories just because they seem to be about turtles, eagles, or even talking daisies. If you've never had a personal revelation through an allegory before, a whole new appreciation may be in store for you. As Grampa would often say, "Just listen with your 'inner ear' and hear your own answers."

To my mom
and to all moms
who inspire love
by being
love

A note about this unique book:

This book is both a novel and a collection of short stories. If you prefer to read the stories separately, they are located for easy access at the beginning of each of the last eleven chapters. Since you'll be returning to read your favorites, this format makes them easy to find. However, if you choose to read the entire novel, chapter one begins with an overall story called "The Orion Connection" that threads all the short stories together like beads of a beautiful necklace. It does this by continuing its story immediately following each of the short stories.

Contents

STORIES
FOR THE INNER EAR

THE ORION CONNECTION

Shawn's thoughts whirred by as the tires on his two-year-old, white Mercedes squealed around the sharp mountain curves. It had been several months since he'd driven the familiar road to his grandfather's cabin. This was his first trip after sunset; usually he drove before dark because he didn't want to miss the beauty of the pine trees against the backdrop of blue skies. Over the sixteen years his grandparents had lived in Idyllwild, Shawn had never found it necessary to drive to their cabin at night, yet his current life crisis propelled him like a cat tossed in a bathtub of cold water. Though he often asked his *Grampa Art* to tell one of his magical stories to help Shawn solve his problems, this was the first time he would be asking in desperation.

Shawn's sun-darkened hands showed few signs of physical labor as they clenched the steering wheel turn after turn. Tiny wrinkles on his forehead hinted that he derived his income from using his head. Though he wasn't losing much of his blondish-brown hair with all those intellectual pursuits and pressures, some strands of gray were appearing after forty-six years of a reasonably comfortable life.

Besides the appeal of his grandfather and the stories, the mountains were always calling him to come and be a kid again. On normal trips he would just let go of the worries and concerns of adult life and regress to the timeless child within, whose inner voice curiously never aged. Because Shawn was so active, his athletic body could pass for a man fifteen years younger; however, this was still not young enough to match how he felt in the mountains— the motherly way his grandmother treated him was also especially encouraging.

Shawn loved pine trees, and though they appeared so warm and friendly in the daytime, tonight their sharp pointed needles and eerie shadows seemed to be saying, *Enter at your own risk.* As the headlights lit up the trees on each curve, their shadows raced by like ghostly figures hiding from view. Deep wrinkles formed on Shawn's forehead as his thoughts focused on the horribly difficult decision he must make on Monday morning at the advertising agency. His whole career was on the line.

A tight curve approached and though Shawn's glazed eyes were looking, they were obviously not seeing. A yellow sign with a drawing of a hairpin reverse curve cautioned 15 m.p.h., yet his silently running Mercedes was climbing to 50.

"Everything was going so great, why am I in such an incredibly awful situation? What should I do?" he asked himself. As he headed into the 180-degree curve, the most expensive car he'd ever owned started straining at what it was being asked to do. As the tires screamed for help, Shawn's eyes widened. His mind was already calculating that the curve was impossible at this speed.

Shawn's white Mercedes entered the switch-back turn with little chance of making it. Unfortunately, the curve's outer edge was not the mountain, but a wide patch of dirt followed by a several-hundred-foot drop-off to the rocks below. As the tires left the pavement and started sliding on the dirt and gravel of the scenic lookout, their screaming changed to a deep grinding. He could feel the vibration as though they were being shredded to pieces.

While his mind roared that this might very well be the end of it all, his long powerful legs, which had supported his skiing, basketball, and backpacking, were now like powerful pistons trying to cram the brake pedal through the floorboard. He pictured himself tumbling inside his car down the cliff to a horrible death, followed by a large explosion and fire. No longer was his important Monday-morning decision very important.

With adrenaline speeding up his thoughts, Shawn pictured his sensitive wife weeping at his funeral and his two teenagers living without a father. Grasping the steering wheel tighter, he shouted, "Oh God, I've got things to do . . . let me live!"

He cranked the wheel hard right and his car spun vigorously clockwise. It also slid toward the cliff for what seemed like forever. Clouds of dust spewed into the air as the car approached a short section of protective railing. Just a few feet away, the railing ended and a large unprotected area opened to the canyon drop-off. Fearing he'd miss the railing altogether, Shawn was relieved to feel the impact of a guard pole crashing into and crumpling his right front fender. With the front of the car now pressing against the last pole of the railing, the rear end spun counterclockwise a half turn before coming to a sudden halt. The force was so powerful, had it not been for his seat belt, Shawn would have been thrown into the passenger's seat.

He sat there trembling in the driver's seat. After a bit of heavy breathing, Shawn paused. There was nothing but total silence, darkness, and a huge cloud of dust. The Mercedes' engine had quit and all the lights were out, even the dash lights.

As Shawn squinted to see why he wasn't tumbling down the cliff, he couldn't see much because his eyes were just beginning to adjust to the darkness. Through the open window on his side, he could just make out a patch of ground illuminated by a nearly full moon. He noticed the smell of dust mixing with the cool mountain air. He looked out the front windshield, squinting again at the bright light of a car passing by in the distance. He couldn't actually see the moving car—there were now trees and bushes between his car and the road— but he concluded that the Mercedes had spun back to face toward the highway.

Once his eyes adjusted to the dark, he could see how far the right fender was bent and pushed up. The guard rail post that saved his life stood triumphantly next to his car.

Shawn felt a chill as he realized that the back of the car must be very near the edge of the cliff. He pictured what must have happened and quickly concluded that the accident might still be in progress. All he could see out the rear window was solid darkness. His stomach turned queasy as he sensed the presence of the drop-off. It was an eerie feeling, reminiscent of when he was a child in his dark bedroom. He used to imagine a monster next to his bed, yet fear of actually seeing the monster kept him from turning on the light. He would finally scream for his mommy and she'd make everything all right. He wished she could just turn on the light and make this all disappear.

Wanting to feel solid ground beneath his feet, Shawn unsnapped his seat belt and reached for the door handle, but something powerful stopped him before he could touch it. A rush of *danger* and *caution* seemed to surround the handle as though it were hot as the sun. From his grandfather's stories, Shawn had learned to trust his intuition. He paused while trying to imagine what the danger could be. His mind flashed with the image of a playground teeter-totter.

Suddenly he noticed an odd illumination on the hood. It wasn't just moonlight reflecting off the white surface. A transparent ball of glowing-bluish light hovered just above the left side of the hood. About two feet in diameter, its presence captivated Shawn. He wasn't frightened of it. Infact, he felt drawn to it. An image of being hugged by loving arms came to his mind. He knew his intuition was telling him to move toward the light.

Ready to make a speedy exit, he looked around the car. His clothes and overnight bag were in the back seat. Then he noticed the journal of stories sitting on the seat next to him. The collection of stories, told by his grandfather and tediously recorded by Shawn over many years, was extremely precious to him. No matter what, he wanted the journal to be safe, so he gently tossed it on the ground through his open window. It landed near the left front wheel of the car. At least that's safe, he thought, reminding himself that there were no other copies.

Tension and fear made him move quickly. To avoid touching the door handle, he raised himself up, slipped his head and shoulders backward through the door window and pushed until he was sitting on the door with his feet still inside the car. Instinctively choosing not to lower himself to the ground, he crawled instead toward the glowing light on the hood. His eyes were locked on the glowing ball as he inched his way closer. He noticed an indentation in the hood, as though the ball of light had tremendous weight. Mysteriously, as Shawn approached ever so slowly, the light decreased in size and intensity. By the time he reached the front portion of the hood, the ball had faded completely out of sight and the indentation was replaced by one caused by his own weight.

Though puzzled and curious about the strange light, Shawn focused on getting his feet back on solid ground.

He carefully began sliding off the car, putting some weight on his right foot. But the car started rising up underneath him like an elevator. Quickly he lifted his right foot off the ground and put all his weight back on the car. It gently lowered and came to rest again. "The car's a teeter-totter," Shawn said out loud, "and I'm what's keeping it balanced!"

He quickly looked back around the side of the car. The center of its dusty white body was resting on the ground, acting as a pivot point on the edge of the embankment. He remembered that the cliff dropped off rapidly along this area of the mountainous road. Getting off the car would almost certainly cause it to tip off the edge and tumble down into the canyon below.

He no longer had an option. I'll just sit here however long it takes until someone comes to help, Shawn concluded. His thoughts went back two years to when he first saw the white Mercedes on the showroom floor. It was love at first sight. He insisted on test driving it, even though the salesman had to move three other cars to get that Mercedes outdoors. Shawn loved the classy white finish, the smell of the new leather, and the incredibly quiet ride. Of course, he never imagined that some day he would be sitting on its beautiful hood, playing see-saw with a 300-foot canyon as a backdrop.

He sat for about fifteen minutes and though several cars went by, none stopped. He could see their lights, but no lights were beaming from his car. They couldn't see him through the pine trees separating him from the road—and they'd never be able to hear his calls.

As he touched the shiny Mercedes hood ornament next to him, Shawn remembered holding a magnifying glass in his office yesterday that was almost the same size. He'd been looking at proofs for a four-color magazine ad, and his assistant was asking him questions. He remembered being a little self-conscious about using the magnifying glass, even though it, or a *loop*, was often used to inspect proofs. His eyes were having trouble focusing on small objects that were easily seen when he was younger.

~ ~ ~ ~ ~ ~ ~

"That should get some attention, eh, Shawn?" The apprentice, a recent college graduate assigned to learn Shawn's successful advertising techniques was eagerly waiting for a response. She had just placed a set of proofs on his desk.

Shawn set down the magnifying glass, looked up at Marleen and said, "Remember, attention is the first step, except we also need . . . "

Marleen interrupted and added, "Interest and desire! What do you think? Do I learn fast, or what?"

Though Shawn liked the youthful energy she brought to the office, he hoped she would know to contain it some around clients. He replied, "Well, let's see. Tell me if your ad does it."

"Sure it does!" she said, not offering an explanation.

He pointed at the powerful graphics and said, "It certainly does demand attention, and it creates interest and curiosity, yet the call-to-action is as lost as I am in the streets of old Boston."

Marleen looked puzzled and asked, "I've never been to Boston. Is it very confusing?"

"Well, let's just say you not only need a map—you need a co-pilot. Also, they seem to double park a lot back there and you have to navigate around parked cars on narrow streets. They talk about us crazy California drivers, but they have no room to complain. So now we're way off the subject. I'm sure the copywriter wanted the special offer to have much more impact than this. The call-to-action gets totally lost due to the impact of the graphics. Did you show it to the copywriter for his comments?"

"No. The 3-D rendering of the cartoon appliances came out so hot, it slipped my mind. I just wanted to hurry and show you. That walking toaster has really cute feet, doesn't it!" I'll get the offer to pop out some more. Do you want to see it again before the client does?"

Shawn didn't say anything, just raised an eyebrow as he looked to see if Marleen was serious.

She was smiling with her head cocked to the side. "Just kidding, I know, I know . . . I'm not cleared to talk direct yet!" Then in a low voice obviously imitating Arnold Schwarzenegger, she said, "I'll . . . be . . . ba-ack!" Marleen laughed, picked up the proofs, and dashed out of Shawn's large and luxurious office.

Shawn's boss and the owner of the firm, Carl, peeked in the door and said, "How's Marleen doing? She sure has spunk, huh? I never see her just walking down the hall. She's like that little rabbit in Alice in Wonderland."

"Yeah, I know what you mean. Come on in, Carl. Actually she's doing fine. With a couple more years under her belt, she could be handling some local accounts . . .

"Got to run," Carl interrupted. "Expecting an important call soon. Something big is up! I may want to talk to you before lunch."

Shawn noticed more energy in Carl's voice than he'd heard in months. As Carl rushed off, Shawn's intercom buzzed. What now? I should be preparing for the photo shoot next week.

The receptionist said over the speaker, "Shawn, there's a John Merland here to see you . . . "

"Oh yeah, send him in."

In a moment Shawn's old school buddy appeared. John gazed around while he walked over to shake hands with Shawn.

"Have a chair," Shawn said. "It's great to see you again. Everytime I think of calling you for lunch—something comes up. How are things?"

"So-so . . . things look good for you, though. Wow. Look at this office! You've even got a view and a large couch . . . is that for your naps?"

Shawn ignored the question, walked over and closed the door before talking. "Well, you know we've cut back a lot over the last year. Got a lot of–well, five empty offices, so I got my pick about a month ago. This recession sure has hit California hard. But as you know, image is important to clients. Carl put the best of everything in my office."

"Tell me about it! Our image was so good it even fooled me. I didn't even suspect what my boss had in mind until the last moment." John paused and then added, "I just got my notice."

Shawn frowned and stood up. "No, don't tell me. You've been there what, four years now? You're one of their best ad men. I can't imagine them letting you go!"

John looked down and said, "Too many corporations are relocating to other states because of California's high taxes and they like their ad agencies nearby. I lost my big accounts, and the prospects for new business don't look good. I was wondering, Shawn . . . Do you think you might be able to get me in over here?"

Shawn was sympathetic to his friend's plight, but knew he had to be honest. "Well, as I just mentioned, we've really cut back ourselves. In fact, I'm a little worried about my own position. If I got cut, I wouldn't be able to relocate. A few years ago I bought that high-priced house—before the bottom dropped out of the real estate market. Would you believe I now owe about twenty percent more on my house than it's worth? Then I'm locked into those big car payments on the Mercedes—to tell you the truth, John, I'm walking on eggshells hoping for new business."

"Aw, you did so well on that national teen-clothing campaign, I'm sure you'll be all right."

Shawn sat down, held both hands up in the air as if bewildered by it all. "My largest account is moving to Colorado and there's a rumor they're switching agencies. Carl might have to carry me awhile on overhead, but no one stays on overhead too long without getting the ax."

The intercom interrupted and the receptionist said, "Carl wants to see you right away. He sounds a bit excited, Shawn."

"Okay," Shawn replied. He stood up and looked at John, but before Shawn could say anything, John was already walking toward the door.

He said, "Give me a call sometime. See ya. By the way, you already know we had an eight-and-a-half-pound boy last month . . . here's your cigar. Better late than never."

Shawn took the plastic wrapped cigar announcing "It's a Boy" and said, "Congrats again, John. I'd like to see him sometime. Take it easy."

John gave a pretend salute goodbye and left. Shawn picked up a folder and slid in a few blank sheets of paper for notes in his meeting with Carl. Glancing up at the door, he picked up John's cigar and unwrapped it. Then he vigorously twisted and shredded it into many small pieces, dropping them into the trash can. He seemed to take pleasure in this activity. When the cigar was completely destroyed, Shawn let out a short victory growling sound, as though he'd just won a wrestling match and was about to slap a teammate's hand. He brushed off his hands, picked up his folder, and quickly walked down the hall to Carl's office.

After the long meeting, lunch, and a short afternoon making the final preparations for next week's photo shoot with live models, Shawn jumped in his white Mercedes and headed home. He was quite happy about the meeting with Carl and looked forward to telling his wife. To celebrate the news of not only keeping his job secure, but also getting a major promotion, he stopped and bought Mary a large bouquet of white roses. His wife loved almost any flower, especially if it was white.

It was an unusually clear day and Shawn was more than pleased to fill his lungs with clean air for a change. Though the reports said smog in the L.A. area was getting better, the major difference was determined by the wind direction. If the wind was coming from the ocean, it was usually fairly clean—especially near the coast.

Shawn switched on his favorite *oldies-but-goodies* radio station. He started singing along to *Heard it through the Grapevine*. Since he couldn't carry much of a tune, he liked to turn the radio up loud to drown out his own voice. Mary didn't know that he was a recovering closet rock star. With all the 12-step programs, especially some strange ones in California, he wondered if there was one for his condition.

He remembered how well the raisin companies promoted themselves using this song and animated dancing raisins. Wish I could have done that, he thought. Then he recalled the giant success he'd had himself, with his teen clothing campaign. Shirts, pants, and even jackets carried silk-screen images of rock stars, models, actors, sports figures, and any other teenage hero he could think of. Shawn got the attention of the nation's teens when he arranged for their heroes to randomly appear at various high schools. First they talked to the student body about issues such as drugs, abstinence, or achieving their dreams. Then, any students wearing the sponsored clothes would be given a ticket to a private party hosted by the rock star, model, actor, or sport's figure. The scheme attracted tremendous television coverage (all free), and it became such a success, almost every teenager in the country owned some of the clothing, even the President's daughter.

As Shawn pulled into the circular driveway that led into what Mary once called their *mini-mansion dream home* in the hills of Pacific Palisades north of Hollywood, he parked in the front instead of using the four-car garage. The tall, black ornamental security gate closed behind him. By the time he reached the front door he was running. From the rather formal entry way he yelled out, "Mary, I'm home! Where are you?"

He found her in the kitchen preparing a dish she had invented herself—Mexican lasagna. He laughed when he thought about how naturally she seemed to integrate her Mexican and Italian heritage.

"Wow, that's about three dozen! What's the occasion, Sweetie?" Mary put her arms around Shawn and gave him a kiss on his right ear lobe. That had special meaning. She once told him that it was reserved to say, "I love you far beyond mere words." Mary's vital energy and Shawn's sensitive nature were a winning combination.

Trying to look smug and *together* despite his excitement, Shawn crossed his legs and put his hand down to lean on the kitchen counter. Unfortunately, his hand tried to rest on a pile of sliced tomatoes. He tried to stop his fall as his hand slid off the counter, but his crossed legs were of no help. Shawn ended up on the ceramic-tile floor which was now newly decorated with tomato slices.

Mary laughed as she helped him up. She said, "This really must be something! You're showing your excitement again!"

Mary couldn't help giggling. Shawn knew his clumsy nature could be a bit uncomfortable at times, but appreciated how Mary took it as amusement. Whenever Shawn was the least bit excited about something, his mind just didn't seem to be coordinated with his actions. She still laughed when remembering their first date. They met for breakfast and he was so excited he poured cream on his pancakes instead of syrup! He looked up with a sheepish smile, observing her reaction, embarrassed and scared that this would end another possible relationship. Other women had left him because of this strange behavior. Mary did laugh, but it was *with him* instead of *at him*. She was pleasantly accepting and even seemed to enjoy a good laugh once in a while. This started winning his love right away.

He rose and grabbed a towel to clean off the tomatoes never missing a beat. Excitedly, he said, "Carl told me it's practically a shoe-in. I'm ninty-eight percent sure of heading up an extremely large national account and campaign. It would mean a promotion, a raise, and other benefits Carl couldn't discuss yet."

"Oh, Shawn, I'm so happy! We won't have to move will we?"

"No. There may be more travel, but we can still live here in our dream home. Isn't this great?"

"Does it involve clothing again?" Mary asked.

"I don't know. Since it's not official until tomorrow, Carl said he'd rather wait before saying any more. Let's tell the kids. Where are they?"

Shawn looked out the kitchen window to the pool area. Usually, Julie would be there with about three girlfriends in those swimsuits he thought were far too revealing for thirteen-year-olds. Actually, even if she were as old as her brother, who was sixteen, Shawn wouldn't like it. At least he and Mary had gotten her to agree to wearing the skimpy ones only at home.

Not spotting his daughter at the pool, Shawn ran upstairs and knocked on Julie's door.

"Just a minute," she hollered. Mary arrived just as Shawn knocked again. Finally, the door opened just a bit and Julie peeked out to see her excited parents.

"Can we come in? Your mom and I have great news."

Julie stepped back. Shawn and Mary, assuming it was all right, entered the room. A distinct smell of cigarettes hung in the air. Two of Julie's girlfriends were sitting on the bed looking at the floor.

"Have you been smoking?" Shawn shouted.

"Well, sort of. But Ron does it, too! We're not the only ones!" Julie put her hand over her mouth and looked at the floor. She knew how much her father hated cigarettes and she feared being a disappointment to him.

Shawn was so upset he was shaking. Mary said, "Julie, please ask your friends to leave now. You wait here. Your dad and I will talk to you in a little while."

Mary tugged at Shawn's arm, pulling him downstairs to discuss what should be done about the situation. He grumbled as they walked down the stairway, "This makes me so angry. How could the kids do this?"

Trying to be calming, Mary said, "I think kids want to fit in, so they experiment. I doubt if either of them have smoked very much."

Shawn sat down hard on the couch. His eyes were distant and cold. Mary sat next to him. "What are you thinking about, Shawn?"

"My father—before he died of cancer. I never told you about the afternoon that I almost lost it. They told him he could extend his life if he'd quit smoking, but he was too heavily addicted. He always said quitting was easy and that he'd done it hundreds of times—it was not starting back up that was the hard part. We were sitting in his living room a few months after he'd had an operation to remove his left eye. He had a patch tied over his empty . . . well, you know, his patch was on like a pirate, but it was white instead of black. As we talked, he lit up a cigarette and to my utter amazement and disgust, smoke leaked out from under his patch. I guess the passages in the head are connected somehow."

"Oh, Shawn, how horrible that must have been, to watch him deteriorate like that. I know there was nothing you could do about it."

"As you know, it took about a year and a half after he called me to say he had cancer, until his painful death. Damn, that was hard to take." Shawn also thought of something even more painful, but blocked saying anything for fear of breaking down and crying—the very last thing he wanted to do in front of anyone! He was forcing the memory of his mother's last days out of his mind. She died still smoking, too, and no matter how hard he tried, he just couldn't get her to stop.

Both of his parents had their lives shortened by tobacco addictions. Shawn hadn't even reached thirty when he experienced the deafening silence caused by their passing, long before he was ready. There were no more questions, answers, or communication, and that hurt him more than anything. Fortunately, Shawn's father was very close to his own father (Grampa Art), and the family spent much time together. Shawn's grandparents became like parents to him as he matured into middle age.

After some silence, Shawn and Mary discussed the situation with their kids. Since Shawn felt he couldn't be very objective on the subject, Mary took the lead this time on the punishment. Julie was grounded for two weeks with no talking on the phone after 9:30 p.m. Once Ron found out they knew about him, too, he promised not to smoke any more and was not punished since he came to them first.

Though this dampened Shawn's spirits for a while, the next

morning he went off to work in a happy mood, looking forward to knowing more details about his promotion. He returned home unexpectedly in the early afternoon.

When he arrived, he just stood by the hand-carved front door and called out to Mary. She met him standing in the open doorway. She pulled him in and closed the front door. He was pale as a ghost and trembling. She followed him into the living room. It was an unusual room for him to choose; he always preferred going into the family room to relax.

"Shawn, for heaven's sake, what's wrong? Did someone get hurt or die? Did you not get the promotion?" Mary finally asked.

He stared blankly into the wood stacked in the fireplace ready to be lit. "Well, I met with Carl. I was so excited at first. He told me he had one of those good news/bad news situations. We met for a long time . . . "

"What is it, Shawn? Just get it out, all right?"

"A major corporation is about to sign up with our firm. Next year alone, the gross income of our company could be several times what we've done in the last three years combined. This is big, very big. We'd have to hire a lot of people—I guess John Merland would be happy because I could hire him. We'd even have to lease another floor of the building."

"So far, so good. Keep going . . . " Mary's lips were pressed tightly together as she leaned forward, waiting for the *bomb* to drop.

"If I accepted the position, I would be the lead on the campaign and almost certainly double my salary next year, not to mention becoming an actual partner with Carl. He even told me of plans for his retirement in a few years, and so far, he said I'm his first choice for running the whole business."

Mary still didn't understand. "Haven't you been feeling concerned about losing your job? What caused the reversal?"

"It was partly the success I had with the teen clothing campaign that caught the attention of the new client. They're extremely interested in the teen, and even the preteen market. I was the head on that campaign, so Carl sees me as a tremendous asset now."

Shawn stood up and started to pace back and forth with his head down and his hand on his chin.

"Shawn, you've stopped talking! What's the bad news?" Mary had never seen him so intense and so worried. It frightened her. She asked him to sit down, but he remained standing. His shoulders sagged as though he were carrying a heavy weight.

Finally, he sat down next to Mary, looked her in the eyes and said, "I can't believe it. The new client is a tobacco company!"

Mary couldn't speak. There was a deathly silence in the room. Her eyes widened as she put her hand to her cheek. "Are they actually saying they're after teenagers?"

"Well, no. They won't admit it publicly, though, of course, anyone who thinks about it knows they are. Carl told me they discussed it only in the most private meetings. He asked that it not be repeated. That part's just between you and me; don't repeat it. Actually they want to attract the preteens, too. And we wonder why we live in a mixed up world! Tell kids to stay off drugs, but then make it legal to promote deadly addictive substances like tobacco and alcohol. Tell them smoking is bad, yet allow billboards with cartoon characters to show how much fun it is!"

Mary remembered all the times Shawn looked the other way when passing those billboards. He did that to avoid getting angry. "Shawn, why don't you just tell Carl you can't work on this particular account? You feel so strongly about all this."

Shawn's voice intensified. "Carl is ex-Navy and they have a phrase for promotion or early retirement. It's called *up or out*. He admitted that without this new account, he was going to be forced to give me notice. And without my background, he might not land the new account. So I either get a large promotion, or I don't work there—nothing in between!"

"There are other jobs, aren't there?" Mary asked.

"At the salary we need, we would almost have to move out of state—yet we can't sell the house in this market. The bad real estate market is a reflection of the bad job market. Did I tell you John just got laid off?"

"So, that's why you mentioned hiring him. Oh, no; his wife must be frantic because she just had the baby!" Mary's voice got softer as she added, "I'll have to call her and see how she's doing."

"Anyway, I can't count on a job locally. Carl tried to rationalize it a bit. He said when he was in the Navy, there were lots of people working in the defense industry, but they were still against weapons. He said if I don't do it, the tobacco company will just find someone else who will."

Shawn walked over to the window to look out at the beautifully landscaped grounds. "We could lose all this and more." He recalled their first view of this house. He'd told the realtor to drive on by because this was more like an estate than a home for them. Neither Shawn nor Mary could imagine living in what seemed like a mansion, complete with circular drive, security gate, and an acre of property.

"What do you mean . . . *more?*" Mary asked.

"Well, we owe more than we can sell the house for. It could go into foreclosure, we could lose our credit rating, and if I couldn't make enough money fast enough, it could even force us into bankruptcy."

"Whew!" Mary sighed. "This isn't going to be easy either way, is it?"

"Nope," Shawn agreed. "There's even something more."

"How could there be *more?*"

"If I quit or refuse to work on the account, Carl could lose the account because my experience with the youth and teen campaign won't be bid on the contract. On large accounts, resumes of key people are part of the bid to establish credibility. Carl's been a good boss and a friend for years. I'd hate to run out on him and cause him to lose a major contract especially since the company is in such bad shape."

Now it was Mary who looked worried. "Then there are the kids' schools . . . They've made friends and are really settled in and doing so well. Oh, Shawn, what are we going to do?"

Shawn hugged Mary for several minutes and then replied, "I think I need to talk to Grampa. I really need to get clear about this decision."

Mary nodded her head. She knew that was a good choice. "I know how your grandfather has always helped you in the past. I suppose you are hoping to hear one of his stories?"

Shawn and his dad had always gone to Grampa Art with their most difficult problems. They seemed to get solved, yet never directly. His grandfather would never really discuss a problem with Shawn or his dad. Instead, after a period of time, when it seemed like Grampa Art had forgotten all about it, he would tell a story. He was so predictable it was almost funny. He would always start his stories in the same way. First he'd settle down in that large chair, sip a little tea while peeking up at you under his big bushy eyebrows that begged to be trimmed, and say exactly the same words. He'd say, "There's a story that comes to mind. Would you like to hear it?"

Though Shawn got much from the stories, never once did his grandfather give Shawn or his dad any specific advice.

Mary had heard a few of the stories. She told Shawn that she loved how it seemed like great wisdom sparkled through his grandfather's eyes, while his deep, resonant voice would captivate even small children. "When do you want to go to the mountains?" she asked as she raised her eyebrows and stared inquisitively into Shawn's blue eyes.

"Right away . . . tonight! It's Friday and I can be back by tomorrow night. Monday morning I will have to tell Carl my decision because he's sending out the contract proposal with the resumes of the proposed staff." He walked over to the window again and looked out as though he were checking how much daylight was left.

"I assume you want to go alone this time?"

Shawn figured she guessed it by the way he phrased what he wanted to do. Mary was good at reading him like a book. Also, he knew she was fully aware that he often retreated from everyone when faced with complicated or emotional situations, though she usually tried to draw him out. This time he detected that she was not going to try to force anything. Not expecting any resistance, he felt comfortable in replying, "Yes, I think I need time alone to just be quiet. You know how the kids are in the mountains! While we get relaxed, they act like they've been on caffeine or something."

"Will you be all right? You know how silent I can be when you need to think. We could leave the kids with the Sanders. I'm concerned about you, Sweetie. But I also want you to know that what you do in your career is mostly your decision, and as a family, we'll just stick together no matter what." She touched Shawn's cheek and kissed his right ear lobe.

"Mary, you're the best thing that ever happened to me. You're so special." He held her close and said softly, "Thanks for letting me work this out. After I get some clarity, we'll talk it all out again before anything is final. It won't be just my decision; it affects the whole family."

"Thanks," Mary smiled. "I guess I just remember what you said your mom used to say—everything always works out for the best. All I know is, you've got to feel good about the decision, one way or the other, or none of us will be happy."

Shawn packed an overnight bag. Mary, Ron and Julie gave him hugs as he left at sunset. No one would have guessed that within only a few short hours he would be sitting on the hood of his car, reflecting back on the last two days.

~ ~ ~ ~ ~ ~ ~

After sitting so long with his legs crossed, Shawn noticed his left leg was asleep. Determined to save his car, he stretched out his leg, being careful not to upset his car's delicate balance. He saw the lights and sound of a big truck down-shifting in the distance. Even a slight sound was magnified in the forest. He remembered once while visiting his grandparents sitting in the kitchen, trying to figure out where a little noise was coming from. He finally discovered it. It was the bubbles popping on the surface of his apple juice.

The moonlight was getting brighter since it was about an hour higher in the sky. Shawn spotted the journal of stories lying near the car and wished he was in his grandfather's living room listening to another story.

After Grampa told one of his stories and left Shawn alone to think, something would click and a solution to his problem would pop up. By the time Shawn was grown, he wondered if this was a clever ploy to get him to think for himself and solve his own problems. His grandfather would always say, "God gave you free will. Who am I to try and control your decisions, anyway? After all, it's you who have to live with the consequences."

He remembered that sometimes his grandfather would retell the same story for a different problem. He was amazed at how the same story seemed to say different things at various periods in life, even though his grandfather would tell it precisely word-for-word the same each time—a mystery Shawn couldn't quite understand since his grandfather even forgot to buy things at the store if they weren't written down.

And the stories were always loaded with a variety of symbolic meanings, metaphors, and analogies. Sometimes they had a style like the parables in the Bible, though often the stories had unusual objects that would come to life, such as mirrors, fences or comets. Or living plants and animals, such as turtles, daisies, grass or eagles would talk. Even an angel or two appeared to help solve problems.

Everyone had a favorite, but Shawn's was the first story he recorded in the journal. It was called *Turtles*. If it hadn't been for that story, he thought, I'd still be struggling to work in a career in accounting that was no longer meaningful to me. And worst of all, I wouldn't have met Mary.

He had heard the story so many times, he could picture it in great detail. To pass the time, he decided to replay *Turtles* in his mind's eye. But first he imagined his grandfather saying, "There's a story that comes to mind. Would you like to hear it?"

Turtles

Willy lived in the ocean and spent most of his time floating around on his back, just taking in the sun. He could see no land, except for islands scattered in various directions.

His main source of delight and entertainment was the girl turtles who would swim by from time to time. He'd swim beside them and they would play, and Willy would swim along for awhile.

They seemed so determined to get where they were going! It always happened that in their eagerness and enthusiasm to get to a particular island, they would leave Willy behind. Without sharing their feeling of excitement, he would tire easily. Then once again, he would be alone.

This happened so much that finally Willy gave up trying to get a friend to stay with him. He got more and more depressed because he was so very lonely. Then he began expecting that things in his life just weren't meant to work out; if something could go wrong, it would!

Just as he would expect, bad things kept happening. One day, he was just floating on his back taking a nap and garbage started falling out of the sky. The messy stuff landed all over him, and he sank from the weight of it all. It turned out that a ship was passing by and the crew had unintentionally tossed the garbage overboard, right on top of him.

Willy cried, "This is just typical: only bad happens to me!"

Again his words came true. A series of unfortunate things happened to Willy. There was the horrible storm, the great white shark chasing him, and then the isolation when he got lost for two weeks with no other turtles in sight.

Finally, he said, "Enough of this! If this is what life is all about, it isn't worth the struggle." Willy was the saddest, loneliest, most miserable turtle . . . and then he heard a voice say, "It can be different, you know!"

Whirling around, Willy found no one. He bobbed his head underwater and checked there. . . but found only greenish ocean water and a strand of seaweed.

Willy thought, Gee, you'd think enough has befallen me; now I'm going crazy hearing voices! Then the voice said, "If you want to find me, it won't be out there."

Willy heard once that if a turtle tried real hard, he could pull his head inside his shell. He was always puzzled about why one would do such a silly thing. After all, the only things going on are outside, so why take a chance on missing out on anything? Besides, it also sounded a bit scary. "What if my head got stuck?", he asked himself.

However, he soon decided that he really didn't have much to lose anyway. Besides, now he was very curious about the voice. So Willy pulled and pulled. Finally, with a little "plop" sound, he managed to squeeze his head into the shell.

It was pitch black, and it was so quiet he could no longer hear the waves, the birds or anything. Realizing he was safe after this bizarre head trick, Willy started to enjoy the peace and quiet. All his worries, frustrations, and depression seemed to drift away. In fact, it was so peaceful—he almost forgot why he came inside in the first place.

The voice spoke again. This time Willy turned his head and widened his eyes, trying to see who was talking. All he could see was darkness. It was blacker than octopus ink at night! The voice said, "Willy, what is your heart's desire?"

"Who are you? . . . Where are you?" Willy snapped. There was no answer at first, and then a soft voice spoke with such a feeling of love, tenderness and caring that Willy was totally and completely captivated. Each word vibrated with familiar tones and inflections. The voice was as comforting as his Mother's, as inviting as his most cherished lover's, and as inspirational as an angel from Heaven. An incredible feeling of peace and safety flowed throughout his body.

The voice said, "I am your friend within. I've always been here, and I will always be with you. I've spoken to you often, but you've never come inside to listen."

"I feel as though I know you. Your voice is so very soothing." Willy barely finished the words when a rush of sadness swept through him. Tears flowed, and his leathery brow wrinkled from the pressure he felt.

The sadness continued for what seemed like hours. The salt from his tears mixed with the salt from the ocean. The voice was silent, or at least if it wasn't, he couldn't tell. The sound of his own thoughts were enough to drown out anything.

Finally, he became aware of a twinkling of a happy feeling starting to grow within. Then it became more than that. It became a mixture of happiness, love and peace. All this joy came to him after he realized that he now had a friend within!

Before Willy could speak, the voice said, "All those times you were lonely and lost—I was there. I love you, Willy, and I can help you, if you will just come inside and visit me." The voice continued with, "Now that I have your attention, there is a most important question I must ask: what is your heart's desire?"

Willy was unable to answer. It had been years since he'd thought about what he really wanted. Content with drifting around and floating on his back, he would just be satisfied with whatever came along. At least he thought he was satisfied . . . "No! That's not right!" he realized. "I've never been truly satisfied. I've only had periods of distraction from the emptiness and despair I have always felt."

He remembered the playful times he had had with various turtles. The memories were usually enjoyable, until sooner or later his friends would swim away toward one of the islands barely visible on the horizon.

Most memories would revert to Milly. She was a beautiful turtle—energetic and above all, quite playful. They would ride the swells together and play tricks on the dolphins.

At night, they would float on their backs and look in awe at the magnificent display of stars. One night they saw two shooting stars at the same time, going in opposite directions.

The next day Milly left.

It was as though the stars signaled that they, too, should go in different directions. Before she left, Milly said, "I want to go to the third island. I've heard of the wonderful sand caves you can build—a perfect place to raise a family." When she spoke of her dream, her beautiful double eyelids opened wide and Willy could hear her heart beat faster.

Milly swam fast and hard. Willy even tried following her for a while, but without sharing the drive Milly's dream gave her, the opposing currents were just too much for him. He soon lost energy and returned to his standard drifting position of floating on his back.

The question returned, "What is my heart's desire?" Before his mind could answer with the familiar, "I don't know," he realized he was tired of saying that. He was tired of drifting. He was tired of trying to live the dreams of others.

Hoping to regain the attention of his friend within, he said, "My heart's desire is to know what my heart desires!"

The loving voice responded, "Dare to dream, for without a dream, it can't come true!"

He asked for more detail, but the voice was silent. Even the ocean was calm, except for the gentle rocking motion which soothed his mind and body.

As his eyelids closed and sleep came, so did images. Images of possibilities, of activities that brought joy to his heart.

He dreamed of the slide on island five. It was made up of a long, smooth rock that formed a 30-foot slide into the ocean. After the rains, water would flow down the slide. All the native turtles would gather to take turns sliding, laughing and enjoying the exhilarating ride, which ended with a big splash in the ocean.

In Willy's last dream, his slide down the rock plunged him deep into the waves with great force. He awoke with a jerk.

Willy realized that going to island five was a strong heart's desire of his, but he had always dismissed the possibility. The trip was very long and dangerous. Two ocean currents met while traveling in opposite directions. That created treacherous whirlpools. These powerful whirlpools drew objects into their swirling holes and sucked them down to depths of many hundreds of feet. It was said that the pressure from the weight of the water could crack the shells of turtles, and that's why no one ever saw them again!

Willy slipped back into his old way of thinking. "It's just my luck. When I finally discover my heart's desire, it's impossible to achieve! I've never heard of anyone making it to island five from here!"

The friend within interrupted his thoughts by saying, "Willy, listen to me carefully. Your own thoughts are more limiting than any barrier formed of earth, water or fire. You are never given a true heart's desire without it being possible to achieve." Just then a giant wave tumbled Willy. It was like the ocean was adding emphasis to what was said—like a cosmic exclamation point!

"But I'm afraid," Willy cried. "I could be crushed or lost at sea forever!"

"You've been feeling crushed and lost for years, Willy. Here's your chance to finally put the joy you want into your life. I'm not saying it will be easy, but if you don't go for what your heart desires, you'll always have an empty feeling inside."

Willy knew it was the truth when he heard those words. Some part of him also knew that he had to at least try to obtain his dream.

Noticing that his neck was aching from being tucked inside so long, he stretched it out of his shell. "What a beautiful sight," he sighed. The mid-morning sun sparkled on the waves, and the puffy white clouds seemed to salute him from the rich blue sky. Amazed at the wonderful feeling he was experiencing, he wondered, "Am I imagining things, or am I the happiest I have ever been? I feel as though the entire world is conspiring to make me happy!"

He shouted as loud as he could, "I AM GOING TO ISLAND FIVE, NO MATTER WHAT! I CAN SEE MYSELF THERE RIGHT NOW!" With that, he immediately started off toward island five.

Willy swam hard for two days and never once even thought of going back inside to visit his newly-found friend.

On the afternoon of the third day, Willy discovered other turtles on a path parallel to his. He found out that they all shared the same dream of living and playing on island five. Their enthusiasm and excitement was contagious, and his energy to swim hard and fast returned.

Though the group worked hard at churning the miles away, they played hard, too. At times Willy wondered if he could possibly be happier than he was right then. He even developed a close tie with an attractive turtle named Heidi.

Though Heidi used different strokes than he and had different ideas about life, they did share the common dream. They became the closest, most loving couple of turtles that you could imagine.

As the group made their way, Willy was so involved with swimming, splashing, and chatting with Heidi that he didn't hear the soft voice inside his shell warning of the whirlpool up ahead.

The group was just on the outer edge of the whirlpool, so no one noticed that their course had started forming a very large circle. That is, until Heidi said, "The sun was in my eyes; now it's on my back. Are we going in the right direction?"

Soon after she said this, the sun was back in everyone's eyes again. At the same instant, they all had the chilling realization that they were being pulled into a giant whirlpool.

Confused and scared, all the turtles started thrashing about, but it was clear that the current was much too strong. They all felt terrified as a vision of being crushed at the bottom of the ocean flashed in their minds.

Willy thought, How did I get myself into this, anyway?

With lightening speed, he remembered being inside and speaking to his friend within. It seemed like ages ago. He had meant to go back and visit, but he had just gotten so involved with everything that he forgot. Since he couldn't do much about what was going on outside anyway, he pulled his head and feet inside to search for his friend.

It was incredible how the shell blocked out the roar of the whirlpool and the yelling from the other turtles.

Willy shouted, "Voice! . . . Voice! . . . Where are you? I need you. Please talk to me." But Willy's heart was beating so hard and his thoughts were flying by so fast, he couldn't hear a thing.

Finally, he tried recapturing the feelings he'd had the last time he was inside by recalling his dream. Though it was hard to hold the image of island five in his mind, familiar feelings of joy and love started to enter his body. Finally, a wonderful sense of peace started to dominate.

Then he thought of how crazy the others would think he was if they knew what he was doing right now. "Here I am in a whirlpool, about to be crushed to death, and I'm dreaming about my heart's desire. Boy, am I ready for the funny farm!"

Just then his friend within responded. "Coming in out of a storm cannot be considered crazy."

The surprise and excitement of hearing the voice quickly gave way to the pressing issue at hand and Willy promptly pleaded, "Oh please, please, tell me what to do!"

With great confidence the voice said, "Your dream is possible by joining with others who share your dream. Hold on to your dream."

"What? I don't understand! What do you mean?" Willy shouted so loud, the words seemed to echo inside his shell. But as he continued to shout, his heart rate increased, he became tense, and the voice faded.

Willy knew his time was limited.

His mind raced over and over what had been said, as though his life depended upon it. What a puzzle: "Your dream is possible by joining with others who share your dream. Hold on to your dream." The more he thought about it, the more confusing it became. He couldn't imagine how this could possibly get them out of the whirlpool.

Finally, he gave up trying to figure it out with his mind and just took action. He forced his head and feet back out into the swirling turmoil.

By now the turtles had started the descent into the whirlpool. Willy was surprised to see how fast things were moving. They were all quite aware of the awesome deep dark hole into which they were being pulled. It was almost hypnotic, the way the water swirled with increasing speed the deeper it got. Just like a funnel, the hole got smaller the further down you went, until *it seemed to get too narrow for anything to fit through. Is that where our shells get crushed? Willy shivered.*

As the turtles went round and round, Willy decided to tell the others what he had learned within, but because he had to shout so loud, the message kept getting shorter and shorter.

He shouted, "We can have our dream, hold on to our dream!" And again, "We have our dream, hold on!" And as Willy got weaker all he could shout was, "HOLD ON!"

Just then Willy felt a click on his shell. Turning his head around, he saw that Heidi had connected herself to his shell by clamping on with her powerful jaws. Of course it didn't hurt, because it was only his shell.

Others started doing the same, until all the turtles—twelve in all— formed a giant chain.

Although this felt a little safer than before, they were still spinning around the vortex and descending rapidly down the whirlpool. Lower and lower they went, until Willy noticed that as the whirlpool hole got smaller, the end of their turtle chain was almost about to reach the beginning of the chain, forming a ring.

When the two ends got close enough, the two end turtles instinctively connected with each other and their circle was completed. Each turtle tightened his or her mouth grip and kept thinking over and over, "Hold on. . . Hold on. . . I'm holding on to my dream!"

Willy noticed something very exciting, though he wouldn't dare open his mouth to tell the others. Their descent into the whirlpool had stopped. The reason was quite simple. Since the diameter of the hole got smaller the deeper they went, and since their circle was solid and not about to shrink— their tight chain could go no deeper.

So there they were spinning around and around like an infinite merry-go-round. Soon the whole group realized what was happening and the pressing unspoken question became, "Now what?"

Since there was no immediate answer, they continued to hold on, until finally the circular chain started to move off-center. As it did, their chain began to exhibit a powerful wobbling motion. It moved back and forth, until part of the chain passed over the center of the whirlpool. By then most of the turtles were so scared they closed their eyes.

As if shot like a giant rubber band from a giant's thumb, the chain of turtles went flying out of the whirlpool. It was almost as if the whirlpool had rejected them because they couldn't be swallowed!

Several minutes went by before they all realized that they were finally in safe, calm waters again. Even so, it took several more minutes for them to feel safe enough to let go of each other.

Willy found himself surrounded by all the other turtles. They were all praising him for the wonderful words of wisdom that had saved them from destruction.

Heidi gave him a big turtle hug, and the love from her eyes almost left him speechless. However, he did have something to say.

He told them the whole story about going within and listening to his friend. Although they were a bit skeptical at first, what else could explain this incredible burst of genius from one whom they had always considered to be a fairly average turtle?

Just as Willy was about to teach them how to go within, Heidi shouted, "Look! It's island five . . . It's only a ten-minute swim from here!"

Every last turtle made the racy swim in just under FOUR minutes!

~ ~ ~ ~ ~ ~ ~

As Shawn sat stranded on his Mercedes' hood, reflecting back on this subtle little story about a few turtles, he remembered how it had changed his life many years ago. He had not been happy for ages. He was bored with working as an accountant, but didn't know life could be any different for him. His tremendous, almost child-like creativity was not being used, yet he held on to the job because it was the best money he'd ever made. It felt safe and secure, so he just put in his required hours and tried to find *aliveness* outside of work.

He wasn't having much luck finding a mate, either. He was just drifting in a sea of singles, meeting new women and saying goodbye to others. He was trying to mold himself into what they seemed to be wanting from him so they wouldn't leave. Everything centered around finding the right woman.

Though he had heard *Turtles* many times before, this had been the first time his grandfather told it directly to him, after Shawn had described his boredom and loneliness. After thinking about the story for almost a whole night, Shawn realized he didn't have any dreams or goals. His life was adrift, and women kept leaving his life soon after entering because he had no direction. He realized that no two people could know if their directions were compatible if one or both didn't know where they were headed.

Shawn decided that he must first find what he wanted to do that brought him joy. Then if he met a woman who stuck around for a while, she was probably on a compatible path.

Dropping the focus on women (since he couldn't understand them anyway) he started exploring what made him happy. First, he took college courses in psychology because human nature had always fascinated him. Then he expanded into classes in advertising and marketing—which he soon realized were really applications of psychology and fishing. He got in touch with a vast resource of untapped creative talents that surfaced when he let himself be more childlike and less structured. He vibrated with a fresh new enthusiasm and excitement for life. Soon he was also attracting many new friends who shared similar interests. He was so happy he had almost forgotten about women.

That's when I met Mary, he remembered. It happened just like in *Turtles*: I got so enthusiastic about going toward my goal and associating with those who shared common interests that all of a sudden there was Mary—my own *Heidi*.

Shawn wondered if *Turtles* had any answers to his current crisis and life-changing decision. No, he thought, I've already reached *island five*. I wonder what story Grampa will tell me? If it's this one again, I just don't know what I'll do!

Thinking of the other stories reminded him of the journal. He looked over the fender and found that it was quite visible in the moonlight. To make sure he didn't forget it, he leaned over to bring it up on the hood with him. Besides, he thought, I need something to occupy my time.

Very carefully, he lay across the front of the car with his arm dangling down near the left wheel. The journal was just out of reach, so he turned around and tried reaching it with his foot. His hand slipped and his weight suddenly transferred to both feet on the ground. The car quickly jolted upward and made about a four-inch sliding movement toward the canyon.

"Aaaaah," Shawn yelled. He grabbed the bumper with both hands and feet, hoping his weight would pull it back down. His posterior extended way out, like a sailboat crewman trying to keep from going over in the water. Finally, the car started lowering again, but because of the slide and new pivot point, it now required him to extend himself to obtain sufficient leverage.

He started to sweat. His muscles were already straining after only a few minutes. Another shift in the car was followed by sounds of small rocks hitting against other rocks as they tumbled down the mountainside. The front of the car went up a few more inches. Shawn also heard the grinding of metal against rock as the undercarriage of the car shifted. His hands and feet were still on the bumper, his rear was on the ground, and his arms and legs were now at about a forty-five degree angle off the ground. The front wheels were off the ground and things looked hopeless.

Just as his muscles were crying out for relief, the story *Eagles* flashed in Shawn's mind . Though he interpreted that particular story as an intuitive signal to let go, he really had no choice. He couldn't have held on for even one more second.

As soon as Shawn let go, the car lifted like a giant ship ready to sink. Horrible scraping, creaking, and grinding noises broke the silence as the rear of the car disappeared below the edge of the cliff. The darkness of the canyon was swallowing Shawn's car and he couldn't do anything but watch. He ran over to the edge just in time to see his beautiful Mercedes slide and tumble down the canyon. End over end at first and then rolling side over side, gathering speed and momentum as it battled with boulders and scrub trees. The loud crunching, scraping sounds were equally matched by Shawn's screams. He never knew he could yell that loud or long.

Finally, exhausted from his vigorous yelling, Shawn stopped. Silence again triumphed in the forest. He continued to gaze down at the tiny crumpled white spot, about three hundred feet below, at the bottom of the canyon. Noticing that there was no fire or explosion like cars in the movies, Shawn wondered if they loaded those cars with dynamite just to make the scenes more dramatic. Then he quickly questioned his sanity for having thoughts like these after losing a car that had cost as much as some houses.

Looking down at his car, Shawn doubted that anyone could have survived the crash. Viewing the whole area of the accident, he wondered how the car came to a stop in the first place. Why didn't it just go over with me inside? he asked himself. An answer popped up in his mind. I must still have things to do while I'm here.

After taking a few steps back, he sat down on the ground cross-legged and put his hands on his head. Sadness swept over him. How could all this be happening? After a few moments of self-pity, he said to himself, I guess I should feel pretty lucky. I don't have a scratch on me, and I know I have plenty of insurance. He put his hands down to the ground to prop himself up, and his right hand came down to rest on the journal. He picked it up and said out loud, "Well, at least you're safe—I can replace the car." Then he thought, I'll have to remember to get a copy made for safekeeping. He got up, dusted himself off, and walked toward the highway.

Just after he had questioned who would pick up a stranger at night, the next car stopped for him. It was an older man in his late sixties and his wife who were coming back home after visiting family down the hill. After some discerning looks through a partially opened window and a few questions about where Shawn was headed, they smiled and told Shawn to get in the car. While proceeding up the mountain road, they asked if Shawn was carrying a Bible. That's why they stopped, they admitted. The man said, "There's a Bible camp in town, and those people often carry a Bible. It might be something they're suppose to do; I don't know."

Whatever the reason they had to trust picking him up, Shawn felt thankful they had stopped. He could have been on the road all night. When asked about what he was doing there on the road, he merely said, *car problems* in order to avoid talking about his ordeal.

During the pauses in talk about the weather and how the town kept changing, Shawn's mind kept returning to the loss of his car. The insurance will replace it; I'll get another one; it will be all right, he repeated to himself. I've got to devote my attention to my decision this weekend, he thought.

The couple lived in the Idyllwild area and took him right up to his grandparents' door. Shawn appreciated the couple's effort because the cabin was remotely located about ten miles out of their way. He thanked them and asked if he could pay for their gas, but they both just waved their hands in a similar gesture—as though they'd rehearsed it. The woman said, "What are neighbors for, if not to lend a hand now and then?"

Shawn walked up the stairs to the porch and waved goodbye to the couple. Trinket, his grandparents' calico-colored cat, had jumped off the wooden rocker and was already saying hello by making stroking passes against Shawn's leg. He kneeled down and rubbed her ears and neck affectionately. His grandmother opened the door and said, "Why Shawn, what a wonderful surprise! Did you just come up to visit Trinket or did you want to come in?" Her warm laugh reminded him that she hadn't lost her sense of humor.

"Hi, Gramma. I suppose I'll come in. Do you want Trinket in or out?"

"Oh, don't worry about her. Your grandfather installed a little cat door and trained her to use it so that she could come and go as she pleases, but the skunks can't. I made him promise that none of those smelly creatures could get inside. Imagine if a skunk got in the house—whew!"

As soon as the screen door opened, Trinket squeezed through first, as though this were all about her. Once Shawn was inside, he gave his grandmother a big hug. With all his attention on his grandfather, he'd forgotten how much he loved his Gramma. She immediately went into the kitchen and began to fix him a snack.

Shawn anxiously peeked into the living room hoping to see his grandfather. He would normally be by the fire, whittling little animals out of soft pine. Though his grandfather wasn't there, he could almost hear his deep voice echoing from the walls. Shawn walked in and looked around for a moment to refresh his memories of the place where so many stories were told and truths about life were revealed. The walls were made out of pine and were stained and varnished to suit his grandfather's desire for a warm, natural look. An open wooden stairway led to the upstairs bedrooms gave a grand view of the living room. The furniture was Early American, and his grandmother had even put little white doilies on the arms of the couch. Shawn didn't like little lacy things because they kept needing adjusting, but he had to admit, he loved being in that room. The end table held a lamp that looked like an old kerosene burner. Thank goodness, he thought, this one is electric. He hated the fumes they produced. The pictures on the far wall were of his grandparents' three children and all the grandchildren. He noticed his picture was of him as a teenager. He wondered if his grandparents still thought of him as being young. Then he wondered at what point are you thought of as being old by anyone much older than you.

Shawn stepped back into the kitchen and asked, "Where's Grampa?" He saw his grandmother slice through a delicious-looking apple cobbler pie.

"Oh, I wish we'd known you were coming," his grandmother said. "As you know, he's almost always here on weekends 'cause he likes to avoid doing things when the tourists are around. But your grandfather got invited on a special trip. He went on a camping hike with friends, and they won't be back until late Sunday afternoon."

"Oh, no—I completely forgot to call first!" Shawn slapped the top of his head and his eyes rolled up. "Everything happened so fast."

His grandmother looked at him and said, "My-oh-my, Shawn. Won't I do for company?"

He laughed and said, "Oh, of course, Gramma . . . it's just that, well, I really was needing to see Grampa. Do you think I could catch up with them?"

As his grandmother set the pie and a glass of milk on the table, she said, "I don't think so. They left early this morning. It's probably best you just wait for them because they're hiking in some pretty remote areas."

Shawn gobbled down big bites of the apple cobbler like he'd done when he was little. In between bites he told his grandmother all about the car accident. Every once in a while she would just say, "Oh, my!" and place her hand up to her mouth with a surprised look.

"There's something else," he continued. "You remember I told you I was holding the car down by sitting on it?"

"Yes," she said.

"Before I could get out there on the front of the car, and before I discovered that my weight now kept the car from tipping, this glowing, bluish light seemed to be hovering just above the hood. It was transparent, and maybe it sounds crazy, but it seemed to hold the car down until I got out there, because I could see an indentation in the metal from its weight. What else would have kept the car from dropping off the cliff? It was certainly out of balance. What do you think that was?"

Again his grandmother put her hand up to her mouth and said, "Oh, my!" Then she just looked deeply into Shawn's eyes much longer than was usual for her and said not a word.

Shawn felt uncomfortable.

She turned to look into the living room and then back at Shawn, as if wondering how to respond. Finally she said, "You know, people sometimes report odd things after they've been in an accident. Maybe it was just a hallucination from all that adrenaline. That was really quite a scary ordeal!"

"But I know I saw this ball of light. It was there," Shawn insisted.

Gramma replied in a calming voice, "Well, maybe it was God's way of helping you tonight." Then she quickly changed the subject by asking, "Should we call someone about your car, the Highway Patrol or something? If you don't report it, your insurance might not cover it."

He had wanted to more fully explore the mysterious light with her, yet her question brought up a bit of fear. "My insurance has a 24-hour claims line; I guess I'll call and find out." Since the phone was right above the kitchen table, he didn't have to move far. After finally getting a live person in claims, he explained the situation and asked several questions.

"What did they say?" his grandmother asked when he hung up.

"I talked to a very helpful woman. She said a police report will have to be filed, but since the accident only involved me and the car is not obstructing anything, they don't have to be called right away. As far as the insurance claim, I have up to a year to file that." He paused to think, then added, "I think I'll hold off until after Monday morning, since there isn't anything that has to be done right away."

His grandmother scrunched her forehead a bit and directed another question to Shawn. "So what's really going on that you drove up at night to see your Grampa? You've never driven here at night before. Is the family okay? How's Mary?"

"Oh, yeah, everyone is just fine. Mary sends her love." Nervous about discussing the true subject, he timidly reached over to slice another piece of pie. Unfortunately, his sleeve caught the edge of his glass, it dumped into his plate and milk flowed, almost covering the little table.

Gramma chuckled, "Oh, Shawn, you never change, do you? That's all right, Honey. I'll get a rag and some more milk." Trinket licked at the milk that ended up on the floor, happy that she finally got her snack.

Shawn looked for expressions or reactions in grandmother's face, yet she was her typical self, acting as though nothing had happened and that she just suddenly had an urge to wipe off the table anyway. She is such a nurturing grandmother, he thought. After his own mother passed away, Gramma was all he'd had for a mother figure. As she leaned toward him to reach the far corner, her eyes twinkled as she looked deeply into Shawn's eyes. As her attention shifted away he noticed the face he had loved since childhood. Though now it had more wrinkles, her face was soft, with rounded cheeks giving a cheery look even when she wasn't smiling. Hundreds of times she had pressed her cheek to his during those good-old-Gramma hugs. That was one of her warmest signs of affection, since she wasn't much on kisses—those were usually reserved only for Grampa.

With all her love and caring, he had always wondered why his grandmother seldom held eye contact for more than a second or two. Her eyes were deep and steady with a magnetic attraction, yet she always seemed to be doing something that drew her eyes away. Just a little while ago, she held the longest contact he could ever remember.

Shawn wished he didn't have this clumsy habit of his, but it had been with him ever since the second grade, when Miss Jenkins had asked him for the first time that year to write something on the chalkboard in front of the class. On his way up, he tripped and fell over the wastepaper basket and sent the class into hysterics. That was bad enough, but the next week the teacher asked him to open a window and he knocked a potted plant off the sill, scattering dirt all over the hardwood floor. From then on, whenever he got nervous, he just naturally got very clumsy. Somehow the two seemed to have gotten anchored together.

Now, with his fresh piece of pie and milk, Shawn decided to

just relax and enjoy being nurtured by his beloved grandmother. He looked up at her, remembering she had asked what was going on. His mouth was stuck. He had always told his problems to his grandfather and wouldn't think of burdening his sensitive grandmother with his current conflict. So gaining his composure, he casually replied, "Oh, there's stuff going on about my career; but I'm sure one of Grampa's stories will help out. They always do."

Walking to the sink, his grandmother raised an eyebrow. "Yeah, he's quite the storyteller. He's so good with his speech and tone of voice, to this day I love to just sit by the fire and hear him talk." As she rinsed off some dishes she continued, "You know, I've never told anyone this, but sometimes I pretend I can't get to sleep just to have your Grampa talk to me for a while. The deep vibrations of his voice are so soothing, sometimes I fall off to sleep before I want to!"

Shawn nodded in agreement, wishing he could hear his grandfather's voice right then. He paused for a moment imagining Grampa's captivating voice. Then he went back to being a little kid again, scooping up oversized mouthfuls of pie, though he wasn't all that hungry. He thought how funny it was that when visiting relatives, he seemed to revert back to being a child. He reminded himself that this trip he must try to remain an adult, with an important decision to make. Friends had told him stories about their family visits, yet many of their stories weren't as cozy and comfortable as his. They often described feeling defensive, getting into arguments, and wishing they could leave just after arriving. Shawn felt very lucky to have his family and wouldn't think of exchanging them.

His grandmother didn't seem disappointed at all that Shawn didn't go into detail about his problem, and he was relieved. She got so concerned about the car, he thought, heaven knows what she would do if she heard my real problem. My lost car is nothing compared to what's really going on. Gramma makes good pies and gives good hugs, but it's the sparkling wisdom in Grampa's stories that I need right now.

After his grandmother retired for the evening, Shawn lit the wood in the fireplace and stretched out on the couch. He picked up his purple journal from the end table where he'd left it, and held it on his chest. Trinket sat near his feet, licking her paws. Shawn had decided to stay through Sunday to see his grandfather, so he thought he might as well relax.

The fire crackled as the kindling ignited the larger logs. It was barely cool enough in the house for a fire, but Shawn couldn't imagine being in a mountain cabin without one. When Mary was with him she would sometimes have to open all the doors and windows to cool it off enough for a fire.

Shawn gazed proudly at the cover of his journal where he had artistically printed the title, *Stories for the Inner Ear*. After recording the stories over the years, he'd come up with that name. It seemed like the stories could be heard by the outer ear like normal, yet the true value came when the "inner ear" truly absorbed the meaning of the stories.

Then Shawn noticed something for the first time. The words *ear* and *hear* were part of the word *heart*. "Oh, my gosh," he said out loud. "It even contains Grampa's name—Art!"

His grandmother suddenly appeared on the top of the stairs. Looking down at him in the living room, she asked, "Did you say something to me, Shawn?"

"Well, I was just talking out loud, but did you know the words *hear, ear, and art* are all part of the word *heart?*"

"No, but that makes sense. True hearing is an art from the heart. Say, I'm turning into a poet, aren't I?" she chuckled as she went back into her room.

Hmmm, he thought. Maybe I should have used the title, *Stories to Hear with the Inner Ear and the Heart from Grampa Art . . .?* No, he laughed to himself, that's too long.

Mary had told him he was one of the few people she knew who could carry on a complete conversation with himself at length. As he pictured their first meeting, the phone rang and shattered the deep mountain silence. It startled Shawn so much he jumped up, sending the journal flying. Trinket was used to the telephone, but she was jolted by Shawn's abrupt movement. She jumped about a foot in the air before scampering into the kitchen. Gramma shouted downstairs to him that it was Mary on the phone, checking on him.

What a coincidence, he thought. Just as I was picturing her, she called. Then he realized he'd forgotten to call her like he usually did when he arrived.

"I've got it," Shawn called up to his grandmother as he picked up the old-fashioned phone in the kitchen. "Hello, Mary?" he said into the little black, round, funnel-shaped object coming out of the wooden box. His grandparents loved the feeling of an antique phone; yet it sure wasn't the easiest to talk on.

"Shawn, you didn't call. Are you okay?"

"I'm sorry; with all that happened, I forgot. Now don't get upset . . . everything is fine . . . I just had a bit of an accident with the car . . . but . . . but . . . I'm not hurt at all." He was trying to avoid getting Mary all upset.

"What happened, Shawn?"

In a rather choppy delivery, he replied, "Well, I sort of spun out on one of the curves. I put a dent in the fender . . . ." Pausing for a moment, he decided that he'd better tell her everything. "Well, actually . . . then the car . . . well, the car . . . sort of fell off a cliff . . . by itself . . . I wasn't in it."

"Shawn! What do you mean it sort of fell off a cliff. How could it do that by itself?" Mary was obviously getting upset.

"Look, Honey; it was balancing on the edge of the cliff and when I got out . . . well, I tried to keep it from tipping by holding it down . . . then it sort of tumbled down the canyon . . . but it didn't explode like in the movies. Remember that movie we saw on cable last week? . . . "

Mary interrupted his diversionary attempt, knowing what he was up to. "I don't want to talk about movies. This is serious, Shawn!"

"Oh, yeah. Well anyway, I'm okay . . . and I know the car was expensive but at least it's insured . . . it can be replaced. I called our insurance company's claim department, and I know what needs to be done. Just please don't get worked up; everything's fine. A nice couple drove me the rest of the way. I'm trying to avoid thinking of the car so I can just work on the decision—it's so much more important. Really, there's not much we can do about the car right now anyway." Shawn softened his voice and tried to lighten things up by saying, "I've already had two pieces of pie. You don't mind if I get fat, do you?"

Mary sighed and relaxed her tone a bit, too. "Yes, I mind. Don't you go back for thirds! Well anyway, thank goodness you didn't go over with the car! Really, Shawn, you seem to be taking this so casually. Some people would think you just didn't care about your belongings. It was such a luxurious car . . . but I guess they should replace it; after all, we're paying incredibly high insurance payments. We can talk more about it later. Has Grampa told you a story yet?"

"Oh, that's another thing. Grampa is on a camping trip and won't be back until Sunday. I'll have to stay over. I'll find some sort of transportation and be home late Sunday night. My meeting with Carl starts at 9:00 a.m., and I can't be late."

"We'll miss brunch with the Sanders on Sunday—but with all this going on, we might have missed it anyway. I'll call and let them know we'll make it another time. Are you going to report the car to the police or anything?"

"Well, the accident only involved me, and the insurance person said I technically don't have to call in a report right away. After Monday morning when the decision-making is over, I'll take care of it. Boy, the car's a total wreck and so hard to get to, but I guess I can be happy it's not blocking the road!" Shawn forced a chuckle at his futile attempt at humor, but heard no laughs from Mary. So he moved on and asked, "How are the kids?"

Now Mary laughed. "It appears Ron is getting a sense of humor. He got Julie back tonight for some of her many practical jokes. While she was out at a movie—it must have been a lot of work—but he filled her bedroom with balloons. She opened her door and out flowed balloons. It took ten minutes of noisy popping before she could even get into her own room! You know how she hates noise! She certainly got a taste of her own medicine tonight."

Shawn laughed. "Who's encouraging the kids now?"

"You were gone, so I needed some kind of entertainment."

Shawn knew this was a sideways joke about his clumsiness, but he didn't mind. At least her attention was off the accident and she was calm.

Continuing to keep the subject changed, he said, "By the way I re-pictured the whole turtle story tonight in my mind. It brought back old memories." He paused, wondering whether to mention that he had been holding the car down while reviewing the story, but his thoughts were interrupted by Mary.

"I love that story. Without it, you could still be working as an accountant and we might not be together! I don't know how you lasted so long doing that. You were dead in that job."

"I really needed to let go and follow my new dream, didn't I? Then I met you in that graphic design class. Wow—was I ever taken with your long black hair, brown eyes, and very kissable-looking lips. And with all that, you really seemed genuinely fascinated with my ideas. Of course, your great tush had something to do with it, too. I still love you, you know?" Shawn felt like a teenager talking on the phone.

"Yes, I love you, too, and I'm glad we're still playing on *island five* together. Just remember: this may seem like a whirlpool again, but hold on to your dream!"

"Except this time, the dream is confronting some dreadful aspects and a major fork in the road. I need a new story. I can't wait until Grampa gets back. I think I'll continue reading the journal. Maybe one of the other stories has some insight for me."

They talked for a few more minutes and then said goodnight.

Shawn poked at the logs in the fireplace before returning to the comfortable couch. He picked up the journal again and flipped a few pages. The next story was another of his favorites. He decided to move to Grampa's chair. As he sat down, Trinket gave a purring meow and jumped up on his lap.

"Oh, I have an audience, do I?" Shawn rubbed Trinket's neck and sat back in the deep-cushioned leather chair. He thumbed through the purple journal, which contained many handwritten stories. They were covered with lots of editing marks because each time he heard them, he would make a correction or two. He recalled how his grandfather somehow told the stories word-for-word, the same each time, and he could recite any of them at a minute's notice. Once Shawn had asked his grandfather how he could do that and he'd just said jokingly, "'Tis for me to know, and you to wonder about."

Shawn had planned to tape-record whatever story his grandfather told him this weekend, but his pocket tape recorder was now resting in peace—or pieces, in his car at the bottom of the canyon.

As Shawn opened the journal to the second story, he imagined his grandfather sitting down with his cup of tea, peering out from under those bushy white eyebrows, and saying, "That reminds me of a story; do you want to hear it?"

"I sure would, meow!" Shawn said in a high voice, pretending that Trinket had spoken. Then he began reading the story *Mirrors* out loud to the curled-up cat.

MIRRORS

High in the mountains of Canada, little Myra tossed pebbles into Mirror Lake. Sitting right at the edge of the water, she could see the almost-perfect reflections of the mountains, trees, sky, and puffy white clouds.

Except for the ripples caused by Myra's pebbles, the lake was almost perfectly smooth. Myra noticed how the ripples made the mountains look wiggly and distorted.

Most people would ponder this only for a moment. Not Myra. She was captivated and full of questions about reflections. Hours would speed by like minutes as she accumulated questions.

This wouldn't be too unusual, until you add the fact that Myra was not a person. Myra was a four-year-old, redwood-trimmed mirror!

I know what you are thinking: "What kind of story is this? I've never heard of walking and talking mirrors!" Upon telling this story, I've often heard people say the same thing. But then again, they've never been to Mirror Lake or the nearby Mirror Village in Canada. Have you?

You've never been there because no humans can find it. It's a mystical, magical place; but it is as real as the reflection you see in your mirror at home.

Myra was so curious, she wished that someone would answer all the questions she had. Just today, she had added three more questions to the list she kept in a special notebook: "Why do the ripples make the mountains look strange? Why do the mountains look upside down? When I toss dirt in the water, why is the reflection hard to see?"

The sun was starting to go down. Her urge to get home was strong since the path through the trees was dangerous without light. One of the worst things that can happen to a mirror is to fall down. Myra had been told that there was no sound worse than that of breaking glass.

Though she had never heard breaking glass, Myra had heard crunching glass. The path back to the village passed by a large gray building with no openings in the walls except for doors. Each time she passed it, she trembled with fear as her hands tried to block the sound from her ears. The sound went crunch, crunch, crunch, tick-tick-tick-tick, crunch, crunch, crunch, tick-tick-tick-tick. It repeated like that 24 hours a day.

Myra felt that something horrible was going on in that building, but no one would discuss it. They'd say to her instead, "Myra, when you are older, we'll talk about it." Of course that would only frighten her more.

The walk home was easy today. Myra enjoyed noticing the trees because once in a while she'd see a woodpecker or squirrel. She liked to catch the sun and reflect it like a big spotlight on the squirrels. This helped to distract her as she passed by that noisy, scary building. It helped block out the crunch, crunch, crunch.

Soon Myra entered the village and felt the familiar cobblestone street under her feet. The high-pitched buildings were pointing to the sky. Myra thought, Maybe they're trying to tell me that the answer to all my questions must remain up in the air.

Myra's mood shifted to frustration. She had never been patient, because of her intense curiosity.

Mrs. Magna Mirror practically tripped over Myra as they met on the street. Compared to Myra's three-foot height, Magna was a giant at eight *feet; that is, if you counted her ornamental brass trim on top.*

"Excuse me," Myra squeaked, even though it wasn't her fault.

"Watch where you're going," rumbled Magna.

Myra decided to ask one of her burning questions. Maybe, by catching Magna off guard, she might just answer. So Myra asked, "Why do the ripples in the lake make the mountains look wiggly?"

"Why ask me?" she snapped. "Who do you think I am? The Prof?"

"Prof" was short for Professor Triple. He wasn't really a professor, but he was nicknamed Prof because there had been a time when he was always trying to teach strange ideas to everyone. He stopped doing that years ago, but everyone still called him Prof.

Myra felt a burst of energy. Could Prof answer my questions? she thought. Why didn't I think of that before? Oh, if only I can get him to talk to me!

The Prof lived on the other side of the village, so the trip to his house had to wait. Myra knew that it would be difficult to sleep that night. It will be just like a night before Christmas, she thought.

After a night of tossing and turning, Myra awoke to the morning sun streaming through the narrow gap in the drapes. It reflected off Myra's surface and made a curved line on the ceiling. "Wow—another question for the Prof," she exclaimed out loud. Excitement rushed through her when she realized that today was the day of her trip to see him.

First she must record today's question: "Why don't I reflect a straight line of sunlight on the ceiling?" As with all her questions, she left about ten blank lines for the answer. Except for the many questions, most of her notebook was blank so far.

Though in a rush, Myra didn't forget her morning grooming habits. She sprayed herself, using the new squirt bottle her mother had bought especially for her. When she was fully covered with tiny droplets, she wiped off her sur-

face with a soft towel. None of the other mirrors in the family were home so she couldn't tell if she'd missed any spots. You see, since mirrors are alive in Mirror Village, no one would consider hanging a relative on the wall just to look at. In fact, except for the mirrors themselves, glass of any kind was not found in the village.

Though none of her friends did stretching and flexibility exercises, Myra had instinctively done them all her life. As mirrors grow older they become rigid and stiff. The thought of becoming stiff didn't bother Myra in and of itself. What concerned Myra was becoming stuck in a shape that she might later find undesirable.

Being in a hurry, Myra only did half of the full mirror bends, corner bends and surface stretches she usually did. She was out the door in a flash, carrying her notebook of questions.

Myra arrived at the Prof's house and found him sitting on an old wooden porch only a few feet from the front sidewalk. She had heard that he sat there most of the day because he loved watching mirrors go by. She noticed a large, cloth-bound journal in his left hand. As she approached, he started writing in the journal as if he were writing about her.

"Are you the Prof?" she asked.

"Yep," he replied matter-of-factly as he continued to write.

"Are you writing about me?"

"Yep," he said, not offering any more information.

"Well, do you say anything besides 'yep?'"

"Yep," he replied.

"Okay then, what did you write about me?"

"I wrote that you are a four-year-old female, redwood trimmed, still flexible, reasonably straight and clean, no large distortions, could be a candidate."

Myra felt a little frustrated. Here she came to him to ask questions and he was stirring up more of them as he talked. "Candidate for what?" she asked.

"Can't tell you right now; depends on things."

The Prof looked very old and fragile, and yet Myra was astonished at the clarity of her reflection when she looked at him. She also felt very safe and loved. She took a seat next to the Prof. She smiled, because she'd almost forgotten about her questions. The happy feelings inside were tickling her and she felt like laughing.

And she did. Her giggles were contagious, too. The Prof and Myra began to laugh almost uncontrollably. They were so loud and genuine that passersby smiled and some started to laugh too—though they knew not why.

When the Prof laughed, Myra noticed three tiny sparkles shining from beneath his surface, like three twinkling stars. When she asked about them, the Prof said those spots sparkled when he was very happy.

Just as Myra calmed herself enough to ask the Prof why she was laughing, he stood up and rushed down the street. Of course she followed, but now she was afraid. Why was he running? Was someone chasing him?

Block after block he scurried, with an occasional dip behind a tree, or a pause in a store doorway. It was now obvious that the Prof was making sure he wasn't followed—by anyone else but Myra, that is. Finally, the Prof sat down on a park bench in the town's central park.

Myra sat down next to the Prof and waited intently for some kind of explanation, but the Prof said nothing.

"What was all that about?" Myra finally burst out.

The Prof calmly answered with a question, "Have you ever noticed the noisy building between here and Mirror Lake?"

"Yes! I hate the sounds. Why?" she asked.

"Well, some make it through and some don't. Those who don't get recycled. The crunching noise is . . . "

"No!" she screamed. "Don't say it. Tell me it's not true!"

The Prof held her close as she cried. He said, "I may not be tactful, but I do tell the truth. It's time you learned the facts while you're still flexible and can do something about them. You're a prime candidate for making it through."

Even though Myra was much too emotional to ask 'Make it through what?' she made a mental note to ask him some other time.

Myra's tears were gently brushed away by the Prof's wrinkled hand. He explained that most of the mirrors in the village were 15 years old or younger. He, however, was 43 and though showing signs of aging, the Prof had remarkable flexibility and clarity.

Myra listened intently as the Prof told her that he knew the truth about Mirror Village and yet hardly anyone believed him, or in fact, even bothered to talk with him. The Prof looked sad as he expressed his disappointment in his failure to convince so many mirrors before it was too late.

He shifted his position slightly. The sun reflected from the Prof's beautifully clear surface and lit up the face of the clock tower. He said, "Time is a funny thing. All these mirrors are steadily getting more rigid each day, and yet some continue to get more and more distorted and further from the true purpose."

"What's the true purpose?" Myra asked.

The Prof looked directly at Myra, and she saw the most clear and beautiful reflection of herself she could ever remember. The Prof answered, "The true purpose is to make a perfect reflection. You see, that's the only way out of Mirror Village. The alternative is the recycling plant outside of town."

Myra detected a sadness in his voice and wanted to know more. He explained that he felt very discouraged and disappointed because he had accumulated much knowledge that could be of great value, yet it just sat within his cloth-bound journal.

The Prof stood, raising his hands. "I've learned the secrets of Mirror Village," he cried. "I know how to reduce the pain and suffering. I know how to avoid the recycling plant. And, I know what's beyond if you make it through! What is really sad is that no one will listen to me. I've gathered so many techniques and so much information; I'm afraid it will all go to waste."

Then the Prof looked past Myra toward the edge of the park. With a frightened look and without another word, he took Myra's hand and walked quickly toward the clock tower. Myra's heart raced with fear and, of course, endless questions rushed through her mind. She almost wished she was back at Mirror Lake with her simple questions. Her life had now become complicated, very intense, and far more confusing than she could ever have imagined.

After a few blocks, the Prof took her to the doorstep of a stylish house that must have been owned by a family of very rich mirrors. He opened the door and told Myra that the family was on a trip and had asked him to take care of the place.

Finally, Myra could take it no longer. The questions were burning and she was so frustrated she couldn't even sit down before she blurted out, "Now! Now! Tell me what this is all about! What's on the other side? Who's chasing you? What are the secrets in the journal? Why won't people listen to you? What's going to happen to you? What's going to happen to me?"

As she shouted out the questions, she got so emotional and upset that Myra passed out, falling to the thick carpet. All the houses had very thick carpets just in case someone fell. The quickest way to the recycling plant was to break your own mirror by falling.

When Myra awoke, she was sitting cuddled next to the Prof on the couch. He had the cloth-bound journal open and was reading some of the quotes. His strong but gentle arm around her made her feel safe and relaxed.

The first quote he read was: "ALWAYS STAY FLEXIBLE."

"Wow," she said. "I've always practiced and knew that to be true. It's amazing that you have it written down."

The next quote was harder to understand. It read: "YOUR VIEW OR REFLECTION, OR BOTH, MAY BE DISTORTED (OR NOT)."

The Prof explained that to make this clear, he needed Myra to know more about how mirrors develop. First, he said that mirrors are formed from perfectly flat glass with a metallic coating on the back. Though these mirrors are very small, only a few inches long, they have almost perfect reflections.

Myra interrupted by asking if they could "pass through" (even though she wasn't sure what that was). The Prof said that new mirrors would pass through to the other side, except that there was a minimum size requirement of three feet tall. Then he added that by the time it reached that size, a mirror could have so many distortions that it would still end up in recycling.

"Anyway, back to the meaning of the quote," the Prof said as he poured Myra some tea. "The part of you that sees is the reflective coating. You see through your own glass first. Then, if you are looking at another mirror, you see through their glass and see yourself on their reflective surface."

Myra completed his thought by saying, "So the quote means that if I see a distortion, it could be either in my own glass, or in the glass of the other?"

"Yes!" the Prof exclaimed, "You catch on quickly. All I would add is that a distortion may be very small, less than an inch, perhaps, or it could be the length of the entire mirror."

"But if you don't know who might have the distortion, or even how big it is, how can you possibly use what is reflected to help make yourself straight?" Myra asked.

"Precisely!" the Prof said as he raised his hand. "By golly, you seem like *you already know all this and all I have to do is remind you! Everyone else just looks at me like I'm weird."*

"But how did you get so straight, Prof?" Myra asked as she saw her own perfect image in his reflection of her. "What did you do?"

"That's a long story, Myra. It's taken me years of research to discover the secrets, yet what is amazing is that unless you are pretty straight your-self, you cannot recognize it in someone else. Even then, you can't be a hun-dred percent sure. That's one of the reasons most of the population of Mirror Village doesn't think I know what I'm talking about. They view me as very distorted because they are viewing me through their own distorted glass."

"It's really a paradox," the Prof continued. In order for me to be believ-able, I would need to twist, turn, and distort myself so that I would appear straight enough for them to accept my word. Yet that would only work for small groups of people, since I can't possibly match everyone's distortion at the same time. If I remain straight, I look distorted to almost everyone, except for mirrors like you."

Myra could see that the Prof was very frustrated by the whole situation. She looked up at him and said in her sweet little voice, "Don't worry, Prof. I'm here now and together we will solve this and help thousands of mirrors. I'm with you all the way! I know this is my life's work, too. I'll always be here for you. We're doing it together."

Hearing those wonderfully supportive words was more than the Prof could handle. He first started to sniff a bit; then one or two tears showed up, and finally he was crying like a baby. It felt so good that someone believed him, someone trusted him, and someone very special was going to help out. And, what was so incredible was that Myra seemed to know the truth already, and he didn't have to spend even one minute trying to convince her.

After about fifteen minutes, they were both laughing and their spirits were high again. That's when the door opened, and the Oval family returned home. Myra noticed that the whole family suffered from many distortions, but the one that was most common was that each one had a large oval curve in his or her midsection. Later, the Prof explained that families often get the same distortion because when they look at each other, they appear straight. In fact, when they looked at other mirrors who were straight in that area, the Oval family thought they had a big, reversed-curve distortion.

Even with the big reversed curve that the Oval family observed in the Prof, they seemed to like him anyway. They were quite friendly and asked Myra and the Prof to stay and visit. However, at dinner the mother whispered to Myra that she should be a bit careful listening to the Prof because "though his beliefs are fun to listen to, he is a bit eccentric and it's best you don't take him seriously." At that moment, Myra realized how challenging it must be for the Prof to get the truth out. Already fiercely loyal, Myra wanted to come to his defense right then, but she felt such a lack of knowledge. Her intuition said it was best to keep quiet.

After dinner, the Oval family showed Myra some pictures from the family album. Sure enough, the oval distortion seemed to have been passed down through generations. One exception was a picture of an Uncle George. He was straight in the center, with a few scratches and one small crack. Father Oval said he was one of the black sheep of the family and never did fit in well. Actually, Myra thought Uncle George had a far better reflection than the entire family, yet they thought he was very distorted.

The Prof walked Myra home that evening. It had been a full day, and Myra could hardly think of any questions. Since the subject had been distortions, the Prof decided to describe some of the distortions he saw mirrors create for themselves. Yes, the Prof did say "create." Since the mirrors started out almost perfect, most of the distortions occurred during their growth to full-length mirrors. The distortions included twists, curves, scratches, cracks, a trapped particle under the surface, dirt, and spots in the reflective surface that didn't reflect any light at all.

The Prof even told Myra about a family of rubber-backed mirrors that he knew. They never held a fixed form at all; they just twisted and turned to provide you with a reflection they thought you wanted to see. The rubber-backed mirrors were always asking you questions and making adjustments to please you. Then the Prof laughed. He said, "They're fun to watch at a party with a lot of different mirrors. They're constantly twisting and curving, trying to please. They look like they're doing some kind of strange dance."

Myra waved goodbye from the door and went inside to see her mother, father, sister, and brother in the living room. It was like seeing them for the first time. Their distortions were now quite obvious to her. She could see the big pebble stuck under her father's glass near the reflective surface. It seemed to grow irritated whenever he was angry but wouldn't admit to it. Now she could see signs of the reflective surface disintegrating. Myra knew not to say anything or he would get upset with her.

It saddened Myra to realize that she was powerless to help even her own family overcome distortions. She felt so much love for them all, but especially for her sister Sparkle. Sparkle never made fun of her, and Myra could tell her anything.

That night, Myra glowed with love and excitement as she told Sparkle all that had happened with the Prof.

Later, Myra awoke to the sound of heavy breathing. Then she saw Sparkle doing stretching and flexibility exercises for the first time in her life. Apparently, Sparkle believed Myra and was practicing step number one, to "ALWAYS STAY FLEXIBLE."

Myra jumped up and hugged Sparkle and they danced happily around the room. Then Myra realized that even though she didn't have all the answers, she was able to inspire someone to start practicing one of the truths out of the Prof's cloth-bound journal!

Her first questions of the morning were, "Will it only work on sisters?" and, "Who else could I inspire?"

She stopped her brother in the hall just as he was wiping himself with his sleeve. She handed him a towel, but he continued to use his sleeve anyway. With a quick yank, she got him to come into the room with Sparkle, where they both proceeded to bombard him with the story. At first he was a bit skeptical. Then, the combined love and energy of Myra and Sparkle pushed him over. He was now a believer; yet he wasn't quite sure what he was getting into.

Since each of them knew two or three other mirrors, they decided to separate and see if they could find others to join in. A meeting in the park by the clock tower was planned by all those who were inspired by the story of the Prof and his knowledge of Mirror Village.

The clock struck 1 p.m., and Myra was amazed to see a gathering of over a hundred mirrors in the park. However, when the Prof arrived Myra noticed that instead of taking a leading role, he stood by the clock tower, and signaled for her to come to him.

It was then that she learned what the Prof had been running from, and why he seemed shy around the crowd. He was avoiding the mirror inspectors.

Myra didn't even know such a thing existed. It was a top secret group of mirrors whose job was to find mirrors to recycle. Some "passed through," but the inspectors were paid more for the ones that ended up in recycling. The mirror inspectors were the ones who caused unsuspecting mirrors to disappear and wind up in that horrible building on the way to Mirror Lake.

The mirror inspectors had warned the Prof many times before not to stir up trouble for them. Now, with a crowd of a hundred gathering, the Prof felt his time was limited. He told Myra that she could continue, but she would need to somehow avoid the mirror inspectors.

"I must answer the rest of your questions now," he said. Then he encouraged Myra to enter the clock tower with him as he bolted the heavy door behind them. It was there that Myra learned the rest of the secrets of Mirror Village, and the Prof's cloth-bound journal became hers.

~ ~ ~ ~ ~ ~

Four years later, Myra had attracted a following of more than ten thousand mirrors, and the numbers were growing rapidly.

Now, instead of 99 out of 100 mirrors being recycled, 99 out of 100 passed right through after having a wonderful, joyful time in Mirror Village. The mirror inspectors were pleased because Myra got the pay scale changed so that they were paid more for mirrors that passed right through. The inspectors even started helping mirrors get straight. They were no longer a secret group but were looked upon with high regard in Mirror Village.

Myra had the Prof's cloth-bound journal published and distributed to all mirrors. She insisted that each copy be cloth-bound in honor of the Prof.

Myra realized that the Prof had done all he could while he was there, and it had been perfect for her to show up when she did. He had done all the important groundwork and had gathered a wealth of information about becoming a mirror with a perfect reflection. Yet, even with all that, he lacked two important ingredients that Myra embodied and radiated so brilliantly. These two ingredients, combined with the knowledge in the journal, totally transformed Mirror Village into a Heaven on Earth.

The quotes from the Prof's journal are printed here along with the final two quotes from Myra entitled: "The Missing Ingredients."

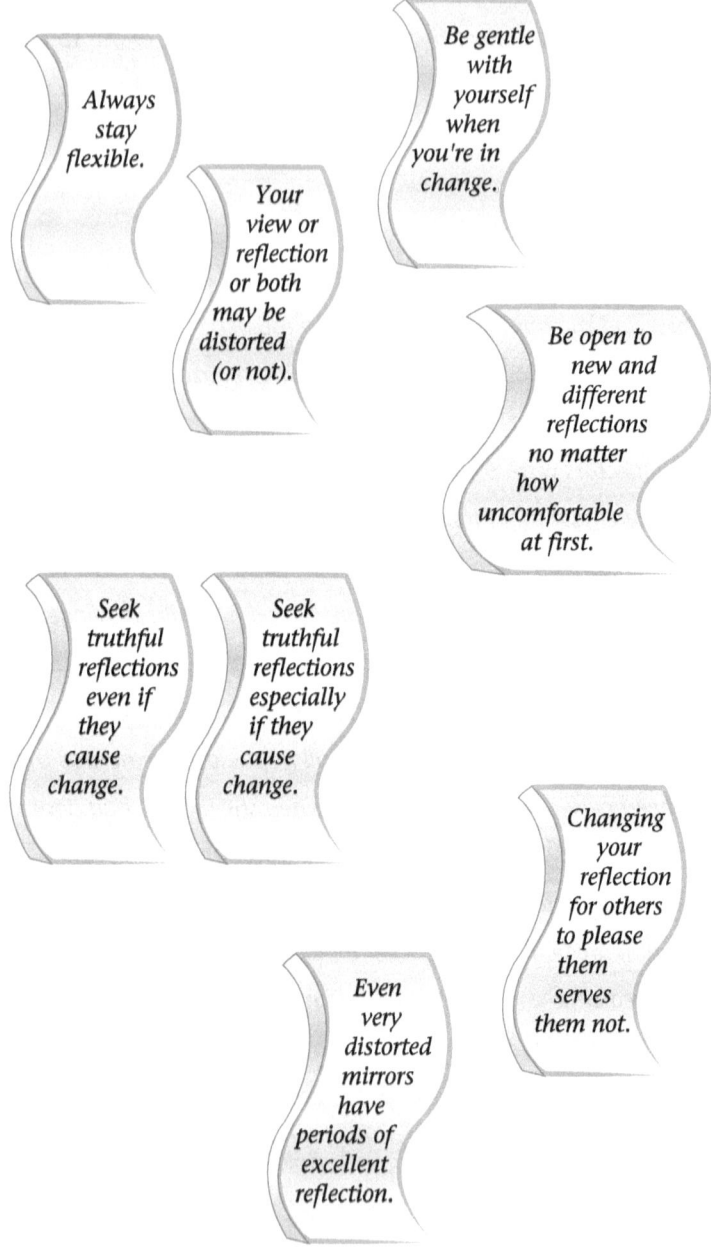

Always stay flexible.

Your view or reflection or both may be distorted (or not).

Be gentle with yourself when you're in change.

Be open to new and different reflections no matter how uncomfortable at first.

Seek truthful reflections even if they cause change.

Seek truthful reflections especially if they cause change.

Changing your reflection for others to please them serves them not.

Even very distorted mirrors have periods of excellent reflection.

No matter how fancy the trim, mirrors are all made of the same basic stuff

All mirrors have distortions, but none know to what extent

A distortion may be in the glass of your own mirror— be not too quick to judge

As you grow new distortions will pop up from stretching in new directions

Seeking to fit in and not stand out leads to wide spread distortions

It's okay to be different and perhaps it's even wise

Argue for your distortions and you get to keep them

Mixing only
with mirrors
who share a
common view
can lead to
many mirrors
with common
distortions

Mix and share
reflections
with many;
fear
not
their view
nor their
reflections

Holding on
to the
tiniest
thing under
your
surface can
lead to a
big crack

Hold on to
nothing
under your
surface—
let it
go

Making
adjustments
based only
on outside
opinion
is
less than
wise

Only
you
have the
final say of
what's right
for you

Chapter 3

"The Missing Ingredients"
Provided by Myra

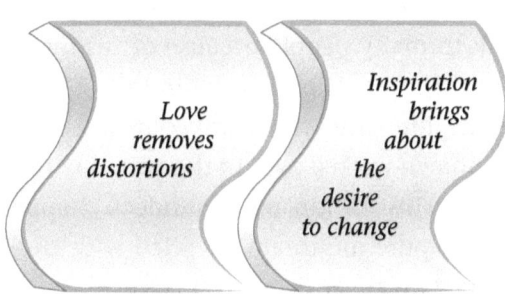

Love removes distortions

Inspiration brings about the desire to change

Epilogue

Myra was often asked if she was sad about the Prof passing through. Her answer was always the same, "Knowing that passing through is a divine blessing into another place of great bliss, I can only be happy for the Prof. Who knows—perhaps we'll hang out with each other again sometime, after I pass through."

• • •

In a human village miles from Mirror Village, Laura Kimberly stood in her beautiful living room, adjusting the flowers picked fresh from her garden. She looked up at the large majestic mirror hanging on the wall and saw something sparkle. "Jim," she called out, "I saw the three twinkling stars again in the mirror. I know I did; it wasn't my imagination!"

Then she said . . .

"You know, it gives me a happy feeling inside."

~ ~ ~ ~ ~ ~ ~

Shawn closed the journal slowly. His eyes seemed out of focus, as though he were replaying scenes in his mind. He felt a special connection to the mirror story, especially reading it aloud, which he often did even when he didn't have a feline friend listening. The Prof reminded him of his Grampa. He seemed to have so much wisdom, yet he didn't talk to many people because of his introverted nature. "He needs a Myra," Shawn mumbled to himself.

The fire in the fireplace was nearly out and was beginning to smoke a little, so Shawn walked over to the pair of windowed, wooden doors opening out to his grandparents' sundeck. Stepping outside, he took a breath of the pure mountain air filled with the fresh scent of pine trees. He looked up at the deep black, clear sky which showed off the Idyllwild stars. They were so bright they seemed unreal. Of course, the first thing he did was to locate the three stars mentioned in the mirror story. Grampa pointed them out one night when Shawn was very young. They were easy to find because of their location in the bright constellation of Orion. In fact, the three stars form the belt of Orion. Shawn had been gazing at those stars for over thirty years. He always had a warm loving feeling whenever he saw what he called *his* three stars.

As Shawn thought over the mirror story, his mind searched for any clues that might help him with his decision. The only connection he could see was that the tobacco companies had been causing mass distortions in people's perceptions for years. They not only promote the idea that smoking is fun and cool but that tobacco is neither damaging nor addictive. He felt frustrated that he was faced with losing his job, career, home, credit rating, financial security, the children's stability in their schools, and the friendship of his boss, Carl. If it comes to a choice, Carl will certainly value his company's future more than Shawn's desire not to spread the tobacco companies' distortions.

Still confused, Shawn put the dilemma out of his mind and recalled when *Mirrors* had been told to his sister. She had been having lots of trouble trying to find her role when she was a teenager. There was one group she wanted to fit into, but they were into lots of parties and drinking. Another group she liked excelled in school activities and were super straight, pre-college achievers. His sister told him she felt like one of those rubber-backed mirrors, always trying to bend to fit in with whatever group she was with at the time. The story had had a big impact on her. She said she discovered she had to find out who she wanted to be, and be that. Then whatever friends she attracted would be attracted to the real her, instead of who she pretended to be. It was so much simpler that way, she'd told Shawn with relief.

Personally, Shawn got a lot from the saying, *Seek truthful reflections even if they cause change.* Before that, he spent most of his time with people who agreed with him and accepted his views. After trying out the Prof's saying, he became much more successful because he was willing to hear other perspectives. That was one of the reasons for his achievements in advertising. Before charging in and implementing an ad campaign, he'd seek out the most adverse comments. He'd even talk to those who hated the product he was advertising. Sometimes he'd modify the entire approach as a result but would end up attracting a much larger buying group.

It was getting late, so Shawn took one more look at the beautiful display of stars and at the trees surrounding the cabin. As he turned to go inside, he didn't notice a transparent ball of glowing, bluish light near the woodshed. It was hovering just like the light on the hood of his car. When he entered the door, the light slowly grew smaller until it disappeared completely.

With a yawn, he closed the doors to the sundeck. When Shawn turned back to look at Trinket sitting on Grampa's chair, he noticed something different in the bookcase behind the chair. He walked over to look more closely at several new books and a folder. The books were about astronomy and the Egyptian pyramids. He pulled out the books and folder and went over to the couch to examine them.

I didn't know Grampa was interested in things like this, he thought. There were yellow stickies marking various pages in the books. In the astronomy books, the marked passages were all about the Orion constellation. In the books about the pyramids, the stickies were attached to photos of the Egyptian pyramids, especially those at Giza.

What do the pyramids have to do with Orion? Why is Grampa so interested in this? Questions kept coming to Shawn as he continued to thumb through the material. Upon opening the folder, he said out loud, "Wow—that's amazing!"

Trinket looked up as though she were being addressed but quickly laid her head back down on her front paws.

Shawn held up two sheets of paper. One had a tracing of the three main pyramids at Giza as seen from directly above—from the air. The other had the three stars from the belt of Orion drawn to scale. It was obvious that the three stars matched the three pyramids exactly. The three pyramids consisted of two large ones in a straight line, with the small, third one slightly off the line. The three stars of Orion consisted of two large stars in a straight line, with the small, third star slightly off the line.

Shawn's eyes got big as he wondered if the builders of the pyramids had placed them in direct alignment with the belt of Orion—his three favorite stars. He also remembered that the three stars kept coming up in the stories, too.

A third page in the folder, contained notes written in this grandfather's handwriting. They said,

"*There is no doubt. The pyramids perfectly match the belt of Orion in size, intensity and relative position. It can't be just a coincidence. Also, the southern shaft of the King's chamber points directly to the belt of Orion. Must pass this information on and ask about it.*"

Shawn had even more questions now. Who was Grampa going to talk to about this information? One of the books was entitled *The Orion Mystery,* and that's how Shawn felt about the apparent connection with Orion, the pyramids, and the stories. He made a mental note to ask his grandfather about all of this as he put the books and the folder back on the bookshelf.

Shawn turned off the lights and went up to his room. His grandmother had left the light on in the guest room, and turned down his bed for him . He felt good about being there. He climbed into bed and noticed that his favorite quilt was on it—a sign of affection from his grandmother. After feeling the flannel sheets against his skin, he turned off the light, drifted gently to sleep.

Shawn always slept well in the mountains. The altitude seemed to make him need a little more sleep the first couple of days, too.

At about 9 a.m., he heard his grandmother shout from downstairs, "Shawn, I've got breakfast cooking . . . better get up now or the food will get cold."

He knew better than to lie around too long after she called. Gramma didn't like to be kept waiting once she got food going. She prided herself on making delicious dishes, and letting them get cold was not something she would tolerate. Shawn usually liked to get out of bed more slowly, but since it was so important to her, he put some hustle into his effort.

It was worth it, too. His grandmother had prepared blueberry pancakes, eggs, bacon, homemade potatoes, coffee, and fresh-squeezed orange juice. The fresh mountain air and the smell of her cooking let Shawn know he was in Heaven.

His grandmother sat down and ate with him, telling him about her new activity in town teaching a group to make quilts. It was good for her because it got her out of the cabin and talking with other folks in the area. Just like Grampa, she avoided the little town during the weekend because that's when the noisy tourists came up, but her class met on Tuesdays and Thursdays.

Shawn was thinking what a simple life hers was, compared to his. He wondered what he would do when he retired. This was something he didn't want to think about, so he starting thinking what he wanted to do on this beautiful Saturday to both enjoy the day and perhaps make some progress on his decision.

He retired to the couch to think about his choices, but instead his thoughts drifted back to the first day he and his family had moved into their dream home. Mary had been so happy . . .

~ ~ ~ ~ ~ ~ ~

"The last box is in, Honey. We're all moved in!", she shouted as she pushed the door shut. Shawn had paused from stacking boxes for a moment to notice what a beautiful woman she was. Though they had been married for eighteen years, her five-foot-five body was almost as slim as when they first met. After two children, she still exercised to stay fit. With her long black hair flying in all directions and no makeup, she looked great to Shawn, radiating sensuality and a feisty energy he loved. Her Hispanic and Italian parents had created a señorita of beauty, with the passion and intensity attributed to those of Italian descent.

For weeks she had demonstrated that passion and energy by rigorously packing for the big move into their dream home. It was everything they had ever wanted, with a few surprises thrown in. They still couldn't get over the fact that it had a lap pool in addition to the regular pool, vacuum sockets in every room and hall (so all the maid would need was a vacuum hose, but no heavy machine), and—what Mary loved most—lush landscaping with lots of trees, grass, and flowers.

Without his first-hand knowledge of accounting, Shawn might never have been open to buying such a lavish home. He had plenty of self-esteem; his ego didn't require material things to pump up his self-image. In fact, if he had his way, he'd be quite happy wearing jeans, western shirts, and boots to work. However, the tax savings gained by writing off the large mortgage-interest payments made it quite advantageous to have an expensive home, and of course he had to dress in very fine suits to impress clients. His company served some very large corporations.

Shawn rushed toward Mary to participate in a celebration hug for getting moved in, but tripped over a pillow. Trying to stop his fall, his hand caught the edge of the moving pad covering the dining room table and pulled all the empty boxes over on top of him.

From behind the box resting on his stomach, Shawn again looked at Mary with the same old sheepish smile that showed off the deep dimple in his right cheek. He always felt so fortunate, that after all these years, she never once put him down or shamed him for his clumsiness. After he met Mary, who treated him the way he liked to be treated, clients were the only critical people he would spend time with, and then only because he felt that was part of the job—kind of an occupational hazard.

Shawn still remembered that first kiss in the new home. He often felt that Mary was like an angel who came just to bless his life. With a big smile, she pushed off the box and straddled his stomach. Their eyes met before their lips, saying without words, "Our dreams of a fabulous life are finally coming true." She moved her legs to lie on top of him, with her face only a couple of inches from his. Beyond being very sensuous, he enjoyed the close feeling of his wife pressed against him by gravity.

They had just touched their lips together when their son Ron came rushing in, yelling, "She did it again! You'd better make her stop!" Ron's dark eyebrows pushed downward, his frown reflecting his displeasure and appealing for sympathy.

Ron was often angry at his sister Julie. That year he was thirteen, going on thirty, and she was ten, wishing she was as old as Ron. He was very intellectual, wore glasses, got straight A's, and was trying on the role of being an adult. All Julie wanted was to be accepted by Ron, though her methods were like pulling on a donkey's tail to get him to go forward. She wanted to be included in his activities with his friends. She pulled devious practical jokes on Ron to get attention and also to rebel, yet he would end up ignoring her even more.

Surprised and a bit embarrassed by being interrupted in such a romantic position, Mary jumped off Shawn, grabbed Ron and Julie by the arms and said, "Stop! Slow down now and tell us what happened."

As she looked at Ron, it was hard for her to keep down a giggle. He had removed his glasses, revealing that his right eye had a thick black circle around it. Mary hid her smile by looking back at Shawn. She could tell he was also doing his best to hold back a laugh.

Ron held up a toy telescope with suggestive markings on the outside. By the words *sexy women* and the outlines of women's figures, you would naturally think that's what you'd see by looking inside.

Ron complained, "You look in this thing and it says 'turn to see sexy women.' When you turn it, it marks a black circle around your eye. See?" Ron pointed to the funny mark around his eye that made him look like Spot the dog.

Julie loudly countered, "Well, if you weren't trying to see something you shouldn't, you wouldn't have a black eye!" Julie laughed her familiar hyena laugh, while nearly falling over a box of towels.

"Okay, you two. There is plenty for you to do. Take your boxes up to your rooms right now!" Mary tried being firm, yet she and Shawn could hardly contain their laughter. Although they didn't approve of some of the more severe jokes Julie pulled, they had to admit, her jokes brought some entertainment to the house. Neither knew how Julie got started with her practical jokes, but both could recite them to friends in great detail—and often did.

After the kids left the room, Shawn chuckled, "Do you remember that night in the cabin, when Julie hid the string under Ron's sheet and then started pulling on it after the lights went out? Wow—I've never seen anyone jump out of bed so fast! Anything that reminds Ron of bugs or spiders just drives him wild. I wonder if he'll survive growing up with his sister?"

Mary said, "Now, Shawn. You're part of the problem. Julie knows you think it's funny, and she's encouraged by you. At least I try and hide my laughter!" Mary looked around the spacious and elegant living room, "I love the Italian marble around the fireplace." Then she became quiet for a moment. "Shawn, do you still think it was wise to spend almost all our savings as a down payment?"

He rubbed her neck. "With the new tax laws, mortgage interest makes one of the best write-offs. In a few years, it will all come back to us."

~ ~ ~ ~ ~ ~ ~

Shawn became aware that he was wasting time, sitting inside his grandparents' cabin, thinking of the past.

One of his favorite things to do was to hike on the trails near Tahquitz Rock. He decided he might as well enjoy himself while he thought over his problem. He borrowed his grandparents' pickup and headed out. His grandmother told him not to be concerned about being out for the day; she didn't need to go anywhere because it was Saturday.

He parked at the foot of the trail leading up the mountain. About fifteen cars were already parked in the lot because it was such a popular spot. Shawn climbed the path for about a mile. The view was so beautiful, he sat down and took a drink of water from the bottle he'd attached to one of his grandfather's hiking belts. He could see the steep slope of Tahquitz Rock and could barely make out tiny images of some rock climbers. Occasionally, he heard distant voices as one person would shout to another. He remembered being brave enough to climb the steep rock surface once, but never again. He'd gotten stuck on one of the ledges, and for a while felt like the eagle in the story *Eagles*.

Shawn had brought the story journal with him. It was sitting on the rock next to him when another hiker walked by and said, "Hi."

"Great day for a hike, isn't it?" the young man asked, looking intently into Shawn's eyes.

Shawn welcomed a chance to visit. After a few minutes of the standard chatter about where each was from and good trails to walk, the fellow noticed the purple journal on the rock and asked about it.

He, too, was carrying a book. "What are *Stories For The Inner Ear?*" he asked.

Since Shawn didn't usually carry the journal around with him, this was a question he wasn't accustomed to answering. As the fellow hiker sat down on a rock, Shawn explained, "Well, my grandfather tells these stories, and, well, they're kind of like children's stories, but they contain incredible truths and discoveries for adults. Actually, I think adults like the stories more than kids, though I haven't read many of them to kids—except my own. The stories have a lot of subtle, hidden meanings and all."

"You mean like the Bible?" the hiker asked as he raised the book he was carrying.

"Is that a Bible?" Shawn asked.

"Yeah, I'm on retreat at the church camp near town, and I thought I'd do my reading on the trail. Got to get exercise, you know." The young man seemed very energetic.

"I guess the stories are kind of like parables in the Bible, now that you mention it. I just never thought of them that way. A couple of the stories even deal with spiritual things." Shawn was hesitant to get into a religious discussion, so he was purposely trying to be vague.

"How about reading me one? By the way, my name is Richard; just call me Rich."

"Hi, Rich," Shawn extended his hand. "I'm Shawn." He noticed that the young man was trying to grow a beard, yet the growth wasn't thick enough. It was like newly seeded grass, coming up very sparsely. Shawn wanted to recommend that he just shave it off but was too polite to ever do something like that. Instead he replied, "Actually, I was going to read them anyway, and I don't mind reading out loud 'cause they seem to have more meaning that way. Since you're interested in God and spiritual things, I could read this short one called *Caveman* . . . Just to give you a bit of background, my grandfather told us this one when the subject came up about which of the many religions was true and which ones have the correct information about how to get to Heaven. Grampa started out by asking a question, 'Could a caveman get to Heaven?'"

Two more hikers approached from behind Rich. Hearing their steps in the quiet forest, Rich turned and said, "Hey, Jack, how ya doing? Hi, Susie."

The couple was awkwardly holding hands as they maneuvered down a trail not wide enough to walk side-by-side. "Rich, what are you doing up here?" Jack responded.

"Thought I'd get exercise and do some reading. Then I bumped into Shawn here, and he was about to read me a story."

"What kind of story?" Susie asked, glancing at Shawn as she reached out to shake Rich's hand.

"Well, it's something about whether or not a caveman could get to Heaven," Rich said. "I guess that means before there were religions, bibles, or even a spoken language. By the way, this is Shawn. Shawn meet Susie and Jack. Jack and I have had some discussions in town, and though we don't always agree, we have some good talks."

Shawn stood and shook their hands and Susie immediately asked, "Hey, can we listen in on your story? It's time for us to take a break, anyway . . . that is, if it's not something private. I love things like this."

Shawn glanced at the two of them. Though Susie was quite interested in hearing the story, Jack seemed more interested in Susie. She had such a beautifully contagious smile, it would be nearly impossible for anyone to not smile back. She looked a bit like what Americans have sterotyped Swedish girls to be: light complexion, long, straight blonde hair, and a pretty face. Jack was a bit more serious-looking, someone who might even be rather low in energy if not around a bubbly person like Susie. Both were wearing shorts and hiking boots. From their rough appearance, it looked like they'd camped out at least one or two nights. Shawn answered, "Pull up a rock and join us. These aren't my stories, though. My grandfather told them, and I just wrote them down."

Rich and Shawn sat down on two small, granite boulders barely three feet high. Jack and Susie dropped their packs near a large bolder and used them to lean against as they sat on a blanket of pine needles.

Jack put his arm around Susie; they looked like they were ready for a campground story.

Shawn thought about how traditional camp stories were about monsters, wolves, or dead people rising from graves. He could never understand why such stories were so popular at camps for little kids—always told just before bed time. No wonder the kids would stay up all night, he thought. Sure, it got their attention, but some of those horror stories were bound to have lasting effects, perhaps even create phobias. He wished they could read his grandfather's stories instead.

Susie directed a question toward Shawn, "So your grandfather tells stories, huh? They must be pretty good, for you to write them down and all."

Shawn explained about the stories and his grandfather. He tried to answer Susie's almost endless stream of questions. They were interrupted by Jack saying, "I thought we got all settled down for a story?"

Shawn was glad for the interruption. Susie would probably have gone on until she had his life's story or until it was nightfall. He picked up Jack's cue. "Like I was explaining to Rich before you two came along, these stories have been told mostly to family and friends. This one usually sparks discussions about religion, so one thing we always have done before telling it is to agree that it is okay to disagree. And, to not expect or demand that others change their beliefs to suit yours. My grandfather says how amazed he is at the many wars fought and deaths caused by people separating into camps of differing beliefs, with everyone believing God was on their side. He always says, 'God's either on everyone's side, or nobody's side, but in any case, those who justify destruction in the name of the Father are as warped as a twenty-year-old wooden shingle.'"

"I think I like your grandfather, Shawn," Susie remarked.

"Well, that makes two of us. Okay, get comfortable and I'll tell you the story *Caveman*. First, let me say that when Grampa tells this story to a group, he divides them up into three groups, corresponding to three strange, frequently-used words in the story. I don't think he liked to say the words since they were supposed to be said with emphasis and drawn out a bit. The words are 'Uhhhggg,' 'Eaaahhh,' and 'Aaaaaahh.' Whenever one of the words was to be said, he just pointed to the appropriate group, and they would say it for him."

Rich laughed. "Audience participation, huh? They sure won't fall asleep that way."

Shawn laughed to himself because he couldn't imagine anyone going to sleep while Grampa told a story. Then he thought of an exception, when one of the more abstract stories, like *Angels*, was told to very young children.

Susie piped in, "Hey, let's do it. Jack, you do the sound 'Uhhhggg,' I'll do 'Eaaahhh,' and Rich you can do 'Aaaaaahhh.' This will be fun!"

Jack and Rich looked up skeptically. Then Jack said with a laugh but also with an undertone of discomfort, "Susie, you're always organizing things." Then, as he looked into her pleading eyes he added, "Oh, why not? Hey, Rich, I guess you're Aaaaaahhh?"

"I'd prefer that over Uhhhggg . . . Uhhhggg!" Rich responded with a laugh.

Shawn, remembering the story, noted that Susie had made good choices by coincidence. Then he said, "I've never done this before, so I hope I do it right. I'll just point to you when you're to say the particular word." He began reading *Caveman* out loud, and instead of saying the strange sounds, he just pointed to one of his three volunteers. Each time he did, everyone laughed. It was a rather unusual way to listen to a story.

CAVEMAN

Uhhhggg was a cave dweller of few words. So was Eaaahhh, his main squeeze. They lived in the caves of a region of lush vegetation and plenty of animals. This was long before civilization as we know it. There were no books, no newspapers, no radios, no clothes, no paper or pencils—nothing.

Imagine finding yourself as though you were dropped on a planet and had to start from scratch. There is no one to tell you what to do, or what not to do. Your language consists of a few sounds that are mostly grunts, groans and a lot of hand gestures. Your main concerns in life as a caveman/woman are how to eat without getting eaten, how to stay warm and not freeze, how to protect your mate for nurturing support and that loving feeling during the long, scary nights.

On one of those scary nights, Uhhhggg was wide awake and laying a bit out of the cave to catch the refreshing breeze coming up from the canyon below. Lying on his back, he could see the stars up above. Though they were quite brilliant and clear, he didn't have the foggiest idea what they were, except that every once in a while one would streak across the sky. Uhhhggg was in awe of it all. On this night he was so in awe, he woke Eaaahhh and brought her out of the cave. He pointed to the sky and made up a new word as he opened his eyes wide and gestured about how large and beautiful the sky was. The word was "Aaaaaahhh." From that day on, "Aaaaaahhh" was known to mean "in awe." In one word, they had found they could express their awe without any hand gestures or anything.

Soon they were using this new word for other things that were awesome to them. Eaaahhh would look at the giant waterfall upstream from their cave and say "Aaaaaahhh." Uhhhggg would look at the power of the tons of falling water and agree by saying "Aaaaaahhh." They would marvel at the wonderful taste of certain fruit and say "Aaaaaahhh." They would see the tremendous power of a thunderstorm with lightning flashes and loud noises and they would say "Aaaaaahhh." They would look into each other's eyes and feel each other's love on a dark scary night. They would cuddle and hold and comfort each other and say "Aaaaaahhh."

Soon the word became to mean much more than just an expression of wonderment, or an expression of amazement—it became a cherished word. A word to describe the indescribable. The word had feeling, power, love, and a richness associated with it that could only be experienced by looking at nature and seeing the thread of commonality in it all. You might say it was one of the first words to describe the infinite, one of the first words to describe that mystical, magical experience of a higher power of infinite knowledge and intelligence, one of the first words to describe God.

One day Uhhhggg was climbing around the rocky cliffs near their cave and his foot slipped. He fell about 18 feet to a ledge below. Although he was not too badly hurt, he did have a problem. The only way off that particular ledge was down the path that led to the sunset. And there, sitting in the middle of the path, was a very hungry lion. Uhhhggg realized immediately, and so did Eaaahhh looking down from above, that the lion had only one thing on his mind—Uhhhggg was about to become a tasty meal for Mr. Lion.

The tension mounted as the lion crept closer to Uhhhggg, slowly and cautiously as if this were too good to be true. Eaaahhh was in a panic. Tears *flowed down her cheeks as she feared for Uhhhggg's life. A life without Uhh-hggg flashed in front of her—alone, scared—and she said NO in her mind. She didn't know what to do, but it was totally unacceptable to her that her mate suffer such a fate.*

Eaaahhh looked up into the sky and screamed the only word she knew that was associated with a miracle—and a miracle is what it would take to save Uhhhggg from an almost certain death. Eaaahhh screamed, "Aaaaaah-hh," and pictured in her mind that Uhhhggg was now safe in her arms and holding her. Because she was afraid to look down anymore, afraid to even imagine what could be happening, she continued to scream "Aaaaaahhh," over and over again. She held her arms as though she were hugging Uhh-hggg to her chest. Her screams of Aaaaaahhh echoed through the canyon below: "Aaaaaahhh! Aaaaaahhh! Aaaaaahhh! Aaaaaahhh!"

Suddenly Eaaahhh felt something touch her shoulder. Uhhhggg was standing next to her, bruised and dirty, but with the biggest smile she'd ever seen on his face .

At that moment, Eaaahhh realized that she knew "Aaaaaahhh." She knew what we call God. She knew that this infinite presence not only ex-isted, but it could respond to her and make things happen—like a signal to her that she was not alone, that somewhere out there, there was an infinite power that she was connected to. A miracle had happened. She felt blessed.

After hugging and tearfully greeting Uhhhggg for many minutes, Eaaahhh looked down on the ledge below to see what had happened. How could Uhhhggg have escaped the lion? The lion was standing where Uhh-hggg had been and was looking up at them.

Uhhhggg pointed to a tree root that was barely visible near the ledge. Neither had ever noticed it, probably because there was never a need for it before. The tree root was just long enough for Uhhhggg to swing from that ledge to the adjacent ledge and then climb up the sloping bank to where

Eaaahhh was screaming, "Aaaaaahhh!"

Eaaahhh made gestures about what she had done. Without having a word for it, Eaaahhh had discovered prayer. And through her first prayer, Eaaahhh knew God firsthand. This knowingness was so profound that it brought great love and bliss to Uhhhggg and Eaaahhh. They prayed each day and felt gratitude for even the smallest of wonders. They created Heaven on Earth.

Early one evening, Eaaahhh and Uhhhggg stood on the cliff near their cave and looked at the spectacular sunset with all the beautiful colors, and they both knew, All is Aaaaaahhh!

~ ~ ~ ~ ~ ~ ~

"Whew, that was great!" Susie said. Her eyes were big and alive with excitement. "They actually discovered God and prayer before there were any religions! It makes you think, doesn't it?"

Jack looked at Rich and said, "That's what we were talking about before, Rich. You're always quoting the Bible, but what about people before the Bible existed; were they doomed? Could a caveman get to Heaven?"

Rich just rubbed his scant beard as he looked out over the treetops to the valley below. Then he said, "Hey, I don't know everything . . . yet. I've only been into this church and this camp for a bit over a year."

"Think of all those people who existed before the Bible and before Jesus," Jack added. "In fact, there are many around the world right now who probably don't know anything about religious teachings." He seemed to be enjoying Rich's apparent confusion.

Susie entered in by saying, "I've always thought of the Bible as a guidebook . . . I mean, I think it helps you find God, but it's not necessary . . . "

Jack interrupted. "Well, some people think it is absolutely necessary and if you don't believe exactly like they do and behave in a certain way, then you are doomed!" He stood up and leaned against the large bolder. "That's why I'm allergic to church. The Bible says so many things, much depends on how you interpret it."

"Like what, Jack?" Susie asked.

"Well, like the phrase 'an eye for an eye.' Many who believe that means the Bible condones taking revenge. Then there's that part that you must believe in Jesus in order to be saved . . . that would mean all those millions of non-Christians are going to Hell."

Rich was quiet and still seemed to be deep in thought. Jack turned to Shawn. "What do you think?"

"There seem to be a lot of different beliefs," he answered. "Some believe that only the Bible has the truth. Some believe that every word in the Bible is to be taken literally. Then there are others, like Susie, who probably feel like it should be used as a guidebook. Like a book about climbing a mountain, it may be helpful but you can still get to the top without it."

Jack wasn't satisfied. "Which way do you believe?" he asked Shawn.

"Personally, I go along with Susie. Yet, I'd go a bit further and say that I think we are all connected to God within. The real secret is communing with God and using your inner, divine voice in guiding the way. The Bible has wonderful insights and knowledge, yet it is obvious from the variety of religions that there are many ways to interpret and translate the messages. Ultimately, unless you give up responsibility for it, you must finally decide what you believe regardless of where you get your information. It's having a direct experience of God that creates knowingness, and that is much more powerful than beliefs."

Susie stood up and said, "You've got it, Shawn. Do you know how to have that direct experience, though?"

"Well, in the caveman story, they had one. I've had it through prayer many times. I've seen things happen that would be far too improbable for them to be just coincidences. Another one of the stories deals with prayer."

Having been quiet all this time, Rich finally spoke. "I'd be interested in hearing that one, if you wouldn't mind. I really would like to have more of a knowingness. I'm feeling a lot of pressure and anxiety with a need to defend my beliefs. I've invested a lot of time in forming them. If I had more pure knowingness, perhaps I'd feel more confident. Perhaps knowingness is the step beyond belief . . . "

"That's a great title for a book," Susie interrupted, *"The Step Beyond Belief."*

Rich laughed. "You know, I bet it would be quite popular. Hey, Shawn, maybe you could write it."

Shawn shook his head and said, "Right now I have my hands full with my career and all. Yet it would be great if people had a guidebook on knowing and experiencing God firsthand. Rich, there are steps to a prayer in the story I mentioned that you might try out."

Everyone sat back down to hear another story. This time, however, Susie wasn't leaning back against her pack. She sat in a more upright, attentive position with her legs crossed. Jack put his hand on her back. It appeared that he would have preferred to cuddle. She asked Shawn, "What's the title of this one?" As she spoke, a hummingbird swooped up right in front of her face and hovered only inches away from her nose. He looked right into Susie's eyes for about two seconds and then zipped away. Susie tilted her head in a cute way and was obviously very happy about seeing the bird up so close.

They all laughed at the hummingbird's prominent appearance. Rich pointed out that some American Indians believe the hummingbird represents joy.

"This is another one of those coincidences," Shawn remarked. "You'll understand when you hear this story called, *Blade of Grass.* Why don't we pass the journal around and take turns reading?"

All agreed, so Shawn passed the journal to Rich and he began reading—*Blade of Grass.*

Blade Of Grass

Once upon a time there was a little blade of grass living in the big forest. This little blade of grass was in an area all by itself. One little blade of grass standing high, blowing in the wind, feeling totally alone.

She was so lonely. She just stood there crying most every day.

One morning the sunshine was particularly bright. A hummingbird flew by, hovered a few feet away, and returned to within a couple of inches of the blade of grass. The hummingbird just hovered there with wings vibrating so fast that the blade of grass could only see a blur surrounding this wonderful creature.

It was the closest and longest view of a hummingbird this blade of grass had ever seen. That would have been surprise enough, but then the hummingbird actually started talking. Well, I don't know if you've ever heard a hummingbird talk, but it is really something special to hear. Each word is melodic and full of vibration as you might imagine. And of course, just like the speed of a hummingbird, the words flow out about three times faster than anything you've ever heard before.

The hummingbird said, "You're the saddest looking blade of grass I've ever seen . . . and I've seen a few in my time. What's your name?"

It took a couple of minutes for the blade of grass to fully comprehend what was said. The words came so fast, they could almost be mistaken for the buzz coming from the fast vibrating wings.

"Well, I don't rightly know," the blade replied, almost amazed to hear her own voice. It had been a long time since she'd had any opportunity to speak. She used to talk to the ants, but the whole colony moved away ages ago.

"Okay," the hummingbird hummed, "then if it's all right with you, I'll call you Joy. Is that fine with you?"

"You just said I was the saddest blade of grass you've ever seen and now you want to call me Joy? I think I should call you Mr. Unpredictable. Actually you have some nerve. Are you trying to make fun of me or something?"

After flying a 360-degree circle around her, the hummingbird said, "No, Joy, not at all. I'm just speaking the truth. Beneath all your tears you are pure joy to behold. Perhaps I can help you let it out. By the way, the name Mr. Unpredictable isn't too far off. My friends call me Randomhumhum. One of my boring friends is called Ohhumhum. Another one of my friends who follows bees to the best flowers is called Beehumhum. Of course, I've nicknamed my girlfriend Honeyhumhum. Oh, and I can't forget to mention my uncle who's into solving mysteries. His name is Dumdeehumhum. And then there is . . . "

"STOP! STOP!" Joy cried out. "Are you purposely trying to drive me crazy? Why don't you just fly off and let me be!"

"I dunno," Randomhumhum replied. "I guess I just haven't done my good deed for the day."

"Well, I can't think of anything that you can do for me, unless you can create miracles."

"Hummmmmmmmm," he hummed as he cleared his throat. "I can do one better than that. I can show you how to create your own miracles. All you need to do is stir up the desire and belief."

With that Randomhumhum flew swiftly through the trees and out of sight.

Joy was terribly confused. All she had were questions. Had she imagined this strange bird? What did he mean, "stir up the desire and belief?" Was he coming back? Could she somehow create a miracle?

Since she didn't have much to lose, Joy decided to give it a try. First I'll work on the desire, she thought. Let's see, what do I really want? Oh, that's easy . . . except it's impossible. I want to be growing alongside hundreds of other blades of grass. I hate being out here all by myself!

Joy tried to think of something else she desired that WAS possible, but she couldn't come up with anything. Nothing else mattered. Then she decided to go with her first desire because, after all, Randomhumhum did promise to show her how to create miracles. "And this would take a miracle," she said out loud.

"Now how do I stir up the belief?" she mumbled. "I can't imagine how it could even be remotely possible. I can't move because my roots are firmly attached in the ground, and there is no time to plant grass around me for I will have gone to seed by then."

The next morning, Randomhumhum came back to find Joy crying again. When he asked what was the matter, she replied, "I feel worse than before. I know what I want, but it is totally impossible."

"Knowing what you want means you are more than halfway there. What do you want?" As Randomhumhum spoke, he seemed to have so much energy he couldn't stay in one spot. He kept darting from one side to another. If Joy hadn't been so sad, she would have almost found it amusing.

Tears flowed down her single leaf as she blurted out, "I want to be growing next to hundreds of other blades of grass. I want to feel them brush up against me as the wind blows. I want to see a sea of green in every direction. I want to be able to talk to others who are just like me . . . but that's impossible and I'm so sad!"

"Why do you think that is impossible?" Randomhumhum asked.

"I can't move because my roots are firmly attached in the ground, and there is no time to plant grass around me for I will have gone to seed by then. Besides, have you ever seen a blade of grass change locations before?"

"Well, I can't say as I have, but that doesn't mean anything. I haven't seen a lot of things, yet I still know they happen." Just after saying that, Randomhumhum flew straight up, stopped, and looked at something. After hovering for about a minute he made a loop around the big tree that was only a few feet away and returned back within an inch of Joy's face.

As Joy just watched, he said, "Yep, I have an example. Remember yesterday how Sally, the big black spider up in those vines, was spinning her little web on one side of the path through the trees?"

"Yes, I saw her," Joy answered.

"Well, she has done the impossible. Her web now stretches ten feet across the path and it is beautifully woven. In fact, I have to be careful not to fly into it myself. Boy, that stuff is sticky on my wings."

Joy was rather in awe about this. How did Sally Spider connect one end of the web to the other side? She couldn't fly.

"I must admit, that does look like she accomplished the impossible." As Joy said this, she still was not convinced that the impossible was possible.

"Well, isn't it possible that the impossible merely APPEARS impossible due to your own non-belief, which is formed by your limited view of things?"

Joy realized that Randomhumhum wasn't a dumdum. She hadn't the foggiest idea what all that meant, yet she knew he was on to something.

Noticing Joy's confusion, Randomhumhum went on to say, "It's like, maybe it's impossible only because you think it's impossible. See that giant tree I just flew around? Well, it came from an acorn that was once only one-eighth of your height. Seems pretty impossible, huh? If you remember that rain we had about three weeks ago, you might think it is impossible that those drops of water running down your blade came from the ocean more than 100 miles away. And, they were lifted from the ocean by some invisible force and brought to you by another invisible force called wind."

Randomhumhum went on to tell Joy of other seemingly impossible things that occurred all around her every day and finally she conceded that perhaps she didn't really know what was possible and what was not.

With that, Randomhumhum shouted, "Then that means, ANYTHING IS POSSIBLE, right?"

Joy shook the topnotch of her blade 'yes' and surrendered to this very persistent and energetic bird.

"I have but one more thing to tell you before I leave you tonight, and tomorrow we'll learn how to create miracles. I once knew this group of 22 fleas that was captured and put into a jar with a lid on top. The jar was sitting on the front porch of the house down by the creek. I could observe the fleas quite easily. Oh, those fleas wanted to get out of the jar so badly! They would jump as high as they could, but they would only bump the hard metal lid of the jar and come crashing down. After about a day of this, I noticed no more sounds of their little bodies hitting the lid. They started jumping lower so that they wouldn't bang against it anymore. Well, the next day I noticed that the lid had been removed. I was so happy because now the fleas could escape. But you know what? They continued to jump only as high as before. They believed the lid was still there. And for them, I guess the lid was still there."

"Well, what happened?" Joy asked.

"Well, when I poked my beak inside to say hi, they looked up with foolish smiles and realized they were actually free to go but just didn't know it. They all jumped out on the very next leap!

"Think about it, and tomorrow if you believe you can have what you want . . . well, who knows what might happen." Randomhumhum barely got the words out and he disappeared through the forest so fast that Joy didn't get to say a word.

Joy's thoughts were flying around as fast as Randomhumhum. They even seemed random. First she would be excited with the thought of having her dream come true. Then she would get depressed in thinking it was impossible. However, each time the thoughts came up about it being impossible, she would purposely think of all the things that looked impossible but happened anyway.

In fact, Carlotta the butterfly fluttered by today, Joy remembered. My, she was happy. It was only a couple of weeks ago that she was fat, hairy and crawled around on the ground as a caterpillar. The fact that she became a beautiful, slim, flying, colorful work of art seemed quite impossible before it happened.

It was finally dawn. Through the night, Joy had thought of many examples of things appearing impossible that weren't. Joy was now convinced. "It IS possible for me to be growing next to hundreds of other blades of grass! I will feel them brush up against me as the wind blows. I will see a sea of green in every direction. I will talk to others who are just like me!"

She had now accomplished the goal of obtaining both desire and belief. "But now, where is that speedy little bird?"

Actually, Randomhumhum usually came later in the day, but today, thank goodness, he came so early in the morning that the dew hadn't even evaporated from the leaves on the tree or Joy's back.

Joy danced back and forth as she exclaimed to Randomhumhum about all that had happened last night.

"It sounds like you're ready to create miracles," Randomhumhum said, but quickly added, "except that YOU really don't do it."

Now Joy was confused. She thought to herself, First he says he's going *to teach me how to create miracles, then he says I'm not going to do it!*

As though he read her mind, Randomhumhum said, "You see, it's like when you are wet, shake yourself, and a drop of water falls to the ground. You may have been the reason the drop left your leaf, but you didn't make it fall to the ground—some invisible force made it travel to the ground. Some call this force gravity. A name helps, but the force is still invisible and still quite mysterious, if you think about it."

"What does this have to do with my situation?" she asked.

"I will show you how to put things in motion now that you have the desire and belief, but I have no idea of how it will come about. However, you put it into motion with five simple steps—once you have the desire and belief, that is. Are you ready?" he asked.

By now Joy was more than ready. She shouted, "Yes!" At this point, Joy didn't even care about the confusing fact that Randomhumhum didn't know how her miracle would come about; she just wanted it done.

Randomhumhum told Joy he was going to demonstrate the steps in such a way that she would never forget them. He proceeded to fly around everywhere. He zipped, darted, and flew in and around the bushes, through the trees, straight up into the sky, and he even dive-bombed into the creek. Upon returning he said, "The first step is to know that there is a divine, invisible Force everywhere, even inside of the ground in which your roots are so firmly planted. So please say that you know this."

Joy said, "There is a divine, invisible Force everywhere, in the ground, in the trees, and even throughout the fibers of my body." Joy was proud of herself. She had even gotten a little creative on her own.

Then Randomhumhum hovered right up next to her and pointed at two droplets of water on her leaf. Just as he pointed, one of the droplets slowly ran down and bumped into the other. The instant they touched, they became one droplet.

Randomhumhum said, "The second step is to know you are one with this wonderful, infinite, invisible, divine Force that is everywhere present. So please say this, too."

Joy thought to herself, Is this bird trying to teach me how to pray? Oh well, why not give it a try? I think I'll even surprise him by mentioning the name of this divine Force.

Joy said, "I know that I am one with this wonderful, infinite, invisible, divine Force I call God."

"Ah, so you've heard of prayers before," Randomhumhum said with excitement. He followed up by saying, "Please keep an open mind to these five steps even though you've tried other kinds of prayers before. I've been all around the countryside, and this really works.

"The third step is to picture in your mind and say clearly what it is that you want as though it's already there. You may even experience what it feels like. Please say this, too," he asked her. Then Randomhumhum flew close to the ground at grass level and at incredible speeds.

Joy found that by not focusing her eyes too well, she could almost picture a field of grass growing in the blurred path that he flew. So she said, "I can see myself growing next to hundreds of other blades of grass. I feel them brush up against me as the wind blows. I see a sea of green in every direction. I feel ecstatic with joy. I am talking to others who are just like me!"

"How else does that make you feel?" Randomhumhum asked. He appeared to be bowing his head with his feet pressed together.

"Thankful?" she ventured.

He congratulated her and said, "That's the fourth step! Expressing your thanks and gratitude, knowing that what you have pictured has already happened, is the next to the last step, and you figured it out. Please say words of thanks."

"Oh, I am so thankful for this. I feel wonderful and I have so much gratitude."

Then Randomhumhum started speeding up the vibration of his wings while hovering in the same spot. Joy thought the vibration was going to shake her leaf out of the ground. Then without saying a word, he shot straight up into the sky. He got smaller and smaller. Pretty soon he completely disappeared.

A couple of minutes went by and he reappeared out of nowhere. He had flown up from behind Joy, just a tiny bit above the ground.

He asked if she could guess the final step.

She answered, "Disappear?"

"Almost. The last step is to let it all go, for you've set it into motion just like when you shook a drop of water from you. Now it is up to the invisible Force to make it so. After this step, you stop worrying about it; you just watch or find ways to see it happen. Please say the final step."

"Okay, I hereby release this to the divine, invisible Force to make it so, and so it is." As she said this, a peace came upon her and she felt so relaxed.

She also felt very grateful for her new friend, Randomhumhum, and told him that she truly appreciated all that he had done, even if nothing ever came of it.

This did not completely please him, as she expected, because he said to her, "Let's not cast a lot of doubt on what we've set into motion. Somehow it is going to work out for the best. And thank you for your kind words."

The next day, Joy was wondering how this wonderful miracle could possibly come about. Like a lightning bolt it struck her. She had a possible answer to 'how.'

She asked Randomhumhum if he could get some of his friends together, and she told him her plan. He said it would take a while and they would have to wait until about three hours after the next rain, but it just might work.

Amazingly enough, the very next day it rained even though there hadn't been any rain for about three weeks. And, just like clockwork, three hours after the rain stopped there was a terrific buzz, unmatched by any sound Joy had ever heard. All around Joy were 33 of the most beautiful hummingbirds she had ever seen. There was Ohhumhum yawning, and Beehumhum, Honeyhumhum, Dumdeehumhum, Yesbuthumhum, Funhumhum, and many more.

After being introduced to each and every one, Joy described the plan that had come to her out of nowhere. How she thought of it, only Heaven knew.

Joy then said, "Ready, set . . . go!" The hummingbirds all left in formation and flew around to the other side of the giant tree in the middle of the clearing.

In a few minutes they returned. Some had little pieces of mud on their beaks. Dumdeehumhum even had a chunk of dirt near the top of his beak that looked like a mustache. When they all giggled, he quickly shook it off.

Then the hummingbirds formed a circle around Joy, and they lowered their hovering circle until they were almost touching the ground. Their beaks started poking away at the moist but firm soil around Joy, until they etched a beautiful circle in the ground. It was good that the soil had a fair amount of clay because their next amazing feat depended upon that.

They all simultaneously dug their beaks into the etched circle in the ground and started lifting. As they lifted, the sound of their vibrating wings became so intense that Joy felt a wave of fear shiver through her blade. She just said to herself, Everything's fine, just fine.

The powerful fleet of 33 hummingbirds lifted the little plot of soil right out of the ground. It was deep enough to include all of Joy's roots.

Bit by bit they lifted. Now they had lifted Joy and her chunk of soil about 12 inches into the air. On a signal from Randomhumhum, they all started moving toward the tree.

When they reached the tree, they made a sweeping curve. Just as they rounded the other side, Joy started to cry with tears of pure joy. She saw where they were taking her.

It was a wonderfully carved hole, the same exact size as the little plot of ground they were carrying. Gently, they lowered her and the soil into the hole made to the perfect depth. Once down, they patted the surface a little, and Joy realized that her dream had come true.

Oh, she was so happy! The hummingbirds started flying in a circle around her, but now they had to fly above her head level a bit. That was because all around her were other blades of grass—hundreds of them. They were brushing up against her as the wind blew, and all she could see was a sea of green in every direction.

She invited all of the hummingbirds to come and visit often, as they flew off in all different directions.

Randomhumhum did a couple of extra passes near her, and he could feel her heartfelt thanks as a tear of pure joy rolled down Joy's blade of grass.

~ ~ ~ ~ ~ ~ ~

The story ended with Jack reading the final paragraph. Rich and Susie applauded the ending, while Shawn was impressed by how much attention and interest they had in the story.

"Shawn, I really liked that story," Susie said, "I mean really, really liked it! Isn't it odd how that hummingbird appeared just before this story about hummingbirds? Quite a coincidence, huh?"

"If we get a chance to read *Angels*, you may get an interesting perspective about coincidences," he replied.

"I'd really love to hear that story too. You know how this story had an unusual way of demonstrating how to pray? I mean, there were five steps described, but I've never been taught anything like that. How did your grandfather come up with that, and does it work? Does it really help in the knowingness area?"

Shawn had been using this five-step method of prayer most of his life. Since he hardly ever talked about religion outside his own family, he wasn't sure how many other people knew about this method of prayer. He told them he didn't want to pretend to know a lot about religious things, but if they were interested he would tell them what he had experienced with this five-step prayer.

"Many of my family members have experienced miraculous things from using this method of prayer. I have, too, and have been doing it for years. Sometimes I just go to sleep doing the first two steps. My grandmother actually showed it to us. She didn't believe any particular religion had all the answers; she just looked for the thread of truth that seemed to be common to many." Shawn looked at Susie, Jack, and Rich to see if he was going into too much detail. All of them seemed to be focused on him, so he continued.

"Grampa told me one time, while he was whittling out a little horse from a piece of wood, that desire and belief were important to lay a groundwork for a good prayer. Then Gramma added, 'If you do the five steps, asking that it be done for the highest good of all concerned, oftentimes it comes about. If it doesn't, it may be that a bigger plan was in store or it wasn't for everyone's highest good.' She then said that people should give up worrying about what if it doesn't come true. That can just put more doubt into the picture, dissolve your belief, and cancel out your prayer." As he said these things, he realized how odd this would sound to Mary, or anyone else that knows him for that matter. Just imagine, here's your husband up in the mountains teaching prayer to three strangers, he thought.

To Shawn's surprise, he suddenly realized that he hadn't done any prayer work for his own challenging situation yet. He used to pray daily for things, yet everything had been working so well, he'd gotten out of the habit. He made a mental note to himself to remember to pray tonight before going to sleep. Immediately, he felt some hope for his situation, for he had many times experienced prayers coming true in his life.

"I don't know," Jack said cautiously, with a glance at Susie. "To tell you the truth, I've had my doubts about whether there is a God or not. I mean, don't get me wrong, I'd like to believe it, but when I see and hear about so many people suffering and having horrible things happen to them, how could a God let that happen?"

Susie looked at Jack as if she either didn't understand him, or couldn't imagine him saying that. She started to say something, but Rich immediately responded by commenting, "That's something I've thought about a lot and have been reading about myself. I have my own theory, if you want to hear it."

"Yeah, go ahead, Rich," Jack said.

"God gave us free will with no strings attached. We are not puppets controlled by some figure in the sky. If we were all controlled by God, perhaps it could be a perfect world, but then again you wouldn't have the freedom to think, act, or react according to what you've learned. In fact, you probably wouldn't learn at all if you weren't allowed to make mistakes. And maybe life is about learning. Without free will, that wouldn't be possible." Rich paused, as if a little concerned that he might be getting on his soap box again—something he'd apparently overdone with friends in the past.

"Wow, that's perfect, Rich," Susie said. "What an excellent way to describe it! I think I've learned more today than in the last year. What you said makes a lot of sense. What do you think, Jack?"

"Well, I don't know. I still can't see why a God wouldn't just let good things happen and delete the bad stuff."

Susie sat up straight. "Jack, really . . . then we wouldn't have free will; you know, we would all have to be controlled like puppets . . . don't you see? It all makes sense when you look at it like this. It's not an uncaring God, but one that respects our free will."

"Well, why do people pray, then? Why don't they just be satisfied with what comes naturally?" Jack was starting to be just a bit snappy in his attitude.

Shawn decided to add something, since everyone seemed to be in on the discussion. "The way I see it is that prayer is another creative tool we've been given. Just as we work to get something we want, we've also been given prayer to help bring it about, if it doesn't jeopardize someone else's free will, go against Divine Will, or perhaps let you avoid some lesson that was important for you to learn in life. I've seen the five-step prayer come true with things so unusual, it couldn't have been a mere coincidence. Prayer actually helped me confirm my faith in a higher power."

"Hey Shawn, that's pretty good. I can tell you've been doing a bit of thinking about this subject, too," Susie said.

Jack started tossing some rocks. It appeared he was no longer interested in the discussion.

Shawn decided to add a bit more. "Grampa told me once that love of all things was the key to Heaven on Earth. Connecting with what you said, Rich, having free will but acting out of love for all people would make things a whole lot better in this world. Perhaps if we all did that, we could end starvation, suffering, and pain on the planet."

Susie got up and stretched her youthful body. Jack immediately stopped tossing rocks. His attention was back on Susie. Though he may not agree with her mind, he did seem to like her body.

She looked at Shawn and said, "You know, a bunch of us locals get together every Saturday night to share poetry, music, or writing. Would you come tonight and share some other stories? Please say yes, okay? Jack, wouldn't that be great?" Susie looked at him to see if he was in agreement. He nodded his head yes, but wasn't as enthusiastic as Susie. Actually, not too many people could match her in that department.

Shawn's eyes went up, as though he were looking to see if there was any reason he shouldn't go . . . Hmmm, he thought, Gramma goes to bed early and there is no TV, and I really don't have any plans other than to read the stories anyway . . .

"What time do you meet?" Shawn asked.

"We start gathering around 7:30, and tonight you could start your stories at 8:00. Since you're from out of town, I'm sure everyone would just love to give you most of the evening—especially if the rest of the stories are anything like what I've heard."

"Each seems to be like a unique flower, with different colors, fragrance, and beauty," Shawn said. "I love them all and never seem to get tired of re-reading them. However, everyone seems to have different favorites. How many people come to these Saturday gatherings?"

Rich piped in, "Yeah, do you think you can fit two more? I'd sure like to come with my friend Carol, if that's all right."

"About fifteen come. We meet in different homes," Susie explained. "Tonight it's at my house. Because of Shawn, there might be more who show up. There's plenty of room though, so please bring Carol along."

Shawn's eyebrows went up. Susie noticed it out of the corner of her eye, but continued without mentioning it. She said with a bit of a laugh, "We've been doing it so long, most of us have heard all of each other's poems and songs anyway. Especially Rhoda and her long poem about mermaids, huh, Jack?"

Jack laughed. Apparently it was an inside joke. "If I hear that poem one more time, I'll just walk out in the middle!" he agreed.

"No, Jack . . . you wouldn't do that to sweet Rhoda, now would you?" Susie tugged at Jack's sleeve and gave him a mischievous smile.

Rich and Jack talked to each other while Susie gave Shawn directions to her house. He confided in her that he was reading the stories for insight into a very difficult decision he had to make, and to please understand if he only stayed for a while. She said that would be fine, yet she was sure he'd enjoy it so much that he'd stay until it was all over.

Shawn sensed that Susie perceived that he was making an excuse to leave if his introverted nature kicked in around all those people. He was beginning to notice that she wasn't an average person: she was keenly perceptive. After saying goodbye to everyone with firm handshakes, he decided to walk up the trail a little more, but he heard

Susie call out as she ran up to him.

"Shawn," she said with a warm smile, "thank you again . . . this has been really special. Can I give you a hug to especially thank you?"

Shawn opened his arms and was grateful to receive Susie's appreciation. It was exactly what he needed right then, and it really picked up his spirits. He felt her gratitude and enthusiasm about the stories.

"Oh, by the way," Susie added, "just to let you know . . . this group of people is a little different from most. We've all known each other for years up here in this mountain community . . . we've laughed, cried, and shared deaths as a group. People speak their minds and their hearts. They're quite open to their feelings, too. It's almost like we've all been in group therapy together."

"Why are you telling me this?"

"Well, we've had outside speakers before, and sometimes they are amazed at how much personal detail some people share about their lives. Just consider we're all family, all right?"

"Actually, that sounds better to me . . . you see, I've got this fear about speaking to groups of people. Maybe if I think of them as family . . . "

"I wondered if you might have a bit of fear about that. Don't worry. You'll feel right at home. Trust me."

"It's that . . . oh, never mind. I'll see you tonight." He decided not to tell her that his fear was compounded by being afraid his clumsiness would act up from all the excitement of being in front of lot of people.

They said goodbye again, and Shawn continued up the hill with an added zest in his step. Most of his exercise time had been confined to sitting on a rock talking, so he was now eager to move a little. Susie rejoined Jack and Rich, waved back at him, and the three of them started off down the hill.

Shawn's heart filled with love for his grandfather. Not only had his stories blessed Shawn's life, but now they were touching others, too. Shawn realized he enjoyed telling the stories almost more than anything else he'd ever done. *Too bad I can't earn a living telling stories,* he thought to himself.

Then he remembered about forgetting to pray for a solution to his problem. *How crazy!* he thought. *I've used prayer all my life with lots of success and here comes one of the greatest crises of my life and I forget to pray for a solution! Sometimes, Shawn, I don't know about you.*

He saw a squirrel climb up a tree, and he remembered Myra the mirror and how she liked to reflect the light like a spotlight on the squirrels. Feeling a bit mischievous, Shawn took out his camping compass, which had a snap-on mirror attached. Finding the sun, he directed the reflection on the squirrel and gave out a little laugh.

Except for not being a female, and of course, not a mirror either, Shawn identified with Myra and her curiosity. He, too, had as much admiration for Grampa as Myra had for the Prof. Then he wondered if Grampa thought of himself as the Prof in real life, with solutions for a lot of human mirrors.

A light sparkled from a small rock, and Shawn picked it up. The rock had a white-ish cast with little veins that looked like gold. He knew it was fool's gold, but that didn't stop it from being pretty. He decided to make this a prayer stone for the weekend. Any time he prayed for a solution to his problem, he would hold this stone in his right hand. It would act as a reminder of his intense energy wanting a solution. Shawn had done a similar thing with a stone when praying for his mother's recovery from a stroke. It worked, and he still kept the stone as a reminder that God answered those prayers.

Shawn could see a long distance up and down the trail. No one was around. It was getting late in the day and he knew he had pretty good privacy, so he could do something he felt was very powerful— pray so loud, the top of the pine trees could hear it.

When he had prayed for his mother, he went beyond the top of the pine trees; he shouted so loud, the clouds could hear him! He shouted, "Mom is 95 percent recovered!" and that's exactly what came about after months of rehabilitation. People used to ask him why he only asked for 95 percent and he would just say, "That's how much I could believe."

Holding the new stone in his right hand, Shawn looked up at the treetops and said his five-step prayer loudly. He said, "God's presence is everywhere. In the trees, the sky, the wind, the rocks. God is infinite and everywhere. God is around me, in me, throughout my body, and I am completely one with this divine infinite Force." Touching the stone to his temple, Shawn continued, "I accept for the highest good of all concerned, including Carl, his family, and myself and family, that I can live my highest dream and fulfill my highest purpose and that we are all healthy, loving, joyful, and prosperous. I accept a wonderful solution to the existing challenge so that everyone's highest good is served, that these things come about as smoothly and gently as possible, and that I am expressing my divine self as fully and as completely as possible; whatever lessons I am to receive are clear and easy for me to understand quickly. I can see and feel this to be true, and I am thankful for the results that are now beginning to show up in my life. And I release this to God, and so I let it be. Amen."

"That was mighty interestin'," said a voice from behind Shawn. It sounded like it came from the trees slightly uphill from him off the path. Shawn looked back and saw a man about the age of Grampa, sitting on a log whittling. Shawn was surprised, because he hadn't seen him sitting there before. He was also a little embarrassed, because he wasn't used to praying when anyone could hear him.

"I didn't know you were there," Shawn replied.

"Oh, make no mind o' me. You wouldn' believe what this ol' man has seen near this here trail. From kids chasin' squirrels to younguns makin' whoopee. Exceptin, I've never seen no flashin' mirrors on squirrels before. Wuz a bit strange if you don't mind me sayin' so. What wuz that fer?"

The old man was wearing a black shirt with the sleeves partly rolled up. He stood up slowly and walked toward Shawn.

"Oh, I was just messing around," Shawn said as he walked closer to the old man. "Say, you whittle just like my Grampa."

"Yer Gramps live in that two-story near Walker's fork?" the man asked.

"Yes, that's it. There are no other cabins for miles around." Then Shawn realized this old man might start telling everyone that Grampa has an offspring who does strange things in the forest.

"Naw, I wouldn' do that. 'Sides, you're not as strange as yer Grampa, anyway."

Chills ran up and down Shawn's back. The old man seemed to have read his thoughts. "How did you know what I was thinking?"

"Well, ya know that story, Mountain out of Ant Hills yer Grampa tells sometimes?"

Shawn nodded in amazement.

"Wal, sometimes I think I'm a some'at like the main character, if ya know what I mean. Actually thar's a 'nother story that even closer fits me."

"Do you try to stay away from people like the main character does?" Shawn asked, forgetting to ask how this old man knew his grandfather's stories.

"Yup, sure do. Sometimes I meet up with yer Gramps along a trail, though. Right nice fellow. Good thoughts. You, too, as a matter a' fact. Boy, ya should hear some of the things I hear—or maybe ya shouldn't! People can get mighty rank! By the way, my name's Jake if ya see your Gramps." With a double wink Jake continued, "And my name's still Jake if ya don't see him."

The old man laughed. He seemed to get a kick out of his own joke. Because he seemed to enjoy himself so much, Shawn felt a little more light hearted, too. He was amazed that his grandfather had shared stories with this old man in the forest. "Have you heard many of Grampa's stories?"

"Yup. I know them all. I gotta go, but I got one last thing to say. Tell yer Gramps I said to tell ya! He'll know what I mean. No more questions; I'm gone. Nice meetin' ya. Things'll work out for the best, you'll see; they do that, ya know?"

For an old man he sure could walk fast. Jake was up the trail and out of sight before Shawn could quit shaking his head in confusion. That was one of the strangest encounters he had ever had. Certainly when he re-reads *Mountains Out Of Ant Hills,* he'll now think of Jake. Shawn wondered what he meant by, "Tell yer Gramps I said to tell ya."

"Tell me what?" he wondered out loud. "Is Grampa keeping something from me? Did the old man mean for Grampa to tell me a special story?" Now, more than ever, he couldn't wait for his grandfather to return on Sunday.

Shawn started back down the hill with his mind swimming in questions. Now he knew what Myra must have felt like.

After the rather short hike down and uneventful drive home, Shawn pulled into his grandparents' driveway. The deep gravel crunched as the pickup rolled up near the front door.

"Gramma, I'm home," Shawn sang out as he bounced energetically in the front door. He felt refreshed from his hike even though some of his experiences were a bit confusing.

"Oh, Honey, I'm so happy you're here. I hate to put you to work, but would you mind cutting a little firewood for tonight before it gets dark? Maybe there's some already cut near the shed. Could you do that, Darling?"

He loved the way his grandmother asked for things. She was so sweet. How could he possibly refuse?

Shawn got excited when he remembered about telling stories on the trail. Hurrying to tell her, he followed his grandmother into the kitchen. Only about three words got out before he tripped. On the fall down, he instinctively reached out to try and stop his descent and caught part of Gramma's skirt. Good thing for her, she was wearing a slip, because the skirt ended up on the floor about the time Shawn did!

"Oh, Honey, if you didn't like this skirt you could just tell me so," Gramma chuckled as she pulled her skirt back up. She'd learned long ago that the best way to cope with Shawn's peculiar, accident-prone behavior was just to laugh it off. She knew it made him feel more comfortable and less embarrassed.

Shawn, still lying on the floor burst out laughing. "What a great sense of humor you have, Gramma! Thanks for being so understanding. You and Mary have a lot in common. I guess I'll always have this clumsy habit of mine. Wait until Mary hears about this one. Oh no, she'd better not. She'll be telling the Sanders I go around pulling my Gramma's skirt off! First she'll have to promise not to say anything outside the family."

He got up, brushed off, and went outside to get the wood. With all the distractions, he'd forgotten to tell his grandmother about his experiences on the trail, telling stories and meeting Jake.

The sun wasn't quite down yet, but the cabin was already in dark shadows. He gathered more than enough wood and placed it in the wood bin on the sundeck. Then he stacked wood in the fireplace, ready to light. The early fall, late summer combination was Shawn's favorite because he loved the summer daytime weather, and the evening chill was just enough for fireplaces. The southern California mountains provided the perfect nip in the air after sundown.

"I fixed you a cup of peach tea with a pinch of cinnamon," Gramma called out. "It won't be long before supper. Why don't you join me in the kitchen?"

"Sounds great," Shawn agreed. As he washed his hands at the kitchen sink and sat down at the tiny table just big enough for two, he looked at the antique phone on the wall. He remarked as he sipped his tea, "We sure have come a long way since those old phones, haven't we? Have you seen the new ones that you just stick in your ear and wear? They're not on the market yet, but I've seen them on TV."

Gramma turned from her cooking and said, "No, don't tell me. You stick the whole phone in your ear?"

"Yeah. It's the size of a hearing aid. It dials by hearing your voice, and you just tap it to answer when it rings." Shawn was proud of how well he kept up with technology.

"What's next, an answering machine in the other ear and a toaster in your pocket?" Gramma laughed.

He didn't want to spoil her fun by telling her that the phone companies offer voice mail now, so virtually half of what she said was already available.

"Oh, I forgot, Gramma. I told some stories on the hiking path, and these young people really enjoyed them. They invited me over to tell some more tonight. You don't think Grampa minds if I share the stories outside the family, do you?"

"No," she said. "He just ain't much on speaking to strangers, else he would probably do the same thing. You get him near people he knows well and you'd swear he's an extrovert, but he's not, of course. They liked the stories, huh?"

He could see his grandmother was very pleased that others enjoyed hearing the stories. He guessed she was very proud of Grampa. Shawn sure was.

Dinner was great as always. He wished Mary would learn some of his Gramma's recipes, but then again, their cooking styles were very different. Mary's food was pretty spicy, while Gramma's was just tasty home cookin'.

They had time for conversation by the fire until a little after 7 p.m. Shawn asked to borrow the truck and said he might be out kind of late. Gramma told him to not get too excited on the way over there; they liked their pickup the way it was. She laughed, but he remembered the old saying that went something like: 'More truth is said in jest than one would think.'

As he drove the old pickup, he thought about his new car crumpled in the canyon. Before letting it get to him, he forced those thoughts out by trying to spot animals. He remembered his dad taught him how to get a rabbit to stop running . . . just a whistle will do it. The trouble was he never learned how to whistle very loud.

When he arrived, Susie met Shawn at the door. Her voice showed her excitement by going higher in pitch as she yelled, "Oh, you came, you came! I knew you would. I've been telling everyone, and we've got about 35 people inside . . . isn't that great?"

Shawn's eyes opened wider, and he took a deep breath. He watched Susie as she bounced enthusiastically in front of him. The words *35 people* kept ringing in his ears. All of a sudden he felt like he'd eaten too much, or like butterflies were flapping in his stomach. He thought, What did I get myself into? I'm not a public speaker . . .

Before he could say anything, Susie grabbed his arm and pulled him inside. Somehow she managed to introduce him to each and every person. She even managed to continue an ongoing conversation with Shawn between each introduction. Talk about being extroverted; Susie could give lessons on the subject!

Shawn started loosening up. Actually, introducing him was the best thing Susie could have done. After he met everyone they didn't seem like strangers, and he never had trouble talking with people he knew. Also, he realized the nervous, excited energy wouldn't be there, so more than likely he wouldn't display something foolish like falling off a chair. Then he wondered if that was why some public speakers stand by the door and meet a lot of people when they come in . . . or maybe some speakers just pretend they know everyone in the audience to make it easier. He never liked the technique someone had told him about, picturing everyone sitting in their underwear—that would make him start feeling embarrassed for them. Hmmmmm, his mind was wandering. I wonder if the word embarrassed came from *I'm bare-assed?*

Shawn's rambling thoughts were interrupted by Susie handing him a cup of hot spiced cider. "Do you know which story you're going to read first?"

Whew, he thought. That's right—"read." I don't have to think or make things up; I'm not a speaker. All I have to do is read! Feeling even more relieved, he sighed and said, "Yes. *Daisies* . . ."

"The story is called *Daisies*?" Susie raised her eyebrows, tilted her head slightly and smiled.

Shawn enjoyed Susie's animated way of talking. "Yeah," he said. "Most of Grampa's stories have very simple titles."

"Okay, everyone . . . . shhhhhhh . . . . hello . . . " Susie finally got the attention of people in various states of rather noisy conversation. "We're ready to begin. There are plenty of pillows on the floor and a few extra folding chairs—and Jim, why don't you pull that large couch around pointing this way . . . "

Shawn was impressed at how Susie could manage the group. She'd told him earlier that she loved being the focus of attention starting at her fifth birthday party. She had long forgotten the birthday gifts she received, but never how she organized her friends to play some games she had made up. Shawn, on the other hand, would rather run away than speak in public.

Then Susie said to the group, "You know, I don't even know too much about Shawn. Jack and I just met him on the trail today. He told us a story about a little blade of grass. It was so great. Before that he told a story about a caveman and we were really excited about some insights it gave. I'm repeating myself, huh? I told most of you this on the phone already. Try and relate the stories you hear to your own life whenever possible; maybe if it's okay with Shawn, we can kind of share any realizations or thoughts we might get out of the stories. How's that Shawn, is that okay with you?"

The room was totally quiet except for the crackling of the large fireplace and the whistle of a teapot, which cut off at that moment. It was so quiet Shawn hated to say anything, but finally words started to come out. "Oh yes, that's fine. Whatever you want to do is fine with me." He heard his own voice in front of all those people and thought, I'm still alive . . . maybe this will be all right. He continued, "As I told Rich, I was going to re-read the stories this weekend anyway, so it's nice to have more people around."

The last part wasn't entirely true because Shawn thought he'd feel a bit more comfortable with three or four people than 35! Good thing ol' Jake isn't around, he thought. Then he looked again to make sure the old man wasn't in the audience.

Susie told a little more about Grampa and the nature of the stories. A woman named Carla in the back of the room asked a question. "I have a seven-year-old girl and a nine-year-old boy . . . you say these are children's/adult stories . . . so could I read any of these to my kids? Would they understand them?"

Susie looked at Shawn for an answer and he said, "Certain ones are good for children, yet others like *Angels* may be too hard for them to understand. I was younger than your kids when I heard the story *Turtles* and some of the others. I enjoyed them, but as I got older they meant much more to me. They're certainly a lot better than some of the classic stories told to kids. Ever notice how much violence there is in them? A wolf chasing pigs or eating Grandma . . . even songs like "Rock-a-Bye-Baby" which has a limb breaking and a baby falling. I guess you shouldn't get me started . . . Well, actually, the truth is the stories aren't published, so I guess you couldn't read them anyway . . . but I hope you enjoy them tonight."

There were no more questions so Susie sat down on a pillow in the front, looking up at Shawn in anticipation. He knew that even if nobody else liked him or the stories, he could always look down at Susie for a warm, encouraging smile. He made a mental note: this might be another good technique for public speakers—find people in the audience who are supportive to look at, or maybe import them and bring them with you, and then look at them when you need a boost.

Shawn sat down in a high-standing, canvas director's chair. Everyone could easily see him that way, although he would have preferred a comfortable cushioned chair which sat low and wasn't so prominent.

"The story is called *Daisies*," Shawn began. "Actually, with all you hikers and trailblazers, this might turn out to be interesting for you. For me, sometimes the value comes from one of these stories days or weeks after I hear it." He said that out of truthfulness, but mostly out of insecurity. He was thinking, if they don't like it, maybe it will pacify them until I leave if they believe it's so sophisticated it will come to them later.

Shawn began reading, but someone at the far end asked if he

could speak louder. Shawn cleared his throat, raised his voice and, again, began reading *Daisies*. Then he stopped and said, "You know, Susie, this is a relatively long story. Perhaps you wouldn't mind taking turns reading it with me?"

Clearly it was more than all right with Susie. She loved the idea. So Shawn, again, began reading *Daisies*.

DAISIES

A daisy growing alongside a little dirt path was stretching to greet the morning sunshine. Its little white petals were well-formed because it had finished most of its growth and was just waiting for more of the spring bees to cross-pollinate her with the beautiful daisies across the path.

She could see them waving as the wind blew through their petals and tiny green leaves. Sometimes she wished she could walk. She would just go right over and get to know them personally.

Her life was not completely boring, however. It was always a delight when an occasional bee would come and land on her. Of course, she could hear him coming from a great distance. The buzz was so loud it made all her petals vibrate in harmony with the bee. Then the wind from his wings would feel like a hurricane upon her delicate but strong petals.

Miss Daisydo remembered the last bee that visited her. As always, when the bee finally landed, there was a wonderful silence. That was like being in the eye of the hurricane because the storm would soon resume when the bee left. During the silence, there was a delightful tickling sensation as the bee's six little feet gently tiptoed over Daisydo's petals. The gentleness was almost like the bee was trying to make up for the giant buzzing sound and hurricane effects just prior to landing.

No, life was not boring to Daisydo. Especially the days, because bees fly *by the light of the sun. When a bee comes in on a low, fast approach it can be downright surprising to an unsuspecting flower.*

A breeze came up, and Daisydo started waving in the wind to her friends across the path. She was surprised when out of nowhere a voice said, "My name is Doublecurve."

First she wondered if one of the daisies over there had a loud voice, but quickly discounted that possibility since it was too far to hear the soft voice of a daisy.

Miss Daisydo looked all around to see who was talking. In fact, she turned in a full circle and when she relaxed, she spun back the other way so fast she was afraid of losing one of her petals.

"Who said that?" Miss Daisydo called out.

"Well, you're always looking across me; now try looking at me for a change. I'm the path that leads to the fruit groves beyond those mountains to the north. You probably don't know of the fruit groves since your view is limited to this area. However, I can see for miles and miles and miles and miles. I am a winding path through the mountains of Nordovia and my total length is almost 100 miles—that is, if you don't get lost. And I can see and hear and feel things every inch of the way." The path said this in a proud, low, and scratchy voice from somewhere near the center of his five-foot width.

Miss Daisydo was shocked! She had heard bees talk, even the nearby trees, but never dirt or a rock or a path. However, Daisydo was very open-minded about things like this. Once she even had a snail speak to her. The snail wanted to assure her that she was safe because he didn't like to eat daisies. Daisydo was thankful for that bit of news. She was too naive to have thought of that possibility.

Now she said in a very friendly voice, "Well, I'm happy to meet you, Doublecurve, but why did you decide to talk to me? You must have millions you could talk to since you are so long? I mean, I'm just a daisy. You could talk to trees, mountains, and even giant boulders. Why me?"

Doublecurve didn't even pause before answering, "You seemed quite friendly, waving to your friends on the other side of me. I thought you might be receptive to a plan I have to save more of those mixed-up humans who travel along me. The travelers who pound up and down my back never take the time to listen to me. If they would, I could save them a lot of time, trouble, heartache, and sometimes their lives. Since they won't or can't seem to listen to me, perhaps you'd like to help me test out my plan. The only hitch is . . . " Doublecurve paused, as if concerned about how Daisydo might respond to a perhaps less-desirable part of the whole idea. Then he slowly said, "You'd have to be picked by one of those humans."

At first, the very thought of being plucked up from ground scared her. However, she had realized early on that her time was limited and that all daisies must eventually drop their petals and merge back to Mother Earth. Thinking about it that way made Doublecurve's suggestion a lot less frightening. In fact, the more she thought of the advantages, the more exciting it became. Perhaps a traveler would place her in the rim of his hat. Wow, what a view she would have! Daisydo was acutely aware that the only problem with being a flower is that your view is fixed. You can't see much of the world while firmly planted, or stuck, in one place.

Daisydo felt this was an opportunity to see more of the world. Perhaps her time would be shortened a bit, but she would gain so much more experience. Also, she reasoned, being picked might even mean more time for me, since I never know when a snail will come by who likes daisies.

After telling Doublecurve all her thoughts and considerations, she said she would be happy to try and communicate whatever he felt was important to the humans. She just couldn't imagine how that could happen.

Doublecurve told her that he would work out the details and that all she needed to do was to memorize certain phrases and tell them to the humans at the right time. He said one of their biggest problems seemed to be when they got off the path and got lost.

Daisydo asked, "How could anyone get lost? If you just follow the Doublecurve path you will arrive at the final destination."

"I know," Doublecurve replied. "It seems so simple, yet those darn humans make it so complicated."

Just then a human stomped by in hiking boots. Being pretty heavy, each of his steps noisily ground the stones into Doublecurve's back. Seeing that Daisydo was concerned, Doublecurve quickly reassured her that it didn't hurt. In fact, he liked it because each step helped redefine him and keep his path easy to see and follow.

Daisydo realized how genuine Doublecurve's desire was to help the travelers get to their final destinations. She was more convinced than ever that she wanted to help out with his experiment.

The human walked up the path a short distance and stopped. Scratching his head, he looked off to the east with a puzzled expression.

Doublecurve said, "Oh no, not another one of those!"

"One of what?" Daisydo asked.

"One of those humans who keep forgetting about their final destination! You see, he is looking over toward those trees on the side of that mountain to the east of us. He's probably thinking they might be as good as the groves where he'd planned to go. Pretty soon, he'll leave the path and march through the valley, across the stream, arriving at those trees—only to find that they don't produce fruit. Then he'll spend days trying to find me again, once he remembers what his original destination was. It's all so frustrating; I wish that I could whisper in his ear one little phrase." Doublecurve sounded disappointed.

"What would you say to him?" Daisydo asked.

"I'd say: STAY ON YOUR PATH! DON'T GET SIDETRACKED BY LOOK-ALIKES: GO FOR WHAT YOU REALLY WANT!"

Daisydo was impressed by this advice and asked why Doublecurve didn't just shout that out to the human who was about to leave the path. Doublecurve said that humans never stand still enough, long enough, to listen to their path. And, when they're off the path they're also out of hearing range. "That's where you come in, Daisydo!" Doublecurve declared enthusiastically.

Daisydo noticed that the human was now well off his path and heading down the canyon to the valley below. Unfortunately, there was no path through that area, and it was filled with jumping cactus and bees. Doublecurve said that when one deviated from his or her path, they were usually met with great discomfort. It was almost like the universe was trying to give you signals to get back on your path.

"How can I talk to the humans if you can't?" Daisydo asked Doublecurve.

"I'll teach you all you need to know tonight. Will you be ready to go tomorrow morning?"

Daisydo agreed and was surprised that evening at how simple it all seemed. The most difficult part, as far as Daisydo was concerned, was how to get a human to choose to pick her in the first place. Doublecurve had an explanation, but it wasn't completely understood by Daisydo. It involved some kind of subtle suggestions that Doublecurve would make to a traveler for several miles before they reached Daisydo. Doublecurve said the human would not be able to resist picking her tomorrow morning.

Sure enough, just after daybreak, Daisydo saw a human walking over the ridge and up the path. This traveler was tall and slim, with dark brown hair. His beard was black and thick, but his very white teeth were clearly vis-

ible when he smiled—something he seemed to do quite frequently.

"Oh, boy," said Daisydo, "a happy traveler." But just then, the human walked right past her.

Daisydo was a bit upset until she saw him stop and pause, turn around and come back to within a couple of feet of her. He reached down and gently took hold of the base of her stem. With one quick motion, she was swept up to an altitude more than thirty times her natural height. Daisydo looked into the eyes of this human, only inches from his face. His eyes seemed to smile as much as his lips. He was certainly pleased with Daisydo.

Just as Doublecurve had described in the previous night's lessons, the human tucked Daisydo's stem carefully behind his ear. This was the second part of Doublecurve's subtle suggestions to the human, and it was a key part of the plan. From that location, even a daisy's soft voice could be heard by the human.

All her petals were free to stretch out and Daisydo had a magnificent view of the world. She was so touched by the sight of everything, her heart filled with love and joy. She almost forgot what she was supposed to do when the first challenge came up. It all happened so fast.

Not far from where they had started, the path formed by Doublecurve's back made a right turn and started going east. The human was quite confused because he knew his destination; the fruit groves beyond the mountains were to the north. There was even a weak little path that headed north, though it didn't have the same well-traveled look that he had been used to.

He started to take a step on the northern path when Daisydo took the first action she'd been trained to do. She said in a loud, clear voice, "SOME-TIMES YOUR PATH MAY NOT SEEM LOGICAL—FOLLOW IT ANYWAY!"

The human shook his head, and Daisydo was afraid she might fall off. He was confused about where the voice was coming from, but he did listen to her words. He stopped, turned, and looked down the path leading to the east—which didn't make sense. After a couple of deep breaths and a sigh, the human made the correct choice and stayed on the path.

It worked! Daisydo thought to herself; he stayed on his path!

The human soon discovered why the path veered to the east for no apparent reason. Just over the ridge was a river. His path led to a log that made a bridge to the other side. He guessed that this was the only place on the river for miles that was narrow enough to get across.

Daisydo felt that this human was now ready for part two of the lesson, so she spoke into his ear, "A PATH MAKES MORE SENSE ONCE YOU'VE TRAVELED IT."

This time the human just said, "Ahhh." He carefully walked the log bridge to the other side. The river below was rushing very rapidly because it was at its narrowest point. He began thinking about that and came up with a lesson for himself. He thought about how easy it was to cross this very dangerous river because he was on the path. It would have been quite a different challenge if he hadn't known about the log bridge. He would have gotten wet, battled for his life, and perhaps never reached the other side alive.

He said his new realization out loud, "THOUGH IT MIGHT BE HARD TO STAY ON THE PATH, IT MAY BE EASIER THAN LEAVING IT."

Of course, Daisydo heard what he said. She was so pleased that he had started inner learning without being told. Doublecurve told her that once this begins to happen, humans will start taking great pleasure in discovering truths about their path. "Later," he said, "they can't help but tell other travelers—that can save a lot of time, energy, and even lives."

After a few more hours of being careful to stay on the path to the fruit groves, the human started noticing something very curious. Every couple of miles or so, he would find a fruit tree just near his path that had one or two *pieces of fruit. At that moment, he plucked a ripe peach from a tree within reach of his path. It was the very same kind of peach he'd been looking for when he headed off for the fruit groves in the first place—just fewer in quantity. Since it was almost evening, he decided to make camp by this particular tree.*

Daisydo was quite pleased at the choice because she felt he was almost ready to discover one of his greatest lessons. Perhaps she would only need to drop a couple of hints.

The human rolled out his sleeping bag and placed his head at the foot of the tree. A nice big root formed a natural pillow. The stars were clearly visible, peeking through the tree's leaves and branches. Almost forgetting about Daisydo, he got back up and gently placed her in a cup of water. Daisydo felt quite pleased at his thoughtfulness. After several peaches and snacks, he settled back down and drifted into a half-sleep dream state.

Though Daisydo was no longer next to his ear, the night was so quiet he could hear her say, "WHEN THE PATH IS EASY—ENJOY; WHEN IT'S HARD—LEARN THE LESSONS."

The human started remembering some of his hard times. He remembered leaving the path out of impatience once. Trying to force a shortcut, he got lost in a maze of thorn bushes, twisted his ankle, and even stepped on a wasp's nest. Unfortunately, he got stung six times before he could hobble fast enough to get away.

The human opened his eyes and looked into the stars. "What is the lesson?" Almost the moment he asked, he realized the answer and said out loud, "Ahhhh—Haaaa!"

Not content with just reciting outloud what he had learned, he now felt he needed to record these lessons because they were becoming precious. Also, parts that were bubbling up were not completely understandable. However, he felt they were great truths anyway and deserved being preserved.

On a pad of paper he wrote:

> *"The fruits of your destination*
> *line the path of your journey;*
> *Enjoy the fruit along the way;*
> *it's your reward for being on the path.*
> *Notice the bumps, the rocks, the hurts, and the detours,*
> *for they signal you to return to your path;*
> *Cherish all your signs, signals, and lessons;*
> *they assist you in being on your path;*
> *Wait not for the destination*
> *to enjoy the fruit of your labor,*
> *for as sure as you arrive,*
> *the journey begins again!"*

He became very happy writing and rereading this. It seemed like a big discovery for him. He realized that if he just focused on staying on his true path, his trip would not only be easier, but he could already begin to sample the fruit he expected to find at his destination.

The leaves almost shook on the tree as he shouted to the sky, "Being on my path is what really matters!"

Daisydo felt little drops of moisture on her petals. The human's realizations and joy had touched her heart so much that for the first time she was crying because of an overwhelming sense of love. She was also crying with appreciation. Her mind flashed on the limited perspective she'd had of the world when she was firmly planted in one place. From her narrow view of life, she had drawn many conclusions and developed many beliefs about things that now had to be changed.

One of her changing beliefs had to do with humans. Her view had been mostly from their big feet stirring up dust on the path, crushing things underneath and being rather insensitive to the world around them. She also thought they had very low intelligence, based on the fact that they didn't seem to be able to stay on their paths. But after being with this human and seeing things from his perspective, she realized that he was sensitive. Many times, he increased the size of his stride in order to avoid stepping on a bug. Daisydo also understood now how humans could get off their paths, not because of low intelligence, but actually the opposite.

Sometimes they over-think and analyze things too much, she thought to herself. She recalled Doublecurve telling her about one traveler stuck at a fork in the road for two days, trying to decide which way made the most sense. If only I could have spoken to his "inner ear," she wished. I would have said, OVERANALYSIS CAN LEAD TO PARALYSIS—SOMETIMES YOU MUST TRUST YOUR HEART.

The night passed quickly and while Daisydo was busy feeling a lot more understanding about the challenges humans face in order to stay on their paths, her human was getting ready to do some more walking. He rolled up his sleeping bag and ate breakfast.

Before tucking Daisydo back behind his ear, he pointed a little black object at her and she heard a click. With the click came a flash of bright light. Little did Daisydo know that her image was forever recorded on film.

It was only about an hour later and about four miles down the path that they came upon five other humans. They were just breaking camp as Daisydo and the human approached them. Daisydo discovered the name of her human host because these people knew him and shouted it out—Jason.

The three women and two men seemed to know Jason quite well. One of the women, Cindy, gave Jason a very affectionate hug. Daisydo felt the closeness of her face and hair as the two hugged. Cindy noticed Daisydo, too, because she said, "Well, I see you're into daisies now."

Jason stopped Cindy's hand from touching or removing Daisydo. He told her it was his good-luck flower. Daisydo was very pleased that Jason was protective of her.

The six of them traveled together along the path for about six miles. They laughed a lot and told stories about the good old days. Jason was obviously very happy to have company, especially old friends.

They all stopped at a fork in the path. A choice must be made. One of the men, Kirk, was a very persuasive person. He wanted everyone to go west to the river and walnut groves. In fact, he had convinced the others to change their destinations and travel with him several days before. Now he was hoping to enroll Jason into his plans.

Daisydo saw what was happening. She knew that Kirk had only selfish motives and really didn't care about each person's individual dreams. He cleverly worded things to discredit their chosen destinations and to create fear about their paths. Then he would sell them on the advantages of joining the group.

Daisydo also noticed that Jason was quite fond of Cindy, and she was the only one without a boyfriend.

Just as Jason started to join the group, taking the path to the left, going west to the river, Daisydo shouted out a phrase: ". . . . ."

Unfortunately, Cindy was walking with her arm around Jason, talking excitedly in his other ear. Jason couldn't hear Daisydo's soft voice. Mile after mile, someone was always talking. Daisydo could not get through to Jason.

However, Jason started noticing something. Though he was with lots of people, especially Cindy, he was feeling more alone than ever. He was no longer following his dream of going to the fruit groves.

He stopped the group and announced a new truth he had discovered for himself. He said to them, "BEING ON THE WRONG PATH WITH LOTS OF COMPANY IS LONELIER THAN BEING ON YOUR OWN TRUE PATH ALONE."

The only person who seemed to understand was Cindy. She nodded her head as Jason spoke of his dream of visiting the fruit groves beyond the mountains to the north. When he spoke of beauty of the trees and the delightful taste of the fruit, Cindy saw that Jason was truly inspired. Cindy encouraged Jason to go back, to get back on his path to the fruit groves. The others just tried to convince him to continue on with them.

It was then that Jason arrived at another bit of wisdom that he would write on his pad of paper later that night. It was: YOUR TRUE FRIENDS WILL GIVE YOU SUPPORT TO STAY ON YOUR PATH.

Cindy was a true friend, and it was hard to say goodbye to her. However, that was soon replaced by Jason's excitement at being back on his path, once he had backtracked far enough to reach the fork. This time he chose the trail on the right, leading north.

Finally Daisydo could be heard again. She decided to give Jason a comforting phrase. She softly said into his ear, "YOU NEEDN'T GIVE UP YOUR DESTINATION IN ORDER TO BE LOVED."

Jason let out a sigh, as though he was relieved to hear that, and someone said, "Who's that?" Jason looked to his right and saw a very beautiful girl his age trying to shake a stone from her shoe. He walked over, and they ended up talking about their common dream of going to the fruit groves.

Lidia and Jason decided to share the journey, except Jason had an unusual request. He asked for an agreement to walk in silence five out of every fifteen minutes. Jason wanted to be able to listen to his inner voice, Daisydo, or both. Lidia agreed, and they joyfully followed their paths together—which happened to lead to the same place.

Jason and Lidia found out that they had each been keeping notes about what they learned while traveling. They enjoyed reading each other's truths about following paths.

*It's been a few years since then. Jason and Lidia are still happily mar-
ried. Though they haven't had any children, they did give birth to something
that continues to help many other travelers.*

*Almost every traveler walking along Doublecurve has a daisy behind
one ear and is carrying a little book with a beautiful picture of a daisy on
the cover. The title is Staying On Your Path by Jason, Lidia, Daisydo, and
Doublecurve. It is filled with wonderful quotes to assist all travelers.*

~ ~ ~ ~ ~ ~ ~

The fruits of your destination line the path of your journey;
Enjoy the fruit along the way; it's your reward for being on the path.
Notice the bumps, the rocks, the hurts, and the detours, for they signal you to return to your path:
Cherish all your signs, signals, and lessons;
they assist you in being on your path;
Wait not for the destination to enjoy the fruit of your labor, for as sure as you arrive, the journey begins again.

Stay on your path! Don't get sidetracked by look-alikes! Go for what you really want!

Sometimes your path may not seem logical -- follow it anyway!

A path makes more sense... once you've travelled it.

Though it might be hard to stay on the path... it may be easier than leaving it.

When the path is easy
-- enjoy,
when it's hard
-- learn the lesson

Over-analysis can lead
to paralysis -- sometimes
you must trust your heart

Being on the wrong path
with lots of company...
is lonlier than being on your
own true path alone

Your true friend will
give you support...
to stay on your
true path

You needn't give up
your destination...
in order to be loved

Though Susie and Shawn had taken turns reading, the journal ended up in his hands for the finish of the story. First there were a few *aaaaahhhs* and then a warm applause—much more than he would have expected, even if he had thought about it.

Once it was quiet again, someone spoke up and asked, "Is this the time when we can share things?"

Shawn was pleased that someone wanted to talk; it took the heat off him. "Sure, go ahead," he said.

He was glad Susie had warned him about the group because there was no reluctance at all on this woman's part to speak out. She looked about twenty-five, with brown hair, and she had a rather plump but healthy appearance. However, if you looked closely at her eyes, there was a sadness about her. She said, "You know, I just realized something from the story tonight. That one saying . . . you know, about if you're on the wrong path with lots of people you can be lonelier than being alone but on your true path?"

She looked around and saw her friends nodding their heads. "Well, all of you are my bestest of friends, but I haven't told you how deeply lonely I am. I've been here since high school just because I love you all so much." Tears started streaming down her cheeks as she spoke. Someone handed her a tissue.

She wiped her eyes and continued, "I know now that loneliness doesn't have to be just for people or even a lover; it can be for something you long to do. There's something I've wanted since I was a little girl."

"What's that?" a voice in the crowd asked.

"I've always wanted to help heal people, but not through conventional medicine—maybe as a chiropractor? But there are no schools here and I'd have to go to a big city—which frightens me . . . and all of you wouldn't be there . . . . But now I feel it in my heart that there is something very important missing in my life."

There was a long silence. Everyone waited patiently as though it wasn't unusual at all for someone to share their feelings so deeply.

Finally, someone said, "Just go for it, hon! Come back later and we'll be your patients!" Some laughed, and other voices cheered the woman on. She broke down in tears, and a woman next to her gave her a big hug. A couple more joined in, and soon there was a big group of people, all hugging each other in the back of the room.

A younger woman, about eighteen stood up about ten feet from the hugging group. She called out, "Linda, if you want a partner, I'll go with you! I need to go to a larger city to see if I can get into modeling. I haven't said anything because I was afraid you all might laugh at me for even thinking I might be pretty enough, but when I heard that part about your true friends will give you support to stay on your path, I thought, what the heck!"

Everyone cheered and applauded, and the two women stepped over people in the center of the floor to give each other a hug. Then they gave everyone the thumbs-up sign and smiled.

By this time Shawn was overwhelmed. He had never seen such reactions to the stories before. He tried to figure it out. What could it be? Are these people always this emotional? Is it because of some sort of group energy? Before he could catch his breath, another person was asking to share.

This time it was a man in a red plaid flannel shirt, sitting on the arm of the long couch. He had a thick beard and was very muscular. Shawn would have picked him as the last person who'd want to share in front of a group of people. He just looked too macho. His voice was deep and slow, and he waited for everyone to get quiet since his voice didn't carry over the chatter as well as the higher-pitched women's voices.

He slowly said, "You know, my wife and I have arguments. We don't talk about them here much . . . Is it okay, Barb, if I talk about us?" He looked down at a very petite woman sitting next to him on the couch. She nodded yes. He continued, "Since this seems to be a night of truth, I want to confess I've really been an S.O.B. to live with . . . and I don't know if I understand everything I'm feeling right now, but I think I'm starting to understand a bit of what Barb has been trying to pound into my thick skull since we got married three years ago."

He looked like a professional wrestler as he stood up and put his hands in his Levi's pockets. Gaining a little more volume, he went on, "Though we look like everything's going okay, Barb's about to leave me. In fact, I'd bet it would be within the week." He looked at Barb, but she just lowered her head and looked at the floor.

Shawn thought to himself, I don't believe this . . . these people must be in some sort of group therapy or 12-step program or something. But Susie had warned him on the mountain that the group might seem like that.

The man continued, "There was a part in there saying your path may not be logical, and it makes more sense after you've traveled it. Barb's pretty emotional and keeps telling me we don't always have to make all our decisions in the family just because they're logical. I've always believed if something ain't logical, it won't work out. I guess I just don't understand people who follow their hearts—I don't know what that means! We have fierce arguments . . . " He paused for a long time, and the room was silent.

Shawn heard his own voice talking which surprised him—he hadn't planned on saying anything. He was asking the man, "Do you love Barb?"

"Yes! She means more to me than anything in the world."

Shawn answered, "Well, I know what you mean about being logical, but you know, in my 18 years of loving my wife, it hasn't been from my head; it's come from my heart." He paused and again there was silence in the room. "If you are wanting to be with Barb, aren't you indeed following your heart? . . . Even though you say you don't understand it, maybe you don't have to. Matters of the heart aren't always possible to figure out, but they're delicious just the same. Just think, man—if we used only our intellects, we would be walking robots."

Shawn couldn't believe he was saying these things to a complete stranger.

The man replied, "I understand what you're saying, I guess . . . " He paused and knelt down in front of his wife. "I want to try and understand what you're trying to tell me. I love you, and I don't want to lose you, Barb."

Barb was obviously touched. She wrapped her arms around him and said in a very Southern accent, "Honey, if'n yer willin' to try, so am I!"

Again the crowd cheered and applauded as the couple kissed. When they stood up, Barb was only about half her husband's height.

Through all of this, Shawn still had time to wonder why it was that tall men seemed to go with short women when there were so many tall women out there looking for tall men! He decided not to ask this question out loud; better leave well enough alone.

Susie stood up and touched Shawn's arm. She said to the group, "Hey you-all, ain't it 'bout time we toss some grub down?" Barb gave Susie a big smile, knowing she was obviously teasing her about her accent. It was clear the two were close friends. "Why don't we take a 20-minute break for cookies, tea, and whatever else you can find in the kitchen? Do you have any more stories after the break, Shawn?"

"Well, sure, if anyone wants to hear some more." There were plenty of shouts of "yeah" and "yes," but it was not a question that needed an answer. This was apparently a valuable experience for not only the audience, but something was happening inside Shawn as well. Something was stirring, but no one noticed the tiny tear starting down Shawn's cheek.

Shawn turned away from the crowd to wipe the tear off and when he opened his eyes, he saw Jake outside, his face pressed to the window. Jake's wrinkly old face was smiling, and he gave Shawn a double wink. Quickly, Shawn wiped his eyes with his handkerchief and looked again. No one was there. He rushed to the window. He could see the entire, empty yard. Toward the back, he noticed something that gave him chills—the same transparent ball of glowing, bluish light he'd seen on the hood of his car. As he watched the ball hover above the ground next to a tall pine tree, it started fading away like it had done before. When it was totally gone, Shawn just stood there with his mouth open. "What is that thing?" he mumbled to himself.

"Whatcha lookin' for?" someone said, tapping him on the shoulder.

Shawn spun around to find Susie smiling at him. Not wanting to discuss the strange ball of light he said to her, "Oh, I just thought I saw an old man outside the window—Jake; do you know him?"

"I don't know any locals who go by that name. Where does he live?"

"I don't know . . . I'm a little confused right now. Please excuse me." He took out his handkerchief and wiped the perspiration off his forehead.

"Are you all right? Do you need anything?" Susie took Shawn by the arm and got him to sit down on the couch.

"I'll be okay, really," he protested.

A few people came up and thanked Shawn for the story and seemed to chatter about things. It was all kind of a blur to him at that point. It was too noisy to think, and even if it wasn't, what he really wanted to think about was that ball of light.

Finally, Susie called the group back into the large room. Shawn went back to his director's chair and picked up the purple journal. As he looked at the journal, he thought, how comforting, there's something familiar that I can depend on. I'll just read another story; everything will be all right.

This time Susie didn't say anything. She just sat down in front and looked up at Shawn with her usual eager smile.

Shawn began. "*Daisies* was the fifth story in the journal that I've re-read while here in the mountains this trip. There are a few more, but I'm sure we won't get to all of them tonight." There was a sound of disappointment from the audience. "Well, we'll see what we can do.

"The next story is called *Angels,*" he told them. He paused, trying to think of something to say as an introduction. He settled for, "This story starts out a bit strange, but if you hang in there, you'll understand soon enough." He opened the journal and started reading *Angels.*

ANGELS

"What's left in this freeze-frame?" Vince wanted to know.

"We currently have only 5,534 hold-flags up. Shouldn't be long now. You're not going to be among the final hundred holding again, are you?" Tara asked her student angel.

"I hope not! I'm not that slow, really. It's just that my guy is one of those challenges, you know? The request involves many agreements per frame, and they're so involved it runs me right up to final. I don't know . . . maybe I shouldn't be doing this," Vince sighed.

"Look, we all had to start someplace. You should have seen me with my first one. Whew! There were times I ended up in the final ten."

"That must have been tough. That was before the fourth-dimensional shift, wasn't it?"

"Actually, during," Tara replied. Though many in the physical were realizing the power of thought and prayer, their confusion created 'hell,' if you'll pardon the expression."

Vince laughed. "I've heard the stories. You'd just arrange the most complicated set of transactions and your person would change his or her mind, and then go back and forth a few times."

"That wasn't the worst of it! With the dimensional shift kicking in, all their projections were amplified a thousand-fold, which caused even the *lighter thoughts to involve negotiations with hundreds of angels! I'm glad the fourth is in solid now. Once you get the hang of it, you'll sail along and stay above the 50,000-flag level."*

"What's the highest hold-flag level you ever released at, Tara?"

"Once I was overseeing a Frenchman as my Earthling, years ago. I remember him so vividly, sitting there at the sidewalk cafe, sipping his pinot chardonnay in the early spring. There was a nip in the air, so people were still wearing thick clothing. He had a 95 percent level of prayer-thought impulse, wanting to find his soul mate immediately. I managed to release my hold-flag at 976,114,258. There were only about 10,000 who released before me during that freeze-frame!"

"That was good! And to think it was with one of those soul-mate requests, too. It's hard enough when they just request a mate. Do they really know what they're asking for when they say soul mate? . . . I mean, there are matching soul vibrations and planet timings—not to mention windows of availability, geographic separations, age differences, and spiritual growth variances!"

"Of course, most don't know. What they are really saying is: 'Give me someone to love, from whom I will not have to learn any earthly relationship lessons, because I'd rather avoid the pain!'" Tara frowned, then continued, "In a large city, a person usually has ten to fifty possible, marriageable soul mates, but they may have ten to fifty thousand excellent marriage partners who would bring them all the joy and love they desire. Plus, they would still be making great progress along the relationship learning path."

"You mean soul mates don't learn from each other as much?" Vince asked.

"Their souls are so harmonious, many of their key issues aren't ever triggered to come to the surface. That area just gets a rest for a while."

"How did you comply with the Frenchman's desire? How many transac-

tional agreements did it take, Tara?"

Tara looked at her student angel, Vince, paused dramatically, then said, "Would you believe only four?"

"No way! How could that be, especially when you consider he was asking for a soul mate?"

"Well, first of all, the Frenchman had already cleared through his assigned major relationship learning tasks with seven women, two of whom he had married. His remaining learning tasks could be accomplished with a soul mate, especially since he had regained his powerful spiritual connection during a long period of hardship," Tara explained.

"That helps. I had to make thousands of transactions to get one woman through three separate heart-breaking love affairs to prepare her for her soul mate. By then, she was so frustrated she swore off men and canceled her request for a soul mate. Instead, she adopted the belief that she was destined to live alone. With such a powerful belief, it was truly all over for her."

Tara looked at Vince sympathetically. "It's tough when their own negativity cancels out the request just about the time you've arranged for it to happen. See, you're actually getting a lot of experience under those wings of yours!"

"It's good that we can do all our work here, where the time illusion doesn't exist. Those in the physical never detect a pause in life's movie, and their clocks appear to always keep clicking. We rush around between frames doing incredible heavenly tasks, but it all flows smoothly to them. If they only knew all the work we get done in far less than a clock-tick . . ."

"Yeah, you remember when I first arrived and you had to explain the whole thing to me? I think what cleared it up was when you said, "Just imagine a movie filmstrip, with all Earth movement completely stopping between frames. Action starts again only when all the angels have completed

all their tasks and released any hold-flags they might have on that frame. The frame does not advance until the very last angel says, 'All clear.' That really helped me understand, Tara!"

"What did you do . . . memorize what I said word for word?"

"It's kind of a talent I have, and it's especially handy being around you. Tara, you're a perfect angel and tutor. Now tell me, how did you keep it down to four?"

"Well, Joanie, who is a much more advanced angel than me, was over-seeing an American sitting behind my Frenchman. The American had made the trip to Paris specifically to meet her soul mate, so Joanie was keeping her close to any souls vibrating within 200 microbands who were also born with sufficiently compatible star and planet timings. She did most of the work by getting the two so close together. Actually, she pulled a future and saw that my Frenchman was about to ask for a soul mate. I made one agreement with Joanie to attempt connection of the American with the Frenchman; a second with the waiter's angel to create a meeting cause; a third to cre-ate initial pursuit interest within the Frenchman; and a fourth to help avoid embarrassment and avoidance due to the circumstances, while at the same time creating an initial interest within the American."

"Oh, this is good," Vince said. "Please go ahead and describe the action after the freeze-frame."

"If I do, you may drop into the hundreds again, but that's okay. I can see you're learning from this." Tara flapped her angel wings, sending a cool breeze toward Vince. She settled down with a twinkle in her eye which beamed that her enjoyment was approaching heavenly level.

Tara described the action before and after the freeze-frame. "The Frenchman placed his very powerful 95 percent-level request. It was so powerful, my wings still shake remembering the jolt of the impulse. It shot straight up from the Earth plane in a cosmic beam larger than I've ever witnessed before. He was quite clear; he wanted his soul mate, and wanted her now. The Earth reality entered a freeze-frame. I immediately made my four transaction angel agreements and was ready to view. I released my hold-flag on the frame. Of course, there were almost a billion hold-flags on the frame from other angels. Once they were all released and the frames advanced, it was fun to watch."

Vince could see that Tara was really enjoying the experience of reliving the scene.

She continued, "The waiter tripped ever so perfectly, sending his tray skidding on top of the American woman's table—thanks to the waiter's angel-thought distractions. The Frenchman turned, saw that wine was starting to spill on the American woman's lap, and rushed to be of help. As he started to blot her coat with his napkin, she became embarrassed, but was distracted by an amazing coincidence. The Frenchman just happened to be wearing a gold lapel pin in the shape of a little mouse, with tiny diamonds for eyes. By coincidence she had admired a pin just like it in a store nearly two years before. That was about the time she started her requests for a soul mate."

"That's clever. Not only did you put them together, the thought of a soul mate was triggered by the memory of the mouse pin. But how?" Vince looked very puzzled.

"Simple; I used a 'retro.' Since I knew the Frenchman was wearing the pin, I simply backed up to the frame when she'd seen the mouse pin in the store and suggested an association of the pin with a soul mate. It was all quite legitimate according to the Angel Code of Ethics. Not once did I change an actual event or try to control her free will! Creating associations by causing certain thoughts to move to the forefront of consciousness is perfectly fine. Its common use, of course, is through symbols in dreams, but I needed something immediate." Tara sounded just a bit defensive; overstepping boundaries and interfering with free will is a serious matter to aspiring angels.

"So what happened?" Vince was anxious to know more.

"The American became curious about this Frenchman who'd come to her rescue and looked into his eyes without any fear. That's what did it. In an instant, they experienced each other's soul vibration, and the resonance kicked in. That's all it took. In two months they were engaged to be married, and it truly became a marriage made in Heaven." Tara had a dreamy look in her eyes, and her smile told of her own pleasure. "You know, Vince," she said in a melodic voice, "soul mates are tough to get together, but once they look into each other's eyes and hear the voice tones, it is like placing a bee near a fragrant flower."

Vince interrupted her dreamy state with another question. His intellectual curiosity seemed boundless. "How many micro-angels do you think were involved?"

"Oh my, Vince, you've been viewing your mechanical lessons, haven't you! . . . Of course you know that each physical object or projection has a main micro-angel supporting it. This micro-angel acts on our angel agreements but still abides by the standard physical laws accumulatively agreed to by humanity over centuries of Earth time. However, even each component has a micro-angel, and by the time you get to the atomic level, there are many more micro-angels guiding the physical properties. In that one scene, there were billions of micro-angels involved. Just remember, though, the micro-angels have not yet evolved to self-awareness."

"When do they achieve that?" Vince went on with his seemingly endless questions.

"Vince, you're already at a holding level of 110. If you keep up these questions, you could end up being the last angel, holding up the entire Earth physical freeze-frame. What do you have to arrange in order to release your hold on the frame?"

That shocked Vince into focus again. He was supposed to be overseeing his Earthling. Just then, Celest flew up and landed next to Tara. Every angel has a higher guide or tutor, and Celest was Tara's.

"Tara?" Celest asked an entire question in one word. She'd come to check on her.

Tara knew exactly what Celest was asking and replied, "You're right. I've indulged in a replay again. But my student angel learned from it!"

Celest raised an eyebrow and communicated a wealth of knowledge. Tara said in a soft knowing voice, "You're right, it could have waited until after this frame. And yes, I realize that Vince is one of the last holds on the frame. I understand, Celest."

With that, Celest rose gracefully with only the slightest movement of her wings.

"Those advanced angels sure are something, huh?" Vince looked up in amazement.

"You should see Celest's guiding angel! She's beyond your vision and imagination. But now, no more distractions. What do you need to do to release your hold-flag?" Tara's voice was determined and focused again.

"My Earthling has put out many 70-90 percent-level prayer-thoughts over the last several years. He wants to come up with an invention that would serve humanity and also support him financially. It's a long-term, mul- tiframe ordeal and . . . "

Tara cut Vince off in mid-sentence with a question, "Is it?" She looked at him with knowing eyes.

Vince stopped and thought. Then he replied, "I don't know . . . "

"Of course, I can't directly tell you. It's your lesson. What have you learned about beliefs?" Tara coached.

"It is given to you as you believe. Beliefs create the self-perpetuating, repetitive thought forms that generate apparent reality, using angels and

micro-angels to carry out the requests to fulfillment."

Tara looked at Vince, amazed and a bit amused by how he approached being an angel so intellectually. To say the same thing, her other student angels would have simply said, "Beliefs are an automatic way of making continual angel requests." But instead, she replied, "That's truly technical, Vince, but it's much more simple than that. Pause and think a little more." Or less, she thought, chuckling to herself.

After a short time Vince looked at Tara and asked, "Beliefs are creative, even in the non-physical?"

Tara nodded her head vigorously and said, "Yes!"

"Oh, no . . . then . . . it could be MY belief that is slowing everything down!" Vince said with some frustration. "My belief that it is a 'long term fulfillment process' is actually making it so. Could the Earthling's request actually be a quick one?"

"I can't say. However, I have had requests fulfilled in one frame that other angels might take thousands of frames to do because they believed it would take that many."

"I've got it!" Vince shouted. "I'll have him meet someone who has learned how fast things can come about. This will help me change my belief about how fast it can happen. It will also help change his belief too, since he has probably started believing it must take a long time also."

Vince arranged with several other angels to start the meeting process, completed all he could do for this frame, and cleared his hold-flag ahead of 79 other angels. He said with relief, "Whew, at least I wasn't the last one to hold up the frame!" To stretch his wings, he flew up around Tara and landed on her other side. She enjoyed seeing her student try out his wings once in a while, though he was still a bit awkward.

Vince smiled and gave her a double wink.

"I know they call you The Orion Angel because your last home planet was somewhere in that constellation. Where exactly is it located?" Tara asked.

Vince replied, "You've heard of the Horsehead Nebula, near the Belt of Orion?"

"No, but I am quite familiar with the Belt—those three bright stars that almost form a straight line."

"That's it. My planet, Nabel, orbits a star about midway between the Horsehead Nebula and the left-most star of the Belt."

"Why did you select Earth for your overseeing angel work, instead of working with the angels assisting your planet?" Tara asked.

"For some reason, I have a strong compulsion to do something for the Earth people. It's almost like I'm trying to make up for something, or correct a wrong. I don't know. Can you find out anything from Celest?"

Tara closed her eyes and spoke to Celest telepathically. When Tara opened her eyes, she said, "Nothing can be revealed to you at this time, except that it has to do with some lessons and karma that are still being resolved in your evolution to higher spiritual realms. Just follow your heart— just as we prescribe for the Earthlings."

"You were talking earlier about time, and it brought to mind a question. I noticed that on Earth—actually, even on my planet—sometimes time seems to move very slowly and other times very quickly. I know that time doesn't really exist, but why would the illusion of time vary so much? Is it because the frames advance at different speeds, depending on how fast the hold-flags clear?" Vince asked.

Tara chuckled and illustrated that she understood his point, "I don't know if you had dentists on Nabel, but time does seem to vary, whether you're sitting in a dentist's chair or enjoying recess at grade school. Five minutes can seem like five hours, or five seconds."

"Exactly!" Vince agreed. "By the way, we had a doctor similar to an

Earth dentist, except the experience was quite pleasant, and we looked forward to it."

"Hmmm . . . maybe we can give that idea to some dentist in a dream. Anyway, to answer your question, it's not the speed of the frames that cause time to seem to speed up, or slow down."

"What is it, then?" Vince asked.

"Fear," she answered. "Fear focuses tremendous attention on each frame, with great trepidation giving the illusion of time slowing down. Love, on the other hand, focuses not on the individual frames, but on the moving experience of many frames smoothly flowing along. Time seems to speed up."

"Okay then, why does time seem to go by more quickly the older humans become?"

Tara rather enjoyed Vince's enthusiasm for learning, so she continued, "Well, realize that though time appears real to Earthlings, it's really an illusion—and a relative one at that.

"What do you mean, relative?"

"It's relative to how much time they've already experienced. For instance, one year to a one-year-old child is 100 percent of it's age. But one year to a fifty-year-old is only 2 percent. Two percent of life seems to pass faster than 100 percent of life. A two-year-old sitting at a dinner table with adults for an hour is equivalent to a twenty-five-year-old sitting and listening to abstract concepts for 12.5 hours!"

"No wonder they can't sit still. Adults would be throwing food, too, after twelve-and-a-half hours!" Vince was excited about his new understanding, and realized the incredible demand parents placed on their kids to sit still.

"This also explains why chronological age differences aren't as important as percent-age differences. A 20-year-old man with a 10-year-old girl is a big difference, since he is 100 percent older. But when he is 50 and she is

40, it's not much of a difference since he is only 25 percent older. Again, the illusion of time is relative. Isn't that interesting?"

"Wow! That's something. Why is it that you can tell me things like this, and yet at other times you say you can't answer because it's my lesson?"

"You answered it yourself. When it's your specific lesson, telling you can sometimes take longer for you to get it. Instead, if you discover it for yourself, even if drawn out of you through questions you ask, your growth is sped along." Tara noticed that Vince's current hold flag was at about 20,000. She didn't want him to get too close to the last angel again.

Vince took action to make about 12 agreements with other angels and released his hold-flag at about 19,500. He loved seeing the result of his work with the other angels. In all, a chain reaction of hundreds of so-called coincidences would occur. Some of them would get the Earthling's attention and stimulate certain thoughts, others were the manifestation of high-thought impulses or prayers coming true—the resulting effect being coincidences or miracles. Of course, it was all God's work, because God is everything.

"Very good," Tara congratulated.

"Thank you. Now, how about another question? A big one."

"You've earned it. Go ahead," Tara said with a laugh.

"Could I actually appear on the physical Earth plane and remain conscious of my angelness? I mean . . . could I be in the physical but still be fully aware of angels, of my connection with God, and still help people grow and learn? I believe I could be of great help to millions of people, but I'd need some greater freedom to interact."

Tara paused for a long time. "Hmmmm . . . I don't know the answer to that, Vince." Then she raised her right wing tip slightly and Celest floated down, making a soft landing next to Tara. She and her angel guide looked silently into each other's eyes for a long time. Celest turned and looked at Vince without saying anything. But Vince experienced her answer.

Celest communicated that Vince could experience firsthand on the Earth plane what he had asked about, but first he must evolve three levels beyond her own high state. She conveyed this without any ego; just letting him know the facts.

Vince knew that some day he would go to Earth with his full angelness intact. In fact, he would have special powers, as long as he followed the Angel Code of Ethics (A.C.E.).

As he usually did when he was very happy, Vince smiled and gave Tara a double wink. Then he picked up the A.C.E. manual and started to read. He was eager to prepare for his experiences on Earth.

~ ~ ~ ~ ~ ~ ~

ANGEL CODE OF ETHICS (A.C.E.)
(This is only an outline of the first four sections of A.C.E.)
Section 1 - Free Will
Each spirit, regardless of physical or astral level, has its own sacred right to free will.

   1.1 - Direct and specific direction is not to be given to those in the more dense planes of existence so as not to violate free will.

   1.1.1 - Dependency on external direction, even angels, can circumvent an individual's free will.

   1.2 - Though each spirit's path leads to the realization of its inner connect- edness with God, angels must not force control over the natural steps and free will to get there.

   1.2.1 - Spiritual growth is far too complex to determine the divine right step for someone else; therefore general guidance, not specific direc- tion, is called for.

Section 2 - Miracles in the Physical Plane

Creating, vanishing, altering or moving objects in the physical plane of existence, or revealing the actual existence of an angel, are allowed only in extremely rare situations in order to save the A.C.E. from being violated, or to assist large groups of individuals in accelerating their steps on spiritual paths.

2.1 - Should this create a situation that has individuals giving up their responsibility for choice and inner direction, steps should be immediately taken to return their confidence in their own free will, and motivation created to give up external dependencies.

Section 3 - Memories, Dreams and Co-incidences

Memories of individuals cannot be altered by angels; however, if it serves to accelerate steps on their spiritual path or to satisfy prayers or angel requests, memories can be caused to move to the forefront of consciousness. Likewise, images and thoughts can be brought forth through dreams, or by placing them in the forefront of consciousness, as long as this doesn't circumvent free will. The third and perhaps most powerful method of getting attention is the use of so-called co-incidences. Use of this technique is freely permitted as long as the results cannot be predicted.

Section 4 - Prayers

Prayer requests are implemented if they:

4.1 - do not interfere with the free will of anyone.

4.1.1 - have at least a 75 percent prayer-thought impulse level and have sufficient desire and belief (greater priority is given to greater impulse levels).

4.2 - are not canceled out by their own contradictory prayer-thought impulses or beliefs.

4.3 - are not canceled out by other individuals' prayer-thought impulses or beliefs.

4.4 - do not alter beliefs, unless they were ready to be changed anyway, or, unless the prayer specifically requests a change in a belief.

4.4.1 - Many beliefs can remain intact if suitable rationalizations are available to explain the occurrence without forcing a change in belief

4.5 - do not cause the individual to avoid a timely or key lesson, or cause a chain of events that will impair learning and spiritual evolvement.

4.6 - do not override micro-angel assignments maintaining standard physical laws, and other widely-held beliefs agreed to and believed in by many.

4.7 - do not create a dependency on prayers.

4.8 - reinforce knowingness of oneness with God, or at least do not diminish it.

4.9 - do not violate previous angel agreements regarding other individuals, unless those agreements can be renegotiated and new solutions found.

Page 1 - - - A.C.E. manual

~ ~ ~ ~ ~ ~ ~ ~

After a lot of applause, a fellow sitting on the floor raised his hand right away. Shawn wondered what the sharing would be about this time, since this story had such deep content.

The man said, "You know, I do think there is more to coincidences than what meets the eye. How many have had such incredible coincidences in their lives that you'd think the odds were a million-to-one against it happening?"

Many people in the room, including Shawn, nodded their heads in agreement.

The man went on, "Well, if you asked the scientists to investigate and come up with reasons, all they'll say is 'it's just coincidence'—but what's that? I think it's a label they put on something they have no way of explaining. It's like asking them how high is up and they answer, 'It's infinite' . . . That's just a label for something we still can't comprehend. I actually think there is something going on that we can't see. Something on the other side maybe; maybe there really ARE angels running around doing things and such."

"Ah, hogwash, George!" said a guy by the kitchen door. He took a drink from something out of a can. The man continued, "You're probably talking about all that metaphysical mumble jumble, UFO's and the like. Why make a big deal over it?"

George sat up straight on his pillow and said, "TV pictures go through the invisible air and appear on screens in millions of homes simultaneously. Yet if you'd talked about doing that a hundred years ago, it would have been put down too as totally impossible and idiotic to think about. Perhaps a hundred years from now, or less, we'll know why everyone experiences things explained away as 'coincidences.' The odds against somethings occurring are so astronomical—like one-in-a-billion odds, they just shouldn't happen—but they do! And not to just a few of us; it happens to everyone I've talked to."

"So I guess you think that story about angels is true?" taunted the man by the kitchen. "The reason there are coincidences is that there's a bunch of angels on the other side arranging things?" He started to laugh.

Big pot-bellied Bob, the owner of the house and Susie's father, looked like he wanted to share something serious. He got in on the discussion by saying, "Well, I have something I'd like you to explain to me. I was living up here long before Susie was born. A bunch of us boys decided we'd go into town at the base of the mountain afterwork to shoot some pool and all. Well, it was just time to leave work when I got a call from Jenny, Susie's mom—before she was a mom, that is. She was quite upset and said she just had to see me for some reason, but she didn't know why. She insisted and said if I didn't come over, it would be the end the relationship. We were just dating, but things were getting more serious. Well, I thought Jenny was just afraid us guys might meet some gals or something, and I didn't want to be controlled. In fact, I was downright angry that she would pull something like that." Bob paused to add, "If any of you have heard this, just bear with me, okay?"

He continued, "I went over to Jenny's house but wouldn't go in. I sat in my truck and made her come out to me. Whew, was I ticked off! We talked for a while, but I could see there wasn't really anything going on. It was just an excuse. She made me come in, and I left about 11 p.m." He paused for a moment, looked up and said, "Oh yeah, it's off the subject but I saw a strange glowing light by my truck . . . never figured out what it was." He continued by saying, "When I drove through the center of our little town, a bunch of people were talking near the pay phones at the closed market. I stopped and they said, 'Did you hear about Sam, Ted, and Charles?' Those were the friends I was going to drive down the hill with. The folks at the market went on to say that a big truck had been stalled on the road in front of my friends and an oncoming van was heading up in the other lane. When my friends swerved to miss the truck and the van, their car went over the side of the cliff. No one survived the terrible crash."

Everyone was silent. Then Bob looked directly at Susie and said, "Sure as hell if I'd been with them, I wouldn't be here right now, nor would Susie there or her brothers! I learned not to be quite so stubborn when Jenny's got a feeling about something."

Susie rubbed her arms as though she felt a chill.

Bob then looked at Dave, still sitting on the couch with his wife, Barb, and said, "You see, Jenny wasn't being 'logical,' but I'm damned glad she convinced me into staying!"

Dave just nodded his head.

Bob wasn't through. He looked over at the man still standing by the kitchen door and went on to say, "Then there's that coincidence stuff. Well, what are the odds that the only time in my life any woman forced me with that kind of threat, it ended up saving my life! Well, I don't know, but I wouldn't be surprised if some kind of angel was working overtime. I don't think it was JUST a coincidence, but then again, I don't know what it was."

The man by the kitchen just shook his head and looked down.

Bob turned to look at Shawn and asked, "You got any ideas, Shawn?"

Shawn was surprised that all of a sudden the ball was back in his court. He didn't feel any more knowledgeable than anyone else, but because he brought the stories, they seemed to look to him for answers. He just said, "I don't know. We each have to form our own beliefs. This is truly an individual thing since it is beyond the physical, or like some call it, metaphysical. I just had an accident on that same road and now that I think of it, there was no reason the car should have paused to let me out before it tumbled down the cliff. I was going much too fast for it to have come to a stop, and yet it did . . . Maybe I had an angel looking out for me too . . ."

Shawn's voice trailed off and he couldn't speak anymore. He remembered the ball of light sitting on the hood of his car, holding it down until he took its place. Everyone was silent as Shawn stared at the floor in deep contemplation, his hand raised to his chin. He couldn't bring himself to talk about something so strange with so many strangers.

Susie seemed anxious about the long pause, so she stood and asked, "Does anyone else have something to say?"

A gray-haired woman sitting on the extra-long couch raised her hand. People became very quiet to hear her soft voice. She rarely spoke in the group, so she had their full attention. "Now, I'm not one to try and force beliefs on anyone else. You all just believe what you want. I myself believe in angels. I never connected them before with coincidences, but it sure makes sense. I mean, most coincidences are like miracles if you think about it . . ." She stopped, but everyone was still looking with anticipation at her.

Susie asked her, "Do you have an example in your own life you could tell us about?"

"Yes, I do, but I just thought of something interesting. We've all had it happen that just as you start to call someone, you pick up the phone and that person is calling you—haven't you?" Many in the crowd ageed. "Well, thinking about the angel story, what if two angels made an agreement that their two *Earthlings* should talk together, but they weren't clear on which was to call the other! Both get the hint from their angels about the same time, right after one of those, what do you call it?—freeze-frames, and they both pick up the phone at the same time." The crowd laughed as they imagined the scene. Shawn was listening with great interest, since before this trip he hadn't thought about angels very much.

"Getting to my example. . . shucks, for never talking, you sure got me started tonight! I guess it's just a subject dear to my heart. I know I have one or more angels looking out after me. I just know it." As the gray-haired lady spoke, she slowly moved her eyes and head, making sure not to miss a single person with her gaze. Though she rarely spoke, it was clear that it wasn't because she was shy.

"Jeremy, my dear late husband after 42 years of marriage, is one of my angels now. I can feel his presence, and I think he puts little miracles together for me. Three years ago, winter was nearing and I had to have a new roof. It was going to take $4,000, and I did not have it. I prayed for a miracle—even talked to Jeremy as though he were right there, too. The very next day I get this phone call from a total stranger on his car phone asking if I wanted to sell my trailer. The renter had just moved out, and I hadn't even made the trip down to Oceanside to clean it up yet. He asked me what I'd sell it for. I had no idea. We'd bought it several years before for $1,500. After telling him to make an offer, to my surprise he just said, 'I can give you a check for $4,000 today!' Before I could catch my breath, he slightly covered the phone and I could hear him yell out, "Jeremy! You get down and come here right now!" Then he explained that his son *Jeremy* was trying to climb over the fence to the trailer. Well, I about fainted with the coincidence of the $4,000 and him actually saying my husband's name, even if it was his son's name too."

The lady sat down glowing with a radiant smile as the crowd applauded, cheered, and let out quite a few *wows*.

Susie looked around the crowd and seemed to sense something. She whispered something in Shawn's ear, and he nodded. She said to the group, "Okay, you know how lots of times when we meet, we sing a couple of songs? Well, I've got one that will get us moving around so we can have a stretch. So . . . everyone stand up, pick a partner, and face your partner . . ."

It came out evenly, so that everyone had a partner. Susie ended up with Shawn. She signalled, "Okay, now . . . quiet . . . shhh . . . okay, I'm going to sing this short song that my friend Karl Anthony sings. You all will hold hands, looking into your partner's eyes, and sing it twice to them. Then give them a hug and find a new partner and do it all over again. Here's the song:

"'Angel, angel, you are an angel; I see an angel in your eyes.'"

"And again the second time, sing it the same way." She sang, *"Angel, angel, you are an angel; I see an angel in your eyes."*

Angel Song

Karl Anthony
Copyright 1987
Excerpt with permission

"Then you give your partner a hug and pick a new partner." Susie was smiling with enthusiasm.

When Susie faced Shawn, ready to start the group singing, he just looked at her in utter amazement. "I think you could get anyone to do almost anything. You have a natural talent with groups, you know that?"

She said with an animated, giggly laugh and a cute little curtsy, "Why, thank you, Shawn," then she hollered to the talkative group, "Okay . . . shhhhh! . . . okay, here we go . . . start! Angel, angel, you are an angel . . ."

Shawn looked into Susie's eyes. His emotions were stirring. He forced himself not to get teary-eyed, but it was difficult because as he sang the song, her presence really touched him, and he truly saw what an angel she was. He noticed that he was having similar feelings with other people too. He changed partners over and over, singing the angel song and deeply looking into each person's eyes. The feeling of love seem to grow with each person, until he felt like he knew each person in depth from a level not of the mind, but of the heart.

After everyone had paired with everyone else, at the end of the song, they all cheered. Susie asked that a big circle be formed. The group seemed accustomed to doing that for they fell rapidly into a circle, putting their arms around the person on either side of them. Susie then asked the group to sing the song to everyone while looking around the circle. A few more rounds of the song were sung, and there wasn't one person without a giant smile.

Susie asked them to make their break short, and after some bathroom visits and refreshments, everyone was back, ready for another story.

Shawn sat down on the director's chair. When they'd returned from the break and gotten totally quiet, he said, "Just by coincidence, I happen to have another story available." The crowd laughed and he added, "I won't say too much about this story except that it has meant a lot to me. The story is cute and yet powerful in a subtle way. It kind of grows on you, if you remember one key phrase from the story."

Before Shawn started, he remembered that this was one of the stories Jake had mentioned in the forest. He wondered if the story would take on any different meaning now that he'd met Jake, since Jake had said he identified somewhat with the main character.

Shawn asked Susie if she would like to read, and of course, she was quite willing. He gave her his chair and took her place on the floor.

Susie bounced up there with her giant smile. Jack gave her the thumbs-up, and she opened the journal and began to read *Mountains out of Ant Hills*.

Shawn got as comfortable as he could on a pillow with no back support. At least he wouldn't be the center of attention for a while, he thought with relief. This had been quite an evening. Just as he thought that, Shawn spotted Jake giving him a double wink through the window. Jake nodded his head like he was agreeing with Shawn. Shawn looked around to see if anyone else was looking at Jake, but they were all watching Susie. Did they not see Jake? he wondered. Or was he not really there?

The next time Shawn looked, Jake wasn't there. Shawn wanted to go look out the window, but he didn't want to interrupt the story.

Finally, Shawn settled down and just listened to Susie. Actually, her vocal inflections and animated style were so entertaining, he quickly got into the story: *Mountains out of Ant Hills*.

Chapter 7

MOUNTAINS OUT OF ANT HILLS

I awoke to the sound of my roommates. They were scurrying around getting ready for work.

Never being the type to move too fast in the morning, I slowly blinked my eyes. It was still dark. Going back to sleep was a great temptation, but instead I had already decided to skip work today so I hardly wanted to sleep the day away.

I didn't tell the others of my plan. They were much too traditional to understand. In fact, they could be pretty hard on me if they knew. I gave up wondering why I'm so different from the others. From my earliest memories, I was always questioning why things were the way the were.

My biggest problem has been with accepting the various roles we play in society. "Why must they be so ridged?" I would ask my brother. I never got an answer. In fact, he never even appreciated my question. He would just say, "You think too much and waste too much time!"

After they all left, I got ready and rushed out only to see that it was an overcast day. Dark clouds threatened to spoil my day of hiking in the country. Since I was already late for work anyway, I decided to make the best of it.

The first half of the day was spent exploring unusual rock formations. They were so magnificent I wished someone had been with me to share the experience. Hardly a chance of that however, I was the only one with enough rebel to do something like this.

The clouds started their wet performance at the wrong time. The climb down from some steep rocks was already a challenge. The rain drops were so large, I was feeling quite battered by each drop.

I slipped and tumbled.

The sun was shining bright when I regained consciousness. Oh, what a headache I had. I must have been out for hours because it was late in the day.

It was that hit on the head that I think caused it. My life changed drastically from that time on. At first, my newly gained power was fun, then I felt cursed. You see I always loved thinking, but this was ridiculous! Let me explain.

I arrived home before my roommates. To keep my day off a secret, I pretended that illness kept me at home. Everything seemed quite normal until Charlie, the more sympathetic of my three roommates, came near me.

I heard Charlie say, "You big faker, you don't look sick to me."

This was not at all like Charlie. I asked, "What did you say?" As I waited for his answer, he turned his head as if he didn't understand the question.

When I repeated it, he said, "I didn't say a word. What? Are you hearing things or something? You must be sicker than I thought."

Then I heard him say with a laugh, "Maybe you have a touch of mental illness." However, this time I was looking right at him and knew that nothing was said out loud.

I was hearing his thoughts!

Wow! I was shocked, amazed, excited, scared and fascinated all at once. Then I heard Charlie think, "Boy am I tired and hungry. That rain sure made the day rough! I think I'll go . . . some . . . the . . . " As he walked away, it was as though I was losing reception of his thoughts. It was like my *antenna wasn't powerful enough.*

Everyone already thought I was a bit weird. If they knew about this, they would have locked me up for sure. Instead of telling anyone, I decided to experiment with my new power. What fun—reading the thoughts of others!

I walked up to one of my other roommates and just as I got within reach, his thoughts came in loud and clear. I heard Jim think, "I really need to strengthen my legs. They're skinny compared to everyone else."

Without realizing it, I responded, "There are some good exercises I learned. Would you like me to show you?" Of course, he was shocked and confused.

Jim said, "What do you mean? Exercises for what?"

Realizing this conversation could only lead to exposure of my new talent, I told Jim that he looked tired, and so I figured that perhaps with the right kind of exercise his work would not be so hard on him. Fortunately, he accepted my explanation though I could tell he was very puzzled about the coincidence of discussing what was on his mind at the time.

As days went by, I rather enjoyed this new power. Everyone I passed at work was busily thinking private thoughts and I was quite entertained. My ability to read thoughts was improving rapidly. I don't know whether it was due to my experience doing it or what, but everyday I was able to pick up thoughts from people farther away from me.

At first this was handy. I no longer had to walk near someone to listen to their thoughts, I could pick them up clear across the room. It was a Friday night that first started changing my mind about it being handy. It was then that I realized I was in deep trouble.

The party was going strong as I arrived in my usual late fashion. Never liking the beginnings of parties, I would just skip them and just be there when things got jumping. This was my chance to try it out on beautiful fe-

males. Just imagine I thought, I can find out which ones to pursue and which to avoid!

That was the last party I ever attended. It was also the shortest, most uncomfortable party of my life. Once inside, I was bombarded on all sides by hundreds of thoughts from everyone in the room.

I know what you're thinking. You're thinking so what's the big deal. When you go to parties you hear lots of different conversations and music too. The difference is that you can be somewhat selective with what you tune into. Move closer to one person and watch them speak and the rest blend into background noise.

Though my new power was quite remarkable, there was no volume control or selectivity. All thoughts of all those within range arrived crystal clear and at the same volume. Add to that the normal sounds at a party, plus the talking . . . well I was about to go crazy before I could get out of there. The two minutes I was there seemed like four hours.

I cried all the way home. I knew I'd never be able to go to a party again. Little did I know that this was only the beginning of something even worse.

It wasn't long before my power had increased to quite a distance. At work I could often hear hundreds of thoughts at a time. I got to where I couldn't tell my thoughts from theirs. It was constant confusion and headaches. My only relief was to stay home from work, but after awhile I even had to take extended hikes. When I traveled far enough and got out of range, the only thoughts I would hear were my own.

On one of my long walks, my single-minded thinking came to the conclusion that I must move away from all civilization. I must be far from anyone if I was going to save my sanity. I sat on a rock overlooking a valley. It felt as though I might fill the valley with my tears. Can you imagine my sadness to realize I must leave all those I love and live my life forever alone?

Chapter 8

It was then that I heard a voice. At first I thought I must be in range of someone and was picking up their thoughts, but I quickly realized that the voice was coming from a lightening bug. She said, "Listen carefully, I can only say this once and you must remember it."

I nodded yes and she said something I'll always cherish. Though I couldn't believe it then, I know now it is an absolute truth.

In a southern accent the lightening bug confidently said, "Everything's a lesson or a 'blessin'!"

She quickly flew into the night. I watched her amber light fade into the dark after only three blinks on and off.

I'd never seen a lightening bug before, much less one that talked to me. By the time the surprise wore off, I became a bit angry at what she had said. After all, how could that be true? Look at my life. I'm condemned to live in isolation. What's there to learn about that? And this certainly wasn't a blessing!

After a few weeks, I silently said good-bye to all my friends and relatives and left. Miles of travel placed me on top of a beautiful mountain. I decided that I had traveled far enough from everyone, so that is where I built my home. It was so incredibly difficult to hike in that area that I felt safe that I could live there for years without contact from anyone.

Fall came, and I prepared for winter. The winter only had about four heavy snowfalls, and I was happy to greet an early spring.

The air was clean and fresh, the sky was clear and beautiful. There was plenty of food and to my surprise, I discovered that though I was a bit lonely at times, the freedom to just be and do whatever I wanted was wonderful. What a blessing to live here in nature and not be confined to the roles of society.

Then I realized that I had been free to do this all along. Had it not been for my problem, I'd probably still be stuck working daybreak to sunset doing the same old thing. What a horrible thought. Then I remembered the phrase from the lightening bug, "Everything's a lesson or a 'blessin'." I understood that my lesson was that the only one truly limiting me was myself. Now, I have the life that I truly love, so the lesson has turned into a 'blessin'.

I wondered if that was true of all lessons—that once you get the lesson, it turns into a blessing. If that is true, then ultimately, everything is a blessing.

These lofty thoughts were interrupted by something very unusual—a thought that wasn't mine. Immediately I feared the worst. Perhaps civilization is going to cause me to move again.

Then I heard another thought. It said, "I wonder if anyone lives around here? I sure am hungry. What's that up there on top?"

I thought, "Oh no, someone is about to find my home." My thought was immediately followed by a foreign thought that said, "If this is your home, come out and greet me, I've been traveling for a long time."

As I looked down the path, I saw the most lovely creature I'd ever seen in my life. She was attractive and very fit. It was hard to believe that a female that beautiful was coming right to my home.

I heard her think, "You're pretty handsome yourself. What's your name? . . . my name is Julie." Without speaking, I just thought my name, and finally realized that she could read thoughts too.

In only a matter of minutes we found that both of us had left civilization for the same reason. I did find it a bit embarrassing at first for someone else to know what I was thinking, but I soon got used to it. One thing I knew for sure, it was going to be one of the most open and honest relationships I had ever had.

~ ~ ~ ~ ~ ~ ~

That was years ago, and we're still happily together. We've made plenty of wonderful tunnels in our home and it's very warm and comfy. Our colony only consists of us two ants, but we don't mind not having offspring. Two thinking as one is quite enough. Could you imagine the confusion of a bunch of quick thinking, six-legged little ones running all through our tunnels?

We thought about it. Then we both thought in unison, "No thanks, two ants are enough blessings to count!"

~ ~ ~ ~ ~ ~ ~

When Susie completed the last line everyone seem to look at each other and laugh. A person next to her said, "What a switch! All along the story was about mind-reading ants instead of people!"

There was a bunch of side talking going on as Shawn exchanged places with Susie. Shawn said, "Let's all give Susie a hand for doing such a good job of reading, okay?"

There was lots of applause and then a woman volunteered to share something. "I guess, Shawn, the key phrase in the story you referred to was, 'everything's a lesson or a blessing'. Right?"

Shawn nodded his head yes.

A middle-aged woman stood up and said, "My mom had always told me everything works out for the best which sounds kind of similar. I was married a couple of times and had several other relationships with some real creeps. I look back now and it's hard to believe what I saw in them. Some how I seem to attract men who were verbally abusive to me and abusive to themselves with alcohol or drugs. My second husband was an alcoholic with a fierce temper and a lot of jealousy. He was so wonderful when sober, I kept thinking he would change. Anyway, one day I came home from the market and paused outside to talk with the new neighbor across the street. When I came in, my husband was in a rage thinking I was flirting with the man. I tried to just go into the kitchen, but he hit me in the back of the head with his fist. The groceries went flying and I fell. Then he kicked me several times. I woke up in the hospital. After the police report, he ended up in jail."

A few people let out a gasp hearing about the abuse she suffered. Then the woman with some sadness in her voice continued, "In the hospital I kept trying to see how being beaten up could possibly be for the best . . . but you know, it truly was. While in the hospital, a woman visited me from a support group for battered and abused women. It started a chain of events that has made my life 1000 percent better and maybe saved my life. To be brief, through many meetings and workshops I built up my self esteem, which was so low that it was really the reason I was attracting such abusive men. I went back into teaching—which I loved, got myself together, lost about 45 pounds and then I met Matt. We've been married now for 8 beautiful years, and I am so very happy." She took hold of Matt's hand and gave him a loving smile. She added, "By the way, Matt isn't like any of the other men. He doesn't drink, smoke or even swear—talk about angels, I found mine!"

The woman started to sit down while people were applauding her, but she stood back up and said after the crowd got silent again, "I guess my lesson was to know I was a much better person than I thought, and that I deserved to be loved. Once I got the lesson—that whole ordeal turned into a blessing. Thanks for letting me share this with you."

She got another round of applause, and her husband gave her a hug as she sat down again.

Another woman stood up that appeared to be in her late 20's. She looked at Shawn and said, "You've been awfully silent about all of this . . . maybe I could get your opinion on something."

Shawn eyes opened a bit wider and replied, "Sure, for what it's worth, but just remember it's just another person's opinion . . . I can't guarantee it will be correct."

"Well you've been around these stories most of your life. I'd be interested to know what you personally think about the story that was read earlier, *Angels,* especially having to do with soul mates. I can't seem to get it out of my mind."

Shawn sat up on his chair and stiffened his legs as if bracing himself. His previous relaxed posture was just for listening. He asked, "You mean about how you can find one?"

She laughed and said, "No, at this point I just want to know if you have had any experience in your family regarding soul mates."

He replied, "I can share a bit of family history. My aunt was divorced and had not even seriously dated for over six years. She came to Grampa in tears. She said she had been praying for her soul mate and nothing was happening. When she finally met with Grampa she hadn't even had a date for over five months. I was visiting at the time, so I got to hear the story *Angels.* After Grampa heard her cry and talk and cry and talk about her problem, he just sat back in his large fold-back leather chair, sipped some hot tea and said, 'That reminds me of a story; do you want to hear it?'"

Feeling a bit more relaxed, Shawn sat back in his own chair and added, "After two months we got a letter from my Aunt. She was in a relationship and they were seeing each other many nights a week. A year later they were married—still are as a matter of fact."

"Was that her soul mate?" the same woman asked.

Shawn smiled and said, "I don't know. After hearing the story she said she modified her prayers to ask for a wonderful mate who may or may not be a soul mate. By *coincidence,* that very same week, a man she'd known for years asked her out for coffee and donuts. During that short time together, she saw him in a whole different light and romance was in the air for the first time in years. Perhaps he isn't her soul mate . . . perhaps he is . . . whatever that is . . . but he does seem to be an excellent match for her. The odd thing is that he was right there all along until she changed her prayers."

The woman said, "Maybe that's my problem. I've been praying for a soul mate too, but to tell you the truth, I'm not sure what that is. I just want to be happily married and start having children while I'm young. What do you think, Shawn?"

"If you were looking for a house to buy, say a three bedroom with two baths and an attached garage. You'd have a lot of choices. If you also specified that it must have been built in 1987, is located within a block of your friend's house, has only been owned by one family who's last name starts with the letter L and has exactly four trees . . . how long might you wait?"

"Are you saying by wanting a soul mate I'm making it that difficult?" the woman asked with a frown and a strained voice.

Shawn adjusted his shirt. He was feeling warm all of a sudden. He answered, "I'm saying I believe in prayer, yet I'm not sure what's involved with asking for a soul mate. I'm very much in love with my wife, Mary, yet I have no idea whether or not she is one of my soul mates. Perhaps if I had asked for a soul mate I wouldn't even be with her, and, after all these wonderful years I don't even want to imagine that." As he said that he pictured his wife giving him a hug when he left home only last night, which seem like a year ago. He was starting to miss her and reminded himself to call her tonight.

"Did you ever ask your grandfather about soul mates?" Susie asked.

Shawn chuckled a bit and replied, "I gave up asking about the stories. Grampa's answer to any question about the stories was always the same, he would just say, 'I tell the stories, you listen to the stories. All the answers you need are right between your ears.'" Then Shawn laughed and said, "I guess that's where your 'inner ear' is located."

Susie was perceptive enough to see that people were getting tired. It was after ten anyway, so she started bringing the evening to a close. First she went up and whispered something in Shawn's ear, and he said something back. She smiled brightly and asked, "How many are tired, but would still like a chance to hear a couple more stories tomorrow?"

Almost everyone raised their hands. She said, "Well, tomorrow's Sunday so most of us don't have work. All we need is a place to meet . . . say about 12:30? Any ideas?"

A woman near the kitchen yelled out, "Why not in the picnic grounds in Idyllwild Park? Most of the tourists are gone for the season, maybe us locals can enjoy the park a little for a change."

Everyone agreed, and they decided to make it a potluck picnic while they were at it. Then everyone seemed to want to come up and either shake Shawn's hand or give him a old fashion friendly hug. By the time he said his final good-bye to Susie and her parents, he was really tired.

He drove through town and saw the little market Bob had mentioned. What a story, he thought to himself. Sometimes life is stranger than fiction.

Shawn started settling down as he neared the fire station and for some reason he turned right instead of heading on up the hill toward home. It was the strangest thing. Soon he arrived at Pine Cove Park. Shawn remembered a giant boulder there that he named Lookout Rock. It has a magnificent view of everything from lights at the base of the mountain to the unobstructed view of millions of stars.

He stopped the truck and walked past the restrooms and up the path to the boulder. Since it was a full moon, he didn't need a flashlight. He'd been there when the moon wasn't out and had trouble finding Lookout Rock.

Soon he was perched on top of the giant bolder. He was going to think about the decision in the office, but decided that he'd wait until his grandfather told him a story. At this point he was just confused about it all. He looked up at the millions of stars and said, "Ahhhhh" like in the caveman story. Looking over his left shoulder he found the belt of Orion. What a beautiful set of three stars, he thought.

"You sure got it rite. Those are quite sumptin' huh! My favorite." the voice came just over his left shoulder on an adjacent boulder. Shawn knew it was Jake even before he turned and saw the old man crouched down like he wanted to sit on the boulder, but not quite yet.

Perhaps it was his smile, his twinkly eyes, or the fact that Shawn was exhausted, but he didn't feel afraid of this old man whoever he was. But he was curious and asked, "Who are you, and I don't mean your name . . . what are you?"

Jake said, "Ah, it don't matter none. You'll be a believin' whatever yer believin' anyway. The question is, who are ya? When ya can answer that one right, ahhh, that's the challenge in life!"

"Are you an angel?" Shawn persisted.

"Isn't everyone?" Before Shawn could think about that, Jake followed it up with, "Look, I cain't be sayin' much. We all have missions in life as well as learnins, and we fit in heaps a lovin' too, and sometimes some of us can make things better for a whole lotta of others."

Somehow the old man was now at the foot of the boulder looking up. Shawn shouted out, "Don't go yet. What are you trying to tell me? I've got lots of questions . . . like what's that bluish glowing light I've been seeing?"

As old Jake walked away, he looked back and just said, "Wat lite, I don't see no lite?" He took a few more steps and added, "Just tell yer Gramps to 'tell ya'."

It was near 11:00 p.m. by the time Shawn got back to the cabin. Trinket greeted him on the porch and acted like she was hungry. The porch light had attracted a few bugs, so he picked up Trinket and squeezed in the screen door trying not to let any bugs in, or make much noise. Unfortunately, three buzzing creatures entered and the screen door banged close, so he accomplished neither.

With a little bowl of milk and some petting, Trinket's loud purring filled the quiet kitchen. Shawn glanced up and saw the old antique phone on the wall and remembered he wanted to call Mary before it got too late. He walked over, leaned across the little kitchen table and reached for the bell-shaped listening object in the cradle. Just as he touched the smooth black surface it responded with a loud ear piercing ring. Shawn yelled! Trinket must have thought he was after her for she wasted no time leaving the kitchen in one long blurry streak.

"Hello?" Shawn asked as he strained to speak into the black round cup while holding the awkward ear piece.

"Shawn? I've been wondering how you're doing. Why haven't you called?"

"What a coincidence, it happened again. I was reaching for the phone to call you! I guess our angels made some agreements for us in that last frame huh!"

Mary sounded puzzled, "What do you mean?"

"Remember the story *Angels*? . . . oh never mind, I'll tell you about it when I get home. I was missing you today."

"Me too . . . and I've been worried about how you've been doing with the decision and all. Have you been making progress?"

Shawn gave Mary a brief version of telling stories on the hiking path, meeting Susie, and the evening of storytelling. After about ten minutes, he started getting a cramp from leaning over the table to talk into the antique phone. When he complained about it, Mary said, "There's a phone in the living room—it looks like an antique car, but it's really a phone. Remember? They got it last year as a Christmas present from your sister."

For years there had been only one phone on the first floor. Shawn remembered that the only way his grandfather had allowed the second one was to disable the ringer, and he liked the fact that it looked like a car he used to own—an old Model "T" Ford. Shawn had forgotten all about that phone, but he was relieved when he switched to the living room. He got comfortable in Grampa's chair and talked for almost an hour more. He mentioned Susie so often, Mary finally asked, "How old did you say Susie is?"

"Oh, Honey, I think she's only 18 or 19. Soul-wise, though, she's probably about a million years old. Not to worry; you'll always be the only one for me. She has just kind of amazed me. She's not only drawn to the stories, but she seems to work naturally with people, and is definitely an extrovert. She's so different from me! You know, we all got into a discussion about soul mates tonight and I—your shy old Shawn—told the whole group that I didn't care if you and I are or are not soul mates; that I loved you and couldn't imagine being with anyone else!"

"Shawn. That's so sweet. I love you, too. Then in Mary's sexiest voice she asked, "Do you know when you'll be coming home? I have a special welcome home surprise for you, if you know what I mean . . ." She added in a lower, softer voice, "Do you . . . want me . . . to tell you . . . all about it?"

He felt a familiar excitement grow as though he were a teenager talking to his girlfriend. "Whew, Mary, you sure know how to get me going! I wish I was there right now. You know what I would do?"

"What would you do?"

"Remember our second night vacationing in Maui?" Shawn could do a bit of teasing himself.

"How could I forget. Okay, I know we'd better stop now before this gets too hot for your grandparents' phone lines."

"I'll call you after I get to see Grampa, okay?"

They said goodnight, and he went right to bed. Shawn was so exhausted he even forgot to turn off the lights which provided good entertainment for the three buzzing bugs. Trinket finished her milk and curled up in Grampa's chair as if to keep it warm for him.

The next morning Shawn woke up to a car door shutting in the driveway. His first thoughts were, *Grampa is back!* He jumped out of bed, and pulled on a shirt and trousers. With his excitement he got his shirt stuck in the zipper. It was stuck half way and wouldn't budge. His shirt wouldn't come out either. Finally, he said "Forget it!" and started downstairs. His left toe caught his right pant leg and in order to keep from tumbling down the stairs, he reached out to grab something. He caught the top of the banister and felt relief. However, he also bumped the potted plant on the ledge above the living room.

In slow motion, he watched the potted plant gracefully leave the ledge and fly off like some alien spacecraft down toward the center of the living room. Shawn covered his eyes just about the time it crashed next to the coffee table down below. It kind of reminded him of the potted plant he broke in 2nd grade, except this one had much farther to fall. Trinket was again frightened by another one of Shawn's noisy episodes and fled the living room as if her life depended on a quick disappearance.

Shawn's head was now throbbing. This wasn't his idea of how to get up in the morning. He walked downstairs and looked out the front door. No one was there. He walked into the living room and looked at the plant, the smashed clay pot, and dirt scattered about on the rug. He was so thankful it missed the coffee table. Grampa made it, as he had most of the other furniture in the house. He used to design and build wood furniture for a living, but now it was just a hobby of his.

Shawn couldn't face cleaning up the mess yet, so he decided to get some orange juice and just relax.

A note on the kitchen table explained the car door. It said, *Dear Shawn, Hope you don't mind, I was invited out to breakfast and church. Help yourself to anything. Go ahead and use the truck, I'm being picked up. Grampa should be home about 5, I'll probably be home around 1 p.m. Love, Gramma*

The peace and quiet felt good. He visited so often that they just treated him like he lived there. That was just fine with him.

The fresh orange juice made every taste bud come alive. Wiping his mouth on his sleeve, he glanced in the living room at the tall grandfather clock with its giant brass pendulum swinging gracefully back and forth. Tick . . . tick . . . tick . . . tick . . .

It was only 8:10 a.m. Trinket peeked cautiously into the kitchen. Shawn laughed and said, "Oh poor Trinket, come on baby, Shawn will be good." Seeing that Gramma had fed her, he decided to give her a little peace by taking his orange juice into the living room. Taking a sip of orange juice, he saw Grampa's chair inviting him over. People generally avoided it when Grampa was around. That seat was reserved, yet he loved sitting there whenever possible.

He sank down into the essence of its comfort. It felt like his Grampa was holding him like when he was little. This was a good time for him to reflect on last night. "Oh no," he said, "I forgot to do a prayer before I went to sleep." On that, he did a short 5-step prayer pretty much like the one he said in the forest. He even remembered to hold his little prayer stone for added energy. Though he didn't go to church much, prayers were pretty common with him.

He thought about the evening and shook his head remembering all the people that shared and how the stories were received. It's wonderful, he thought, when you can share something you love and then have those people love it too. Maybe I'll just quit my job and wander from town to town reading stories. Sure, I'll be a gypsy and forget about a dream house. What AM I going to do on Monday? Do I let go of everything or do I help promote something I hate? Then he thought, It's kind of like voting—you get to pick the least worst of the two candidates. Then he steered his mind away from politics because he wanted to stay calm. He hated how no one sees that the system must be changed, or at least no one does anything to change it so that special-interest group money doesn't have so much influence. He felt strongly that we must change what motivates elected officials otherwise the system just molds the frisky, bright idealized candidates into robots serving those wielding power and money.

The phone rang. Somehow he knew it was Susie. She sure is an energetic little gal, he thought as he walked toward the kitchen forgetting about the phone in the living room.

"Hello," he said as he leaned over the table to talk into the little funnel-shaped mouth piece. Then he realized why his grand parents didn't talk on the phone too long. It was too uncomfortable! Just as he remembered the other phone in the living room, he heard Susie's melodic and perky voice.

"Hi, Shawn?"

"Yes, hello, Susie."

"Hey, you recognized me. Great. Hey, I wanted to talk to you about the thing at 12:30." She talked fast like she was in a hurry to leave.

"Oh yeah. Say, where in Idyllwild Park is the meeting area?"

Susie said to follow the road to where it loops around the picnic area and not to worry about bringing anything to eat because he was bringing the entertainment—the stories. Then she asked what stories were left and how could people hear the ones they missed.

He said, "Well, there are three stories left—*The Playground Fence,*

Comets, and *Eagles*. Then he thought silently to himself, . . . and if I'm lucky, Grampa will tell me a new one.

He continued saying, "As far as hearing the stories they missed, I don't know, we're kind of running out of time and Grampa always frowned when I talked about giving anyone a copy of one the stories. I don't know, maybe he plans on publishing them some day. Actually, I really didn't get his permission to even tell them in public, but Gramma says she knows it would be all right."

"Well then, you'll just have to come back soon for another visit!" she enthusiastically pointed out.

"I'd really like that more than you know, Susie. I've loved telling the stories, and I want to thank you for putting this all together. Say, how many people do you think will show up . . . probably about half of what was there last night?" Shawn guessed half based on general invitations and no shows and his own desire to keep it small and comfortable.

Susie said to his surprise that she thinks the number will be closer to 60 or 70 because the word seems to be spreading. She also said that she's in a hurry to get some kind of loud speaker prepared just in case.

All of a sudden, Shawn felt like he had just eaten too much again. Perspiration started appearing on his forehead as he imagined speaking to the whole town of Idyllwild with a P.A. system, maybe spotlights, ushers, a band, flags, baton twirlers . . . .

"Shawn?" Susie interrupted his thoughts.

He shook his head trying to shake off the scary image of him addressing a few thousand people with perhaps the governor flying in to listen.

"Oh Susie, I'm sorry . . . I guess, well, you know I've really never been in front of very many people. I used to be an accountant, and now I may give a presentation to at most 6 or 10 people, . . . I just don't know about this . . . "

"Shawn, just remember all you have to do is read, or delegate the reading. Besides, I have something planned for the sharing. I've been wanting to learn how to lead workshops, so maybe I can practice. The difference between a workshop and a lecture is that you get the people involved doing things. There may be more people wanting to share than we have time for, so if it's okay, I know how to split them up into little sharing groups. What do you think?"

He was quite happy she wanted to get so involved and told her to just plan it all and that he was going to try to not think about it.

After eating a snack and cleaning up the potted plant mess in the living room, he felt like he was ready for bed again. Settling for a hot shower instead, he started to remove his clothes—the only ones he had since the overnight bag was still in the car at the bottom of the cliff. However, the shirt was seriously stuck in the zipper. About 3 inches of the shirt tail protruded from the front of the pants, which would certainly attract lots of attention in front of 3 thousand people. Shawn corrected himself—60 people.

"I've got to get out of these clothes," he said to himself. Locating some scissors in Gramma's sewing room, he drew in his breath and slipped them carefully inside his trousers to cut off his shirt tail. Trinket rubbed up against his leg with a purr, but Shawn was too preoccupied to show any attention. Though he missed pertinent personal parts, his shirt tail was not the only thing cut. He now had a nice odd shaped hole in the front of his trousers, but at least he could take them off.

Shawn and his grandfather were about the same size, so he went clothes shopping in his closet. This is funny, he thought, here I'm going to be wearing Grampa's clothes, reading his stories in public, sleeping in his house and driving his truck! It's like I'm becoming Grampa! This is not what I expected this weekend.

Finally, he arrived at the park about 12:15. He was wearing a dashing large-square, black and red plaid flannel shirt, accented by blue-jean coveralls with button-down straps crossing in the back, and a timid nervous smile. He even remembered to bring the purple journal which added an accented touch to his color co-ordinated outfit.

Shawn had never worn coveralls before. He felt loose—kind of like he wasn't fully clothed or something. It was almost like the first, and last time, he'd worn boxer shorts. If the right clothes are said to add confidence, this outfit made him want to leave the country. Grampa's regular pants wouldn't fit, they were just too big. The coveralls were too large also, but it was harder to detect.

Wanting to check things out first, he had purposely parked about a half mile from the meeting area. He walked up the hill and paused behind trees and bushes. When he came over the top of the next little hill he saw about 90 people gathered in the clearing complete with microphone and speakers. Shawn had trouble swallowing.

"Remember," he said to himself, "all I have to do is read. Nothing else. All I have to do is read." He kept repeating this as he finally went down to talk to Susie.

As soon as Susie saw him she started waving to come over. He shuffled over and tried to hide his nervousness by pretending to be very calm. As he talked to Susie, he crossed his legs and put his hand down on the table. However, he missed and hit the extended edge of a paper plate containing about 40 stacked marshmallows. The plate flipped, and the little white fellows went flying all over like fluffy golf balls.

Before Shawn scrambled to pick them up, Susie said, "What fun. Hey, what would it be like if the sky hailed marshmallows instead of ice?"

He just looked up at her, smiled and said, "I guess there'd be a lot of happy kids roasting them." Susie helped and hardly anyone really noticed since they were all setting out food and talking. Somehow Susie had a way of making him feel comfortable, yet ironically enough, he thought, she's the one always getting him in these difficult spots in the first place.

Barb and her husband, Dave, were there. Shawn looked around to see who else he could recognize as he munched on a celery stick. He said hi to the future chiropractor. Though there were many new faces, those he recognized were like old friends after singing to each one of them last night. Bit by bit, he started feeling more comfortable and actually started enjoying himself.

Too bad he wasn't hungrier because there was a ton of food. Those Idyllwild people go wild with their homemade chili, bar-b-q meats and all sorts of extras.

Shawn heard Susie's voice over a speaker system. The sound carried quite well. In fact, people not in their group farther down in the park were looking toward Susie. This did not comfort him.

Susie did a great job of reviewing what has happened, an introduction about the stories, Grampa, and a good acknowledgment to Shawn for telling the stories. She also said, "Many of you meet regularly and don't need any encouragement to share your feelings and all. In fact, some go on . . . and on . . . and on . . . " There was some laughter. "However, those of you who are new to this, please just feel comfortable to listen or share as much as you like. She also had them select groups of about 5 to 8 people which would be their sharing partners after a story was told. She told them they would first share within their little group about what they realized out of the story and perhaps what they may have discovered about their own life. Then she said, if any have a pressing need to share something with the large group there maybe time for a few.

She handed the microphone to Shawn, and he got a round of applause. When he thanked Susie, they also applauded. He said a few words to convey how he appreciated everyone's friendly reception and enjoyment of the stories.

Then he said, "The first story today is called *The Playground Fence*. I don't like to say too much before a story so you can form your own impressions, so I'll just begin." Besides, he thought to himself, I'm too scared to think of anything to say anyway!

He opened the journal and found a new challenge already in how to hold the journal and the microphone and turn pages and try and relax too. He sat down at a picnic bench and laid the journal down in front of him. This also accomplished a goal of not being so prominent and visible.

Shawn began reading *The Playground Fence* while gently setting his foot down on an escaped unsuspecting marshmallow.

THE PLAYGROUND FENCE

I stand as the border surrounding the playground for God's little children. My steel wires weave a scary barrier to prevent children from leaving before their time. My low profile allows the Father or the Mother to lift a child in or out, yet I have no open gates that a wandering child may find.

All day long I stand, surround the playground and observe, yet I long to speak. There is much I would tell the children of God to make their short stay much more rewarding.

Each child responds differently when placed inside this wondrous and diverse playground.

Some act as though this were their first visit. I notice them more because they cry, scream and try to climb up my wireside to escape the feeling of abandonment.

I long to speak and say, "Dear child, you are placed here out of love for only a short while. Play, love, learn and enjoy yourself. Sooner than you think, you'll return to the other side."

OOPS, here comes Mindy again. Her feet are already running when her Father places her inside. Sure enough, she's heading right to the slide. Mindy loves the slide so much she never tries out the swings, merry-go-'round or even the miscellaneous toys.

I long to speak and say, "There is so much to experience in the play-

ground, your limits are self-imposed."

Bobby is sitting under the slide with a few other kids. He's teaching them all sorts of things. Listen carefully and you can hear him say, "I've learned the secrets of this strange place. The only way you can ever go home is to do as I say. Before you go on the slide you must always tap it three times and ask the slide to forgive you for using it."

You can see Bobby's followers all over. Look, there's Joanne using five taps for the swing and then bowing to the east. I guess this can be considered just another children's game, yet it consumes much of their time and attention. Look at their faces. Most of them are doing it out of fear—not love and joy.

I long to speak and say, "There is nothing you need to do, dear children. Just learn and love one another and don't hurt yourself or others."

Ah, there's Jim on the grass with a pile of toys. He thinks the playground is all about seeing how he can possess the most toys. Unfortunately, with all the time he takes gathering them and protecting his pile, he hardly has a chance to play.

I long to speak and say, "Play with whatever toy you have, don't hoard toys because you can't take them with you. They stay in the playground."

One of Carrie's followers is sitting on the grass leaning up against one of my poles. Carrie teaches that the way to get home is by not playing. "Just sit still," she says, "don't look or play with anyone and soon you'll be picked up and taken home."

An almost opposite teaching is spread by Allen being pushed on the swing by Janet. Allen tells kids that he knows someone on the other side and if they don't push him on the swing, they'll be kidnapped and hurt. Sometimes Allen hits them to show how they could be hurt if they don't do what he says.

Oh, I long to speak and say, "Learn to treat others with honesty, caring and respect. Toys and other children to play with is a privilege and could be taken away."

Why is Cindy just sitting by the merry-go-'round and pouting you ask? Well, Cindy thinks she shouldn't have to do anything. She says she shouldn't have to climb the stairs to go down the slide, or pump herself in order to swing. Often she waits by the merry-go-'round until others are pushing it, and then she takes a free ride.

There are others like Cindy. They're the toy stealers. Instead of finding their own toys to play with, they grab others' toys and run. Sometimes they just destroy the game others are playing because they don't feel they could win.

Yes, I long to speak and say, "This is not the only playground, dear children. There are others far more fun and enriching, and, there are others which have only broken toys. You reap what you sow. The next playground you visit will be exactly what you need, not as punishment, but for your own learning. Play, love, learn and enjoy yourself."

I see that Martha is about to be picked up after many, many times visiting this playground. She has learned to play with most all the equipment and toys, has loved the other children and treated them kindly. She even teaches others the principles I would teach if I could speak. Martha is as close to an angel as they come.

I long to speak and say, "Remember Martha, she learned to always treat each person as though it was their last day in the playground."

As Martha is gently lifted, she smiles to all around. She waves and wishes all her friends love and joy. I happen to know of the next playground planned for her. It's filled with much greater wondrous toys and even a fence that talks.

~ ~ ~ ~ ~ ~ ~

There was a bit of silence at the end, followed by gentle applause. Shawn knew people were doing some thinking. He handed Susie the microphone. She asked that people take turns sharing within their groups, set the microphone back down and clicked it off. "Shawn," she said with an unusually soft voice and eyes puffing ready to cry, "do you want to join our group? We only have four so far . . . "

Though he was concerned about Susie, he didn't mention anything. He just patted her back sympathetically as he sat down next to her. Susie said, "Shawn this is Mark and next him is one of my very best friends, Nadine, and next to her is Cindy . . . I think you met her last night. After nodding hello to everyone he glanced around at the rest of the crowd and saw them moving closer together in small groups in order to hear each other. In no time the area was murmuring with gentle voices. He shook his head slightly as he was amazed at how Susie could orchestrate the activities of a group of people so smoothly. They just seemed to naturally follow her.

He noticed that Susie had her head down and was avoiding eye contact. Though she really got attention when she wanted, a new talent for becoming invisible emerged. Mark volunteered to be the first person in the group to talk. Susie sighed with her breath ever so slightly and appeared relieved that someone else was going to speak. He was a young man in his late 20's wearing very stylish sunglasses pushed up on his head, which gave the message he was cool. He was dressed in nice clothes without any wrinkles, was wearing a very expensive watch and his big-city grooming seemed just a bit out of place in this small mountain town.

Mark said in a low voice, "There's a T-shirt that says something like, 'He who owns the most toys in the end wins' . . . I've been so busy collecting toys like in the story, I haven't spent much time thinking about what life is all about. It hasn't been easy. I've been working two jobs now for a couple of years and come up here for visits to de-stress. I don't want to think about death or morbid things like that, it's kind of creepy you know . . . I guess I use my car and boat and high-tech stereo to distract me from thinking about what I'm really doing here.

Is there a purpose to life? Do we continue on after we die? Or, is it a one-shot deal where we go around seeking pleasure, avoiding pain, turn the lights out and never wake up again? . . . I guess the story just stirred things up a bit . . . I'm feeling a lot confused."

No one had any comments, but after a pause Mark looked at Susie and said, "Your turn, Susie."

Susie kept her eyes low and said, "To be honest I'm feeling quite sad right now. I'm sorry, Mark, I don't even know if I really heard you." Her normally bubbly voice was soft and thoughtful as she shared, "That last thing in the story about Martha treating each person as though it were 'their' last day . . . well it reminded me of Denise." Nadine reached over and took Susie's hand and cupped it in both of hers. When Susie looked up at Nadine, both had teary eyes.

Nadine said in a very caring voice, "Susie, hon, I know what you are feeling. You were so close to Denise."

With that, Susie started crying, and Shawn handed her a napkin that had survived the picnic. After composing herself a bit she said, "Maybe people wouldn't carry around anger and resentment as much if they realized they may never see that person again. It happened to me last year . . . I was angry at my very best friend, Denise, and stopped speaking to her. We were so close, we often said the same thing at the same time. I could read her face like a book. I knew whenever she raised her right eyebrow just the slightest she was about to make fun of something. Anyway, she had borrowed an outfit of mine, got permanent stains on it and never offered to do anything to make it up to me. She didn't seem to respect my clothes just as she didn't hers. In a childish way that I'll regret forever, I thought I'd teach her a lesson. I passed her in the school hall one Friday and gave her the cold shoulder and looked the other way when she said hi. She didn't even know why 'cause I also wasn't speaking to her. On Sunday, her mother called me to say Denise was in the hospital in a coma. While rock climbing the previous day near the very steep portion of Lily Rock in Tahquitz Park, she took a bad fall. She never regained consciousness, and I never got to say I was sorry and patch things up. I can never tell her how much I loved her. It still hurts . . . " Susie started to cry again, and now Nadine traded places with Mark and hugged Susie. Nadine also had tears in her eyes.

In a few minutes, Susie recovered, dried her eyes and said, "I'm okay now. Thank you all for listening. Actually, I feel deep inside that Denise understands. Personally, I believe only our physical body stops at death. I think we pass to the other side and can still see what's going on. Have you read some of those stories about people who died and came back? I think that's true."

Our group was happy to see how Susie rebounded from her sadness and soon we had all shared. As a conscientious workshop leader, Susie excused herself and walked around to see how much more time people needed to complete. Since some had larger groups than ours, she gave everyone a few more minutes. She didn't notice that Nadine was also visiting each group.

When Susie picked up the microphone and asked for every one's attention, instead of becoming quiet, they all started singing 'Row row row your boat'. She immediately looked at Nadine with a smile bigger than Texas and shook her finger at her. Different groups even came in at different times and Susie started waving her hands like a conductor.

After it was over, Susie looked at Nadine and asked, "Did you put them up to singing my favorite song?"

Nadine nodded her head yes while saying to Shawn and their small group that the song has great spiritual meaning to Susie and she thought it would pick up her spirits a little. He immediately asked Nadine, "What do you mean?"

Instead of answering his question, she turned toward Susie and said loudly, "Hey, Susie, Shawn would like to know why you get so much meaning out of that song. Tell us all, okay?" Then Nadine whispered to Shawn and the small group, "If Susie explains it, I think she'll be even more uplifted . . . she really has a thing for that song."

Susie beamed a smile as she looked up and said, "Some of you have heard me say this before . . . do you mind hearing it again?" The crowd applauded and many yelled out, "Go for it, Susie." "Yeah, tell it again."

"Okay, but this time Nadine you got to help. Come on up here."

Nadine got up and went and stood by Susie with her hands behind her back.

Things flowed almost like it had been planned long in advance. Susie somehow managed to involve everyone in the process. Again Shawn was surprised at this girl who was barely out of high school with such great presence and natural instinct in front of people. Susie told the group, "Okay, here's how we'll do this. When I raise my hand, the whole group will sing one line of the verse. Nadine and I will alternate in describing what it means. Okay?" Some people said yes and others nodded yes.

"I have no idea who made up this song, but I think it is much more than a silly kid's song. I think the person who wrote it was quite advanced. A friend of mine first told me about some things he got from the song. I added some other interpretations to it. Well, here it goes . . . " Susie whispered something to Nadine and then raised her hand. The group all sang, "Row row row your boat," and Susie started explaining the first line, "The boat is your body which temporarily houses your invisible spirit, which is the real you. It is YOUR boat and it belongs to no other spirit or person. God has given you free will and you may do whatever you choose with this boat. Of course, you will also reap what you sow. You know, 'what you put out, you get back'! The song is telling us to 'row, row, row'. Although we have been given a boat, a body, we must not just sit and do nothing. A boat with no power or rowing is merely adrift in the stream and is then subject to crash into rocks, getting stuck, or hitting the rapids and turning over damaging the boat. Many times I hear people complain of terrible things happening in the world and they say things like, 'If there is a God, how could He let such horrible things happen?' Well, I believe that He has given us creative abilities, a giant playground called Earth and most of all, free will. How much heaven or hell we collectively create with that is up to us."

Susie raised her hand again and handed the microphone to Nadine. The group all sang, "gently down the stream," and Nadine started to describe the phrase as Susie took a hold of her hand and moved the microphone closer to her mouth. "Which direction should you row? In the direction of the stream." Nadine looked at Susie and continued, "Going against the stream wastes a lot of energy and in the long run, the stream still wins out." Nadine paused and looked at Susie again and then said, "Oh yeah, going back and forth across the stream ends up with a lot of stops and starts. So the direction is with the stream, but 'gently'. You needn't force your boat or make it stressful. Just row gently, guiding your boat to avoid collisions with rocks, other boats and obstacles so that you can continue gently down the stream of life."

Susie smiled and raised her hand as she took the microphone back. The crowd sang, "merrily, merrily, merrily, merrily." Susie said, "This word is repeated four times for emphasis. Our journey down the stream in our boat is meant to be merry. Perhaps by grasping the larger picture of reality, even the rapids can be taken with a bit of merriment in our hearts. Let go of stress, experience the true joy of the journey down the stream in your boat. If you're not, perhaps you're taking the voyage a bit too seriously. Since we're all suppose to be merry, we should row our boat in a way that best helps everyone achieve a smooth trip—merrily. You know, like the win-win philosophy except globally, too. Until all people have adequate food, shelter, education and others aren't forcefully trying to control and manipulate their free will, we may not be fully satisfied, but we need not deny ourselves the joy of living."

Again, Susie raised her hand and passed the microphone. The crowd sang the next phrase, "life is but a dream." Nadine said, "As your boat reaches the end of the stream that returns back into the great ocean, the boat eventually dissolves and your spirit ascends into the heavens like a water droplet completing this dream." Nadine paused, handed Susie the microphone and said, "You have some more, but I don't remember it exactly."

Susie said, "Personally I believe each one of us is eternal. If that's true, how long, in comparison, is this life you're living? It's like a flash or a second. If it's that short compared to eternity, isn't this life more like a dream in which we've forgotten our eternalness? . . . If that's a word . . . " Susie could see everyone was deep in thought. Then she continued, "Okay, everyone, just start singing the whole song in rounds like you were doing before."

After a few rounds, she held up her hand and got them to get quiet again. Then she said, "There are many religions and millions of people in the world who believe we keep coming back to learn more lessons. I guess they probably feel that just as the song keeps repeating, so do the dreams. Your spirit descends from the heavens like a water droplet. Another boat is launched on another stream so that you may merrily row again. When the first group starts the rounds, it's like a new generation is being launched. As another group starts in its like the next generation is launched."

A burly huge man in the audience stood up and said very loudly, "It sounds like you're talking about reincarnation! I never read nothing in the Bible about that. I think when it's over it's over, then there's judgment day and you either go to Heaven or Hell. What about that?"

Susie didn't get defensive, she just said in a calm voice, "I don't know if I personally believe we keep coming back, I don't know what's true for sure, but I believe in God, and, I have an open mind to how it all works. I have heard that references to reincarnation were in the Bible at one time and removed in the early centuries because church leaders thought it would be too dangerous for people to think that way."

The man's eyebrows scrunched together as though they would help retain his sacred beliefs. He replied, "Well, I don't buy it."

Susie explained, "I'm not trying to convince anyone, or change their minds. Like . . . have you ever thought that Heaven or Hell may be a state you experience moment to moment? . . . that it just depends on how much love or fear you're experiencing? That would mean part of what we're doing on Earth is to be able to love all things and all people. I think Jesus even said something like that. "

Some of the people nodded their heads yes.

"Well, I still can't buy anything about reincarnation," the big man replied.

Shawn cleared his throat and was a little reluctant to get into a discussion that can get people so stirred up. Then he offered, "I think what Susie is trying to say is that whether it's true or not, it's just another belief. We can use our beliefs to separate from one another, perhaps even get angry and fear others, or see our commonalty in knowing God exists. Our finite minds may not be able to conceive of the infinite workings of the universe, but if we're not too attached to our beliefs about how it all works, we can still feel togetherness in our exploration."

Susie nodded in agreement and said, "I'm in awe of the universe, the stars, our planet, life . . . like did you know there are more stars in the sky than there are grains of sand on Earth? It's like to be in awe is to know God. If anyone wants to discuss things like this or anything else just see me sometime today. But right now why don't we take a snack break and come back for another story, okay?" Susie clicked off the microphone and set it down.

Shawn went up to Susie and said, "I think you handled that so professionally, Susie. Have you had any training leading groups?"

"Not this life time," Nadine, Shawn and Susie all laughed together. Shortly afterwards, Shawn raised his hand to his chin and seemed to be deep in thought. If there was reincarnation, could people have developed talents in previous life times and had them carry over to other lives? Maybe that would explain child prodigies.

While everyone got more to eat, Shawn got Susie's attention and asked her, "Susie, I just noticed that Jack's not here today. Wasn't he coming?"

She tipped her head slightly and bit her lower lip before she replied, "We kind of had a falling out last night after everyone left. It seemed like he only has one thing on his mind . . . and our discussions after the stories yesterday showed how different we really are. I'm going to take a break from guys for awhile."

"Well, I'm sure it's all for the best, Susie."

Somebody called to her, and she said, "See ya in a few . . . "

Shawn scooped up some chocolate-chip cookies and sat down to review the next story *Comets*. He ended up reading it all since it was so short.

COMETS

Lonely are the days that I speed through the universe. Days I say? I don't even have days to call my own for I orbit no particular sun. I visit several solar systems, yet the very freedom to be on my own path that I cherish and love, leaves me with blank, black sky in all directions. Yes, there are millions of sparkly lights reminding me that I'm not alone, yet I can only visit them briefly and leave.

If I leave a trail, perhaps another will follow, however, it has not worked in hundreds of years. Now I realize that should another catch up, it would be because their speed is faster than mine. Alas, I would be quickly surpassed and left alone in their trail of misty comet dust.

At least I have gratitude that my trail brings love and joy to most that I visit. The dust I spread is true angel dust for it is given with love, and throughout the universe it creates awe among all observers. They watch, ponder and search for a reason for my trail. In doing so, they absorb the love I've spread in search of another.

To be in awe, is to know God. Perhaps I'll call myself minister to the stars.

Recently, I had a burst of hope. Passing through a twelve planet solar system, I was told by one of the moons of the largest planet that I was the second comet with exactly the same path, speed and relative size. It took this moon several centuries to realize there were two comets instead of one because everything was so similar. He said our angel-dust trails, which are comets' outward expression of personality, were almost identical. One of us passes by every 111 of his solar system's years.

Excitement filled my heart. I immediately wished upon a star that we could travel together. Oh, what fun it would be! And, since we're on the same path there wouldn't be the disappointment of having to go separate ways. We could talk about the mysteries of the universe. We could sing in harmony about the delights of the stars. We could weave our trails together and make a cosmic event that would generate so much awe, the love of God would be spread even to star groups never reached before.

Love heated my ice crystals and vaporized a few before I realized that though we are on the same path, we must be on opposite sides of the large elliptical orbit through the universe. In fact, for the first time, I now knew that it takes me 222 years to make one trip and return to my new found moon friend I named "Cupid."

"What a dilemma," I shouted out loud. "Now that I've found my soul comet with the same path and speed, we are 111 years of travel apart!"

"Well, at least you found someone!" The moon let out a little of his own dissatisfaction. "Can't you be happy just knowing that your soul comet exists?"

Before I could answer, I realized I was getting too far away to be heard. I shouted, "Oops, I got to go. Please tell my soul comet about me and say how much I wish we could travel together . . . good byeeeee . . . " My voice trailed off as I started my next 222 year journey though this time, I knew it would not pass fast enough.

Since the life of a comet is in the tens of thousands of years, one orbit is not all that long. However, this particular trip seemed endless. I tried to occupy my time by counting quasars, black holes and other unusual celestial events, yet my mind would return to a haunting question. "How can I travel with my soul comet?"

All that would pop in my head was the 111 years that separated us. Somehow that time needed to become 0, but how?

A passing meteor told me there are three steps to travel with any other in space. First locate who you wish to travel with, second communicate thoroughly, and third . . . ask for Divine guidance.

The first step took thousands of years, yet at least it was accomplished. The second puzzled me though. How could I communicate thoroughly? I can't even see my soul comet in the vast darkness of space!

Then I realized, everywhere I go, my soul comet goes. We have so much in common. I left messages everywhere from then on. Every nearby star, every planet and moon I passed kept a greeting of my love, well wishes, insights, desires, and blessings. I delighted in knowing that though the first message from Cupid the moon would take 111 years, the messages from now on would be continuous and ongoing.

Up ahead I saw Cupid's solar system approaching at last. Is there a message for me? What kind of response was there?

Finally the distance was just barely close enough to talk with Cupid. "Cupid, talk to me. Did you speak to my soul comet?"

"Yes, and as I expected, your soul comet has the same desire and wish as you. Unfortunately, we didn't have any solution to the dilemma and in 111 years of thinking about it, I haven't a clue for an answer."

I told Cupid about the three steps revealed by the meteor and how I have initiated the second one by leaving a constant trail of communication throughout the entire path. Then I realized in my haste and intense involvement leaving messages I had forgotten about the third step . . . asking for Divine guidance.

After departing from my dear moon friend, I focused on three stars in

the deep black sky. I think they're called the Belt of Orion. I chose them because each one together reminded me of 1 1 1. The 111 years representing
my dilemma, which is now our dilemma.

As I stared at these three beautiful stars, I prayed for Divine guidance.
Though I knew of no solution, I got in touch with the awesome size of the
universe and how anything must be possible with a Creator that could design such a magnificent display of wonderful celestial jewels.

For several years, I sped gazing at these stars in prayer. I was particularly noticing the center star of the three that formed almost a perfect straight
line. Then I noticed it wasn't a straight line. Two of the three stars form a
line yet if extended straight out, it misses the other star slightly.

My intuition told me this was the Divine guidance I had asked for. God
had answered my prayer. I just didn't know what the answer was exactly.

I left messages all along about the discovery to my soul comet. Perhaps
the two of us could figure it out.

The meteor had been correct in saying the second step was to communicate thoroughly. Neither one of us had the complete answer to the
dilemma. It was only through intense communications through many orbits
that finally the solution came to us.

~ ~ ~

Now, we joyfully fly through space side by side. Our angel-dust trails
weave together creating a fabric of glowing material that generates tremendous awe among all that can see. Oh, what joy to finally be traveling
together!

Oh yes, what was the solution you ask?

I told my soul comet, Sparkle, about the three stars not quite in a
straight line. Sparkle said maybe it meant not to go straight along our orbits,

but didn't know anything about changing course. I knew that by generating a lot of love, tiny ice crystals heat up on my surface giving off vapor which results in a push.

We coordinated a plan through many orbits and a great deal of patience. Love was focused on Sparkle's side that was facing in toward the center of our orbit. I sent love to my surface that was facing away from the center. This widened Sparkle's path to an orbit that takes 233 years and narrowed my orbit taking 211 years. Every orbit I was advancing 22 years closer. Years later we heated up the opposite sides and came back to our perfect 222 year orbit, yet now we are side by side. We realized the importance of communication and Divine guidance. We also realized it was the power of love that literally brought us together.

Now we spread the word that: "Love is an invisible force, like gravity, that brings heavenly bodies together." Yet, in reality, we both believe there is no separate thing called gravity, there is only love. When you feel gravity on your planet, you are feeling your planet's love pulling you closer and closer.

~ ~ ~ ~ ~ ~ ~

For some reason, this story seemed different than all the others. It wasn't anything major. *Comets* was still a good story, but in all his experience with the stories this was the first time something didn't seem right.

First the story was much more intellectual than normal, but then again all the stories varied. The key was the three steps communicated by the meteor. "First locate who you wish to travel with, second communicate thoroughly and third ask for Divine guidance." Shawn knew that the first step should have been to ask for Divine guidance! He was sure he had written it down correctly, yet he'd never noticed it before.

Something was wrong, and he didn't want to read it to the public until he understood. He felt a responsibility to make sure it was correct. Just then he heard Susie over the speaker system getting people's attention back. Quickly, he glanced at the next story. This one he knew was perfect to read.

As Shawn started to move, he noticed his right foot feeling stuck. Closer inspection showed a squished marshmallow was attaching him to the concrete slab under the picnic table. "How do I manage to do these things!", he said to himself as he scraped it off with a stick.

No one had anything to say to the large group except Bob. He pointed over to the swings and slide and said, "I guess I'll remember this story now when I see playgrounds!"

Shawn remembered telling Susie the names of the stories he was going to tell and was concerned people may be expecting something titled *Comets*. So he picked up the microphone and said, "The next story was going to be *Comets*, but instead I think I'll skip it and go on to *Eagles*."

A few people made a disappointing sound but he countered with, "But . . . I have a surprise for you. After *Eagles*, I'll read my all time favorite story of them all."

"Which one's that?" Susie shouted out.

He looked at her and thought to himself, I'll bet she's one of those people who can't wait to open her Christmas presents either. Then he said to her with a smile, "It wouldn't be a surprise if I told you, Susie!" He opened the journal and paused before saying, "I remember the first time Grampa read *Eagles,* it was to my uncle Ned. He was in a lot of trouble for the first time in his life. Nothing that worked before was working then--from severe financial problems, a relationship that went sour, death of loved ones, . . . well, you name it, Ned was going through the worst time of his life, not to mention a mid-life crisis and a career that was no longer working. After we finish sharing, I'll tell you what this story did for Ned, but for now let's just read it."

Shawn sat down and started reading *Eagles*.

EAGLES

Bumped from the nest by a rambunctious brother, the baby eagle fell and tumbled down the earth cliff. From a protected warm nest to utter chaos, fear and pain, the eagle sought survival.

Though his wings were too fragile to fly, he made a futile attempt. Finally, his claws caught a branch growing straight out from the cliff, and it stopped his fall.

What a scary experience that was. A quick shake of his feathers removed most of the dust. Upon opening his eyes, he had to shut them to not be overcome by fear.

The tiny eagle was perched thousands of feet high on a branch that barely supported him. If he fell again, it would be disastrous.

As he sat clutching and shivering a voice said, "Hold on, you'll be all right."

Curious to where the voice came from, the baby eagle opened his eyes just wide enough to see a beautiful owl sitting on a branch nearby.

"Help me," the eagle cried.

"If you just hold on long enough your mother will rescue you," the owl said matter-of-factly.

The eagle held on tightly and again shut his eyes. Sure enough, his mother soon flew up and scooped him off the branch. She was careful that *her claws merely wrapped around his small body. Within minutes, he was back in the safety of his nest. There was food, warmth and joy.*

The baby eagle grew, and his wings became strong enough to support flight. He was a fast learner and soon developed many skills. He could fly, dive, glide, soar and land on the smallest of perches.

He was also a teacher and loved to show other eagles fantastic maneuvers and high speed dives. He also shared the lesson he learned as a baby eagle from the wise owl because it saved his life. He would say to them, "If you're in severe trouble, land somewhere, hold on, close your eyes and wait to be rescued."

A few years past, and the eagle became quite talented in flight. He learned to use the updrafts near the cliffs and started to depend on the constant flow of wind up the mountain.

One warm summer day he had exhausted all his energy and strength diving and climbing high. After completing his last dive for the day, he connected with the normal updraft to take him up to his favorite resting spot for the night.

Midway up, however, the wind not only stopped going up, it started going down. He had never seen that happen before. The sudden down draft dropped him hundreds of feet and flapping his tired weak wings didn't help a bit.

He remembered what he learned as a baby eagle and reached out, caught a branch and held on.

It was quite a coincidence that he caught the very same branch as he did as a baby eagle. Unfortunately, the branch had not grown as he had. In fact, it was barely attached to the cliff by dry roots.

When the mighty eagle caught the branch it bent. He flipped upside down and was slammed against the dirt cliff. The branch drooped from his weight and was slowly starting to pull out from the crumbling dirt wall.

What a predicament he was in. Hanging upside down with his wings pressed against the cliff he could not fly away in that position. Even opening his eyes only gave him cause to tighten his grip —his view was down the slightly sloping cliff to the rocks far below.

He remembered the lesson he had been teaching other eagles for years, so he held on, closed his eyes and waited to be rescued.

He hung and waited. He waited and hung.

Time went by, and then he noticed that the branch was still slowly pulling out of the cliff. This frightened him so much he clenched his claws tighter.

His thoughts went to the last time when his mother rescued him from that branch before. He thought of his nest that had long since vanished due to rain and wind and time. He remembered the last time he had seen his mother years ago. Then he wondered how he could be rescued again, since long ago she had left the area. Even if she hadn't, she couldn't possibly carry him any more.

As fear continued to spread through his body, he felt the branch slip out a little more. His head was now pressed into the dirt, and dizziness was setting in from being upside down so long.

The giant majestic eagle became as frightened as the baby eagle he once was. He felt weak, powerless and even guilty for being so frivolous with his energy. "If only I hadn't allowed myself to become so weak, I could have flown out of the down draft!" he thought to himself. Now his only security was a little branch that was eventually going to pull out from the cliff.

Even if he didn't follow what he'd learned as a baby eagle and let go, the slide down the cliff may cause him to tumble, break a wing or worse yet, his neck.

So there he hung —afraid to let go, yet realizing the branch could not continue to support him.

He felt powerless to solve his problem, so he did something eagles rarely do because they are so strong, so capable, and, so full of ego.

The eagle prayed. In fact, he prayed and prayed and prayed.

"Save me," he prayed, "and I will show other eagles what I've learned from this!"

Finally, he stopped and began to listen. At first he listened for any more slippage of the branch. Then he found himself just being in silence.

Just then a voice asked, "What have you learned?"

Thinking that there was someone out there talking to him, the eagle managed to open one eye. The other was pressed into the dirt. When his vision cleared, he saw the wise old owl on the same branch just as before years ago. Of course the owl appeared upside down from the eagle's view.

The eagle assumed the owl had asked the question, so he said to him, "I don't know what I've learned, please tell me!"

The owl replied, "I wish I could, but as wise as I'm thought to be, I'm doing well just to grasp my own lessons. Besides, no one has the same perspective of the problem as you do."

"But you told me what to do before, why not now?" the eagle cried desperately.

"I was much younger then. I thought I knew the answers for everyone else. What I can say is that a solution to an old problem may not be a belief to live by." The owl watched as the eagle's branch slipped out a little more.

"Great," the eagle thought, "the wise owl not only tells me his old advice may not always work, but he can't advise me with new advice because of different perspectives. Well my perspective is upside down, dizzy, and I'm scared!"

The eagle shut his eye, and a tear dropped to the rocks far below. He was remembering how he used to soar to such great heights. He could almost feel the wind and how it supported his majestic body. How he wished he was there now, but now it's like a fading dream. If only he would get another chance, never again would he take it for granted.

A black crow flew up and landed on the top side of the eagle's branch. His weight caused the branch to sag a bit more. Quickly, the eagle asked the crow, "What should I do? Oh, what should I do?"

Instead of answering, the crow just laughed and asked, "How on earth did a powerful eagle like you get in such a ridiculous position?"

The eagle didn't bother trying to explain, and finally the crow flew away eager to tell other crows about the eagle's odd situation. Unfortunately, the guilt stayed, and the eagle tightened his grip a little more.

A butterfly landed. Again the eagle asked the pressing question, "What should I do?"

The butterfly answered in a very sweet and delicate voice, "Just let go and fly, my dear."

"They don't understand," the eagle said to himself, "it takes several good full wing flaps before I can get my heavy weight into flight, and my wings are not even able to unfold. It's different for butterflies —they're so light."

The owl was right, the eagle realized, no one knows my own situation better than me. No one can see it from exactly my perspective. But my view is upside down and confused.

The eagle felt that no one could help. It was hopeless. If he holds on or lets go, either way he believed it was going to be disastrous.

He decided to pray again, but he even had mixed emotions about that since praying for a solution to an insolvable problem seemed useless too.

He prayed and prayed for an answer– for a solution. Then, just as before, he listened and listened.

Sure enough he heard a voice again. The voice asked, "Does the belief serve you?"

This time he knew the voice wasn't from the owl, the crow or the butterfly. He felt the voice come from deep within his feathered chest.

He had already given up the belief that all he had to do was 'hold on and be rescued', but he had taken on a new belief. The new belief was that this was going to end in disaster and that there was no solution. Being quite moved by hearing a voice coming from within, however, the eagle started to doubt the belief. "Maybe," the eagle thought, "maybe there is a way out."

Without much further consideration, he took the only action he thought possible. He let go and released his grip.

Though his muscles relaxed, nothing happened!

His sharp claws had been clinched so tightly they had buried themselves deep into the fibers of the wood. His powerful claws were embedded as though they were nailed to the branch. Without strokes from his wings the claws could not be torn loose!

What a dilemma! Now that he is willing to let go, the branch won't let go of him.

At least there was relief. Being willing to let go; being in a state of surrendering to whatever happens, allowed him to relax his muscles and tension. Peace and clarity came over his troubled mind and things became clearer.

For the first time, fear left his body. Since there wasn't anything he could do anyway, he didn't even fear making a mistake any longer.

With his new belief that 'maybe there is a way out,' thoughts and creative ideas started to flow through his peaceful mind. He even thought of unusual questions that hadn't occurred to him before. "What if there was another choice between holding on and letting go? Could there be other possibilities?"

The eagle started putting attention on what he could do instead of fearful thoughts and what he couldn't do. He found that with his relaxed muscles he had some flexibility to move his wings even though they were folded up. By pushing and pulling on his wings against the cliff wall, he could actually get his entire body to move. As he did, he heard cheering come from all around.

The owl, the butterfly and even a whole flock of crows were praising his movement. He never knew he had so many friends.

The eagle kept pushing with his wings until one wing overlapped a rock extending from the cliff. With one giant push, the eagle righted himself on the branch.

For a minute or so the eagle sat shaking his head and adjusting his mind to the view of a right-side-up world. Then the twisted branch pulled out from the cliff, but that was now no problem for the eagle. His giant wings spread out, and within a few powerful flaps he was soaring high and proud again.

With a powerful thrust from his wings and a shake of his claws, the branch was easily discarded.

The eagle was free at last to fly, soar, dive and of course continue to teach other eagles the valuable lesson he learned, and now he was very clear about what he had learned.

On special teaching days you can often overhear the great eagle's advice to others about what to do if they are in severe trouble. Some having heard the story might think the eagle would have changed his lesson from "Hold on, close your eyes and wait to be rescued," to "Ask if a belief from the past serves you now."

However, you'll most often hear the eagle humbly say, "Let go of your ego, pray often and listen within."

~ ~ ~ ~ ~ ~ ~

There was enthusiastic applause following this story. As Shawn glanced out over the audience, he saw someone peeking around a tree. Sure enough it was Jake with a big smile giving a thumb's up sign!

He gave the microphone to Susie, and she started getting people set up to do their sharing. Shawn had one thing on his mind—he wanted to talk to Jake. He excused himself and told Susie he'd be back in a few moments.

Jake was still behind the tree when he ran over and looked behind it. "Jake," he said, "please, you must answer some questions, all right?"

With a long piece of grass straw in his mouth, Jake leaned against the tree with his shoulder and said, "Shawn, settle down, fella, with all that energy ya might do one of them there tricks, ya know. I loved the marshmallow thang, by the way." After a small pause, the old man confidently continued, "Yer doin great readin' of them stories ya know . . . and ya passed the test too."

"What test?" Shawn demanded.

"Why, if'n I told ya that, it woodn' be a surprise. We cain't have that can we?" Jake was having fun teasing Shawn, yet there was something odd going on with his eyes. Strangely enough, his left eye seemed jovial and mischievous yet his right eye seemed all knowing and piercingly serious. "What I can tell ya is: the answer to yer prayers may not appear to be yer answer. If yer lucky, yer Grampa will tell ya somethin' today." He smiled and gave Shawn a double wink.

Shawn glanced back to see if Susie was needing him yet. When he looked back at Jake his view was of the tree and a few ants on the bark. Looking down he saw a dim ball of light quickly fading away. "That ball of light is Jake," Shawn said out loud, " . . . then it was Jake who rescued me in my car that night!" And that double wink, he pondered, it's like the double wink in the story *Angels* . . . He started feeling dizzy as so many thoughts flooded his mind about what all this meant.

"Shawn.. . . Oh Shawn . . . Where are you? We're ready for you." His thoughts were interrupted by hearing his name over the loud speaker.

Upon coming back over to Susie, a very old man named Arthur, at least in his 80's, wanted to say something to the entire group. Though he didn't want to use the microphone, his voice was too soft for everyone to hear. Susie finally persuaded him to talk into it, but he wouldn't hold it. Susie held it in front of his mouth as he said, "You know I'm old enough that I've lived through a world war and the big depression. Just before the depression hit I was a mighty rich man, at least with money. The bottom dropped out of the stock market, and maybe you thought it was just made up stories about people jumping out of building windows in New York, but I lost a couple of buddies to suicide. They saw their life fortunes disappear as the old ticker tape did its ticking. I can't say it didn't cross my mind, but I thought what the heck, I got my health, I'll just start over. Though most of my friends up here don't know it 'cause I live a moderate life style, I went on to do it again. The next time I diversified, and I also put a lot of time into helping others. Money without a heart is like an eagle that can't fly. I had a lot more appreciation for people having hard times after that. When we were sharing I heard a couple of people say they were in hard times right now. To those I just want to say, remember this here eagle story, it's got good advice. Especially the last line, lord, you don't know how much I prayed—that's truly the way to experience God—through prayer. Thank you. That's all I got to say."

The people stood up and gave him a standing ovation. The old man took his seat a few feet away.

Susie asked if anyone else had something to say. There were no hands going up, so she returned the microphone to Shawn.

"Whatever happened to your uncle?" Someone asked.

"Oh, yeah, Uncle Ned. Well, the eagle story was perfect for him. He had so much disaster in his life. He got into a victim role of just waiting for someone to help him. By the way, he told me it's okay to tell people this if it could make a difference for them. A year after he finally started getting his life back together, he could look back and see what happened. He said he was so down and out that what he really needed was love. He was waiting for someone to help him as a sign of love, yet everyone had already overextended themselves. He took the eagle story to heart and let go. He filed bankruptcy, let his house go into foreclosure and just started focusing on rebuilding his life one step at a time, and, he said he started praying a lot. With support from friends and church members and lots of prayers, he got rid of the guilt which was just weighing him down. At the same time his confidence started building."

Shawn paused a moment, then continued, "He got his expenses down real low and started a job in an office with structure instead of his freelance career that wasn't working. To make a long story short, within a year the eagle was flying again and within two years he was soaring."

"If you're having a hard time, maybe you'll like the saying my Grampa told me. 'Don't take life so seriously, after all it's just a temporary condition.'"

A few people laughed, and Shawn went on to say, "If you have time for one more story the next one is my favorite. It's called *Turtles*. However, my voice is getting a bit tired, so I wondered if Susie would read this one."

Susie jumped up and said, "I sure will!"

He opened the journal to its first entry, *Turtles*, and handed it to Susie. Her eyes lit up like she'd received a gift on Christmas morning.

As he sat and listened to Susie's animated voice read *Turtles*, he felt like Willy in the whirlpool about to be crushed by the tons of water. Reflecting on his problem, he remembered the story saying 'hold on to your dream'.

Is that telling me to hold on to my job? he thought to himself. He continued to listen to the story while drawing a blank as to what to do.

The crowd really loved this story. As Susie finished there was a lot of applause and even some cheers. Shawn sat in with a group for sharing, and the turtle story seemed to really draw a lot out from people. There was someone who was in a relationship with someone wanting to live in San Francisco yet he loved living in Idyllwild. He said he would have to take a serious look at whether they were wanting to go to the same island. There was another person who didn't know what his dream was. Susie even shared that she wasn't yet living her dream.

Shawn didn't feel comfortable sharing his major problem and decision, so instead he shared how the story gave him the insight and courage long ago to change careers; which in turn brought him his mate. He was now with his *Heidi* and loving every minute of it. He spoke with so much love for Mary he started missing her smiling face and the way she always rubbed his arm or back when she was being supportive.

Susie said over the speaker to people very involved and talkative, "Hello? If I can have your attention . . . Sorry to interrupt, . . . thank you .. . . perhaps if you have more to talk about you can continue later. I know some folks need to be going soon, so I kind of need to just wrap things up, at least the formal part. Remember there's still lots of food left! Does anyone have anything to say to the group?"

A hand went up and Shawn recognized her. It was Carla from last night who had asked about whether she could read the stories to her kids.

Carla came up to the microphone and turned to address the crowd, which was actually closer to a hundred now because some of the people in other picnic groups were invited to join in before the second story. She spoke with very strong conviction. "After hearing these stories, I'm more than ever convinced I want to tell them to my two children while they're growing up. Plus, I want to re-read them for myself, and maybe to a friend when they need some insight." She was interrupted by some cheers and shouts of "me too!"

She turned and looked directly at Shawn and said, "Shawn, I don't know what it will take, or what you got to do, but I'm voting that you get these things published and share them with the world!" She turned to the audience and asked, "So, who agrees with me?"

Everyone stood and applauded. Chills ran up and down Shawn's spine, and he was absolutely overcome by this unexpected demonstration. Tears welled up inside as he tried to force them back. This touched him deeply. He loved the stories so much that to feel others loving them this much was beyond ecstasy—he was in bliss.

He rose as everyone sat down, yet another person came up to speak. Carla handed Joanne the microphone and she said, "Shawn, these stories are so vivid, so real, I see them as an animated movie . . . Yeah, like a Disney movie!" Again, there was applause and cheers of agreement from the people.

Arthur passed Shawn his card. "Call me," he said very seriously, "I know people that can get things done in the animation business!" He tucked the card away in his Grampa's pant's pocket.

Finally things settled down and Shawn spoke.

"You all have really touched me. Carla, I will ask my grandfather if we can pursue this. And, Joanne, you know I never thought of the stories in movie form, but now that you mention it I can see them all in my mind from turtles to the mirrors in Mirror Village, to daisies and even the eagle hanging on the cliff!" Shawn paused to let the vision sink in. The microphone was shaking from excitement.

Carla and Joanne put their arms around Shawn as he promised he would get back to everyone and let them know what Grampa says.

The rest of the afternoon was a blur as Shawn got hugs, ate more food and visited with all the very friendly people who had now become his friends. In all the years he had visited Idyllwild, he had only met a handful of people since his purpose for being there was usually to retreat from the world in the first place. He realized his hideaway would never be the same from this weekend on.

Shawn said a warm good-bye to them all, especially Susie. He asked for applause for Susie, and they all stood up for it. After it quieted down and people started cleaning up and talking to each other, he said to her, "Susie, you have been so special. You've really been a catalyst for everything. How can I ever thank you enough?"

Susie looked up with her big blue eyes and simply said, "I want to help you with the stories some how. They are a part of me . . . they really touch me inside."

Shawn could see how sincere she was. He gave her a big hug. "If there is anything possible, you'll be the first I call, okay?"

She smiled and gave Shawn a squeeze.

As he walked slowly to his Grampa's truck, he paused to look back at his new friends. Then he slowly turned and walked hesitantly away from the group. Just as he pulled the truck door and it creaked open, he heard a familiar spunky voice say, "Shawn! So how ya getting back down the hill to your home?" Sure enough he turned to see Susie's smile and big eyes with her head cocked to the left just slightly.

"I don't know . . . I haven't figured it out yet."

Susie came up within two feet and looked intently in his eyes and said, "Well I have! I'm driving you . . . I mean . . . if you don't mind. I have my own car, it runs good and I've got the free time."

After a short moment to think about it, he took her hand and said, "That's so nice of you, and you know, I can't think of a more enjoyable way of getting back down off the hill. Except, I don't know when I'm leaving, and I have to be at work early in the morning. I haven't even seen Grampa yet . . . and afterwards I'm sure I'll need to think some . . ."

Susie interrupted and added, " . . . and, all those things will still be true regardless of who drives you, so it might as well be me. I will drive you no matter what time, and if you need quiet to think about your decision or something, I won't even talk, okay?"

He looked at her wide excited eyes and surrendered, "That's great, Susie. We have a beautiful guest room, maybe you can stay a few days and meet Mary and my kids. We have a pool, too. Do you swim?"

"I sure do." Susie raised her arms and shouted, "Yes, yes, yes! This is going to be so cool!" She gave Shawn a big hug and said, "Just call me, I'll be waiting to come and get you and I already know where your Grampa's cabin is." As she turned and walked away with a skip in her walk, he shook his head and said to himself, "How can she seem as young as my kids at times and yet so extremely mature in front of an audience?"

He knew Mary would be relieved at having his transportation

solved and was thankful he'd have something to tell her next time she asked. He pushed in the clutch of the old pickup and started the engine. As he shoved the gearshift into first gear, he thought, after all these years of driving an automatic it's funny how I automatically remember how to drive a stick shift. I don't even have to think about it. My body just seems to shift this old floor shift as though I do it every day.

It was 3:50 p.m. and he didn't feel like going straight back to the cabin. Instead, he headed back up to Lookout Rock. He needed some peace and clarity after mixing with all those people.

He was sitting on the giant boulder realizing he wasn't appreciating the beautiful green pine trees, the puffy white clouds and the birds. For some reason he was sad. He hated that feeling, so he tried thinking thoughts that would make him feel better. He replayed all the people standing and cheering about the stories and the wonderful time he had, yet a melancholy, depressed feeling continued to dominate him. Instead of avoiding it this time, he closed his eyes and went inside to ask what it was all about. Tears he'd been pushing down for years started bubbling to the surface.

This time, maybe the first time in his life, he finally let go fully and the tears began to flow. He cried and cried. He couldn't even control his verbal cries. They were loud and agonizing. Then he recalled his dad and his death. He missed him so much. Then the crying intensified greatly as he realized what he had really been suppressing was grief for his mother. He never spoke about her and her passing because it was so incredibly painful. She was so loving, so wonderful, "Why did she have to die!" he shouted to the sky in anger. He remembered how she used to hold him and take him for rides in the car and how she always told him he was such a good boy. He felt like the very depths of his soul were being cleansed out of every drop of built-up remorse.

He remembered how she used to visit very old friends in convalescent homes. She was so compassionate, tears once came to her eyes as she told Shawn, "So many in there are never visited by their own relatives. How sad and lonely it is for them, just as they need attention the most in their last years, months or days. If you ever know someone whose relative is in a home, tell them to go visit them while they can! It may be hard, but it is worth every minute."

Shawn's mother was recovering from a stroke and a heart attack years earlier, but could still not abide by doctor's orders to quit smoking. Shawn was so frustrated in not being able to persuade her or help her add years to her life by quitting. He recalled how he had spent 50 hours in the hospital room with her while she was in a coma breathing rapidly for her life. Her eyes were partially open, and he wondered if she could see him. He placed his hand on her forehead and told her he loved her. His saddest memory was at the funeral when she was lying so still in the coffin. There was no rapid breathing, only infinite silence. He placed a little paper gold heart on her chest and said goodbye knowing that he would never see her again.

His emotions flowed out for over a half an hour, when finally he paused, blew his nose for the 50th time and started catching his breath. He realized the worst of it all was the deafening silence, and never again being able to ask her any questions about his childhood or hers. No longer was she there to call at night. No more questions, no more answers . . . just silence, that deafening silence. God, if people only knew, there would be a whole lot more talking going on while loved ones are still alive. He paused and thought some more— most of us live in denial that it is going to happen to those we love, and that denial is costly in love unexpressed. Oh, how I wish I had hugged and kissed my mom more. If she was here now, I'd take more trips to see her . . . Then he remembered his friend, Karl Anthony, and his wonderful song, *May There Always Be Sunshine*. Four lines of the refrain were written by a Russian child in 1928 who was only four years old at the time. The little boy's powerfully touching words wished that there would always be sunshine, blue skies, mama, and me. Shawn sang the melodic lyrics out loud many times while imagining Karl's guitar in the background.

Shawn raised his voice to the heavens and cried, "Mom, wherever you are . . . I love you . . . always."

"Close yer eyes Shawn. Go inside and talk at her. Ya can ya know!"

Shawn looked around for Jake because it was obviously his voice, but didn't see him. He did as he said. For about five minutes, he just sat in silence praying and picturing his mother. Then he tried talking to her out loud as though she were right there.

"Mom, I love you. Speak to me . . . "

A voice inside his head spoke, he could hear his mother's voice, and it was just how she phrased things, "Oh, hun, I love you too. Please don't cry. I'm okay."

"But I couldn't stand it seeing you lying there not breathing." he burst into tears again.

"Honey, listen . . . " But Shawn was crying too loud to hear.

"I can't stand the thoughts of you buried under all that ground not breathing . . . " Shawn cried with agonizing pain over the vision of his mother's grave site.

Some laughter from his mother caught him off guard, and he listened. After she laughed a bit she said, "Don't go crying over that. That's not me, honey. That was my body. I'm not there, I'm up here. I'm doing fine flying around. Your dad's here, and we've even been dancing. Can you imagine that?"

Shawn could, he pictured his mom and dad like they looked in their prime– dancing and smiling. He knew he wasn't making this up with his imagination.

"Son. Everything is just fine. You showed me so much love, you called me once a week for years, not to mention all the other things . . . there were so many. You couldn't have been a better son in any way. I want you to not be sad any more. Everything is wonderful here on the other side, really."

They continued the conversation for some time, and Shawn felt an inner peace he'd never experienced before. He felt like he could finally give up the grief he'd been carrying around for so many years. His mom and dad were all right.

Chapter 11

He slowly opened his puffy eyes and saw a yellow butterfly land on a little branch growing out of the crack in the boulder. He felt love from the butterfly as though it were telling him, "It's okay, Shawn, it's okay." A breeze blew through the tops of the pine trees and made that familiar whishing sound he loved so much.

He watched the butterfly as it sat peacefully on the branch just slowly opening and closing its beautiful wings in the sunshine. He could swear the butterfly was looking right at him and waving. The wings seemed to be saying everything's all right, calm down, feel love, see beauty, know that God is with you.

He thought of the butterfly in the eagle story and imagined himself as the eagle whose mother had long since left. If that story was the right one to guide him, should I let go of my job? he thought. Then he wondered, does Grampa's specific selection of the stories help with the answer, or is truth, truth. Hmmm . . . After all that emotional release, Shawn felt calm inside and felt drawn to just observe nature rather than think. He took a walk through the dense pine trees and purposely tried to notice and observe each little detail as though the beauty in nature was being presented to him as a divine treat. A squirrel darted across his path and he thought of Myra the mirror. He looked for daisies along side of the path but couldn't find any.

When he returned to the cabin, there was a grand treat awaiting him. He couldn't help smiling when he saw his grandfather waiting for him on the front porch in the old wooden rocker.

His heart raced with excitement. Finally, his beloved Grampa was home at last! He pulled up on the door handle so hard, it came off in his hand. Not wanting to do anything embarrassing in front of his Grampa, he paused and took a couple of peaceful breaths and tried to fit the handle back on the door. Grampa walked over to the edge of the porch waiting for Shawn, but just saw him curiously sitting in the truck. The harder Shawn tried to attach the handle, the more futile it became. Finally, he slid over and went out the opposite side of the pickup. He jumped from the truck and didn't even shut the door. Like a little boy, he ran to the porch and wrapped his arms around his grandfather like he hadn't seen him in 10 years. "Oh, Grampa, you don't know how good it is to see you!" Shawn shouted.

They hugged for a long time and then looked at each other. Shawn loved every wrinkle and every beautiful gray hair on Grampa's head; even the gray hairs in his bushy eyebrows. Grampa had a giant smile and held Shawn by each shoulder as he looked with admiration.

"Grampa, how long have you been home?" Shawn asked.

Grampa frowned and pointed to his throat. Gramma came out on the porch and said, "Your Grampa caught a cold yesterday after a chilly night in the woods Friday. Unfortunately, he spent the second night anyway not wanting to break up the trip. Now he has a very bad case of laryngitis! He sounds worse than one of those big frogs down by the creek. At his age, he could damage his voice box permanently if he strains it, so he's not saying a word."

Gramma put her hand on Shawn's back. "I'm sorry, I know you were really looking forward to a story."

Shawn was really confused and bewildered. He was happy to see his grandfather, yet this was not at all what he expected. He was depending on a story. He was starting to feel despair.

They all went in and sat by the fireplace and Gramma served some hot peach tea with a pinch of cinnamon. Grampa of course settled down in his favorite chair while Gramma and Shawn sat on the New England style couch. There was already a fire going to keep it nice and warm for Grampa as the evening set in.

Grampa motioned for something to write on. Gramma handed him a pad and he scribbled out a little note which said, "Shawn, Gramma says something is bothering you. Go ahead and tell us about it."

Shawn glanced at Gramma. She also read the note. He decided to go ahead and talk about it with Gramma present.

He told them the whole story about how the job market is almost non-existent, how his friend John just got laid off, how he owes more on his house than it's worth and yet he is being offered security, a great promotion, partnership and even more when his boss retires.

He also told them the down side of having to work for a major client that wants him to promote tobacco to teens and pre-teens. They were already quite familiar with how much Shawn hated anything to do with smoking, so he didn't have to go into that.

He looked at his grandfather for some sort of reaction to the greatest problem he had ever faced. As usual however, Grampa Art just sipped some tea and though he was attentive, he didn't seem very worried. Of course, he never did when someone told him of their problems.

Gramma showed a little more concern. She was deep in thought with her hand on her chin like when he told her of the car going off the cliff.

Since Grampa couldn't talk and Gramma wasn't, Shawn talked in more detail about the conflict. He even told about telling the stories that weekend and how well they were received. Then he remembered Jake, and stood up.

"Grampa, do you know Jake?" he looked at Grampa with intensity.

Grampa nodded his head yes and nodded at Gramma. Gramma said, "You might say we're pretty close with Jake. I guess you've seen him a few times now?"

"Yeah, he keeps popping up, but he leaves quickly. Did you know he can just disappear? Did you know that I think he saved my life when my car spun out? There was this big ball of light sitting on the hood holding the car down. It was the same ball of light I saw near Jake a couple of times. Oh yeah, and Jake said something odd . . . he said to tell you to 'tell me'. Tell me what?"

Grampa raised his big bushy eyebrows, tilted his head to the side and looked intensely at Gramma. She did the same with him. There was a pause that stretched seconds into hours as they seemed to be talking through their eyes to each other. Shawn figured they'd lived together so long, they could probably do that.

Finally, Gramma leaned back and sat up straight. She closed her eyes and just sat there silently. With a finger to his lips, Grampa motioned Shawn to be silent and then with a couple of waves of his wrinkled old hand, motioned him to sit down.

Shawn thought to himself, this is really strange. Grampa couldn't talk, Gramma isn't talking and I'm not supposed to talk—yet I have more questions than Myra the mirror.

After about a 5 minute *hour,* Gramma opened her eyes and rose slowly. Then Grampa rose and took Gramma's hands. It looked like they were doing a little two-step dance as they traded places. Shawn just sat with his mouth open.

Grampa sat down on the couch next to Shawn and patted him on the leg. Gramma sat down in Grampa's sacred chair—the first time he'd ever seen her sit there. She smiled and looked at Shawn with eyes that sparkled with clarity and a sense of wisdom. She said in the most incredibly confident, mellow and comforting voice he had ever heard from his Gramma, "That reminds me of a story; do you want to hear it?"

Shawn could not be more amazed if you told him that Madonna had become our next astronaut. He looked at each of them back and forth. Then with a puzzled look he slowly asked, "What's going on?"

All in great silence, Gramma looked at Grampa. He just nodded his head and smiled as he looked at her. Then he motioned with his hand like he wanted her to continue.

She said, "Shawn, there's something we'd like to tell you, and we hope you'll understand. If Grampa hadn't gotten this unusual case of laryngitis, we probably wouldn't have ever said anything, even with Jake's encouragement. But you obviously need a story, and it looks like Jake wants us to reveal much more than we expected."

Shawn was sitting on the edge of his seat listening. She went on to say, "I've never been much for talking or telling stories. Your Grampa on the other hand, loves to tell them. He does such a wonderful job of that. The stories come to me, and I give them to your Grampa in a way that he never forgets a single word. However, if people knew that the stories came from me, they'd naturally be asking me to tell the stories. So, when the first story arrived, which was *Turtles,* I gave the story to your Grampa and let him tell it with one condition—he must never let on that the stories came from me and to just go ahead and pretend they were his making. This was the most difficult thing your Grampa ever did in his life, because as you know, he is incredibly truthful and forthright. I can tell he is sure happy this is finally being said." Grampa nodded his head 'yes' to that while raising his thumb up in the air.

Shawn just sat there with his mouth still opened in amazement. He flashed on all the years he gave credit to Grampa and so greatly underestimated his Gramma's talent and wisdom.

Gramma continued, "He's done so well, too, even though many times he wanted to tell everyone the truth. I'm sorry if this causes you any misgivings or bad feelings. Once you start telling people stories, it's awfully hard to stop. Ooops, I mean fib-like stories, you know . . . like that saying, 'oh what a tangled web we weave when first we practice to deceive.'" They all laughed at the double meaning of stories, though Grampa's laugh was quite muffled.

Shawn worked on gathering composure and then asked, "Well, how did Grampa remember those stories so well? Nobody would have ever guessed."

"Shawn, you have a couple more extremely major surprises in store for you which involve Jake, but I think you're ready for them, at least Jake thinks you are. Those may be revealed after the story, but I might as well start by saying you are the only person to ever write the stories down, therefore, I know you have a particular affinity for them. Yet, I have a special way of, let's say, transmitting the story once, so that a person remembers it word-for-word, forever. All the stories Grampa tells were only told to him by me one time. He'll never forget a single word as long as he always starts the story with initial words you've heard so often. Without any more questions right now, I think you came up here for a story, and a story you shall get if it's still your chosin', except this time it will be from the horse's mouth. Shawn, from now on, whenever you tell a story, just say these words . . . 'That reminds me of a story; do you want to hear it?'"

Shawn said, "I sure would. Please tell me a story . . . Gramma." He settled back into the couch and looked at Grampa. He was smiling and was obviously quite happy. His shoulders even seemed higher like he was finally relieved of some big burden.

Gramma looked directly into Shawn's eyes and began telling a story he had never heard before called *Beads*. However, after a few minutes of hearing her comforting voice, he noticed that her lips were not moving! The story was being told directly into his thoughts and mind only. He looked at Grampa and could sense that Grampa was hearing the story as well.

Resigned to the fact that he didn't understand Jake or lots about this weekend, he decided to just listen. He didn't hear the story with his outer ear, only with his "inner ear."

BEADS

It wasn't until I had strung several spheres that I realized that I was alive.

Though I was aware and conscious, I had no idea what life was all about. Many questions came to mind: What are the rules? What's the goal? How do you win? What's it all for? Where did I come from; where am I going? Who am I?

Having no answers, all I could do was observe. I couldn't even move. So I just laid there looking straight ahead.

A bright yellow sphere moved closer to me, and I noticed its center had a hollow opening that extended clear through to the other side. Without being able to move, there was no choice other than to enter the yellow sphere and hope for the best.

Once inside, I was feeling quite joyful. The sphere seemed to radiate joy. The inside was as bright yellow as the outside because light was emitting from whatever it was made of.

As I moved through the sphere, I felt a soft tickling sensation along the surface of my body. The experience was so enjoyable, I wanted it to last forever. However, I soon protruded through to the other side.

Once outside, I saw other spheres approaching. There were red, blue and orange spheres coming rather fast. However, only the blue sphere had *its hollow opening pointing toward me.*

As I entered the blue sphere, I felt calmness and peace instead of joy. Instead of a soft tickling sensation as I passed through, there was a pleasant brushing sensation. Though I preferred the yellow one, I liked the blue one, too.

Again, I was exiting and looking eagerly ahead for new experiences of life. I was hoping for another yellow, but instead there was a very dark gray sphere destined to envelop me. Compared to the beautiful, almost phosphorous colors I was used to, this sphere looked ugly, dark and scary.

As the opening approached, I instinctively wished I could avoid it. Something inside me moved and although I still entered the opening, I had managed to move off center a slight amount.

It was horrible inside. It was cold and sharp, rough objects scraped my surface. I felt fear and even terror before I finally reached the opening to the other side.

Thank heaven that's over, I thought as I looked up ahead. No spheres were approaching for quite some time. I was relieved to have a break to recuperate.

Remembering my slight movement, I tried again and was able to shift to the left and then to the right at will. I was immediately thinking up uses for this discovery like avoiding gray spheres and going toward yellow ones.

After some practicing, I got to where I could move to the left or right the width of two spheres without a great deal of effort.

By stretching far to the left and turning slightly, I got a view of my body for the first time. It was very long and round like a tube. It extended as far as I could see until it disappeared into the last sphere I'd just left. Apparently my body was so long it was still passing through the spheres of my past.

The outside color of my body was transparent gold and was filled with the same material. It was like I was a long golden string threading my way through these objects.

BEADS

"Rather poetic," I said followed by, "What now?"

"Start choosing," a voice responded.

I twisted from left to right and saw another long golden body just like mine. Except now I could see what was on the end. Besides a brilliant glow, the tip was just the end of the tube. However, the tube was not empty, it was solid like a piece of spaghetti.

I was happy to find company and so I shouted a friendly hello.

Each word spoken by the other body made the glow from its tip twinkle. The words were stern and quick, however, with a bit of tension thrown in.

"Start choosing," my new found acquaintance repeated, "It's either choose or be chosen."

Just then, he shot up in the air going over a gray bead, shifted to the left and smoothly entered a bright orange sphere. Amazed at this display of movement, I just gazed in that direction for some time.

Before I could see what was coming, I realized what being chosen meant. I started experiencing the pain of going through another gray again. It was terrible. This one had ripples of abrasive objects scraping against my golden body.

I exclaimed, "Ah Ha," when I went out the other side. I had learned the lesson of choosing. I immediately started getting prepared for the next sphere since this process seemed inevitable. This time I wanted to choose instead of being chosen.

With a glance back, I noticed something strange. Both gray beads that I had past through had changed colors. One went from gray to violet and the last one from gray to red. They were now beautiful. How strange that was.

Quickly, I moved to the right just in time to catch a bright green sphere. After thoroughly enjoying a gentle experience of warmth and nurturing, I popped out looking for my wise and more experienced friend.

With no spheres immediately before me, I searched for him to my right.

I found him streaming his gold body through the air just above the tops of the spheres. He told me how to maintain that for awhile at a time which made time for an enlightening discussion.

The spheres, I found out, had a name. They were called beads. Each color gives off a different experience. He said there are thousands of colors each having its own particular kind of experience and feelings upon passing through it.

"Oh my," I said, "How will I remember them all so I'll know which to choose?"

"Well, I can give you some general guidelines that will help," he offered and proceeded to say, "But first know that there are no bad beads, they are all good. Actually, I just heard this and haven't experienced it myself, but its on good authority. It must be true, yet as you can see I avoid those grays with a passion."

My mind immediately flashed to the two gray beads that were horrible. When I asked him how they could possibly be good, he said, "It's a mystery to me. If you find out, please let me know, too. I think it has something to do with lessons. What did your first gray teach you?"

"Well, I learned that I could move." then I mumbled, "that was quite useful."

"What color did it change to?" he asked again.

"Violet," I answered, "and the last one changed to red when I learned that I can choose or be chosen."

I remained in silence for sometime just thinking about it all. Finally, I said "Ah Ha, I think I've got it. The grays are some sort of learning beads. They teach you something, and if you get the lesson they change to a beautiful color. That means that all beads are gifts and are good. They are either enjoyable to experience or they present a lesson gift."

My friend said, "For a newcomer that's pretty good. In fact, I've noticed that all beads of that particular lesson that lie before all of us, and those you've already strung, will also change to a beautiful color simultaneously. Of course, there are millions of subtle color differences and lessons."

"Hey, lets call them 'Ah Ha' beads," I shouted, "because when you get the lesson, you usually say, "Ah Ha."

"Ah Ha," my friend responded as he proceeded to avoid a gray and shoot into a row of three bright colored beads.

I thought to myself, that's interesting. He still avoided the gray bead that would have given him another Ah Ha.

I was straining to remain up above the spheres but was starting to drop when I heard him tell me the draw back to those "Ah Ha" beads. He said, "If you forget the lesson, they all change back to gray, yet even darker and more intense inside. And, if you've strung beads that were changed to a beautiful color by an Ah Ha of someone else, it also will return to gray if they ever forget their lesson.

I dropped down and felt fortunate to be able to choose between a lemon color and a pink. I wasn't ready for another gray yet, and since lemon was the closest to the yellow I cherished before, I directed myself inside. It was quite wonderful actually, it was crisp and refreshing, but this time when I was ready to pop out the other side, I immediately entered a gray bead. The beads were sitting so close to each other, choosing one automatically chose the other.

Once through the rough and painful gray, I wondered—what was the lesson in that? I twisted to look back at the gray and it remained the same shade. I then realized that some choices come with unexpected consequences and that choosing something I call good sometimes automatically comes with something I call bad.

Just then the gray bead shifted to a beautiful turquoise Ah Ha bead. I also felt my radiance brighten. My tip projected much more light than before.

With more light I wondered if I could see farther when I stretched above the beads. Upon trying this, I saw farther ahead than ever before.

Just as I was gaining confidence that I had the game figured out, something seemed to bump or jar what we named the moving conveyor belt, and the beads up ahead got all mixed up. One patch of bright colored beads that were approaching me that I was fondly looking forward to, now had a variety of different grays mixed in. As I looked in amazement, my friend said, "That's why you teach what you learn to others."

"What do you mean?" I asked.

He said, "We all share the beads up ahead, I've found that the more we each learn, the more the grays are changed to delightful colored Ah Ha beads."

As I said, "Ah Ha," and learned from what he said, I saw several grays up ahead change to bright colors. One gray switched right in front of us and a gold thread was able to enter a colored bead instead of a gray one.

"We're all in this together," I said as I raised high enough to see many other golden threads like me weaving their way through the maze of beads.

I raised up even higher to see only part of the seemingly endless conveyor belt filled with beads as far to the left, right and in front as I could see.

There were grays changing to bright colors, but unfortunately, I saw some bright colors changing to gray, too. I figured somewhere one or more golden threads had forgotten a lesson.

Wondering how many grays I had, and how far back my thread extended, I twisted so fast my tip didn't follow. I found myself peering down through the inside of my golden, yet transparent body. My light was illuminating everything. I could even move my presence, or light, back down through the inside of the tube of my long body.

I noticed I was going back through the last bead I had passed through, the turquoise one. I twisted very fast and was facing the other direction.

I saw my tip was several bead widths away. It was like I was in this long golden tube which I called my body. Since I could move about, I concluded that whoever "I" was, it wasn't my body.

I twisted again and went through the turquoise bead, the lemon, violet and red. As I went through them, I had only slight sensations of what I felt as I originally passed through them. Some were hardly detectable, perhaps only five percent the original feeling.

Without doing anything, I suddenly found myself, my awareness, back at the tip!

The tip had just entered a pink bead. Apparently, I was automatically drawn back there to experience it.

Once on the other side, I raised to view future beads and positioned the tip away from entering beads for awhile. I was far too interested in discoveries back inside to be distracted by entering more beads.

With a quick twist and a thrust, I was quickly passing back again through the turquoise, the lemon, the violet, the red until I reached a gray.

Because of possible pain, I was afraid to pass through at first. After deciding to continue, I found it was uncomfortable and distressing emotions came up, yet it was certainly not as rough as the initial ride through at the tip.

As I neared the other side of the gray, I realized the lesson it had originally presented to me, but had apparently missed. Just as I said "Ah Ha," the bead changed to a beautiful orange. I said "Ah Ha" again when it dawned on me that it's never too late to learn a lesson from the past and convert a prestrung bead to a beautiful color.

I then understood that when I go back and discover lessons it not only changes that particular gray bead, but hundreds out on the conveyor belt awaiting all the golden threads. This gave me another feeling of Ah Ha, and I noticed the radiance of my light brighten. My learning affects everyone

*else, and their learning affects me. We're certainly all in this together, what-
ever "this" is. I felt a closer kinship with other golden threads.*

*Continuing back through my golden thread body past many beads, I
came upon a black bead. As hard as I tried, I could not enter this bead. It
was as though it was the end of the line, or, perhaps the beginning. Also, my
light could not illuminate any part of the bead nor could I see any light from
the other side. My intuition told me this is where I started and before that,
I assumed I didn't exist. That brought up some fear about going through a
black bead up ahead. Would I then cease to exist I wondered.*

*Deciding to suspend these internal investigations, I journeyed back to
the tip. There I raised high and viewed the thousands of beads on the conveyor belt. Though I hadn't really noticed them before, I saw that the vast
array of beads were sprinkled sparsely with black beads.*

*To my surprise one black bead was in my path of possible beads. I
quickly found my friend and asked about the black beads.*

"Should I avoid the black one?" I asked.

*He answered, "I do. I have the sneaky suspicion that they're different
from all the others. I've been told not to worry too much about it. I tried
once to string one, and it moved away. Yet, someone I knew tried to avoid
one, and it moved to become unavoidably strung. My theory is the black
ones select you, but I still won't test it by poking around at them. If you do
string one, it's your last bead! All of you and your strung beads are pulled
backwards until you're off the conveyor belt."*

*I was quite frightened to hear this. There was something about "the
end" that didn't appeal to me. I decided to find out all I could. To do this I
must learn, change gray beads to Ah Ha beads, and continue to increase my
luminescence and brightness so I could also increase my visibility. Perhaps
then I could see what's outside the conveyor belt, either in front or in back.*

My friend laughed at my plan. He said it was futile and to just enjoy stringing as many colored beads as I could. I realized that regardless of my purpose, I and all my golden thread friends, were destined to string beads.

As time went by and I collected many beads, I became much better at stringing, yet I found I needed this improved talent the further down the conveyor belt I got. Either the belt was moving faster or the beads were closer together, I couldn't tell which. However, without improved skills, an overwhelming number of gray beads could be accumulated.

By observing other golden threads, I learned much about life. It was a double bonus for as I learned, gray beads were changed to color, and as I taught, other gray beads changed too. The more we all learned, the better off we all were and the less number of those challenging gray beads there were. Also, the more that knew a lesson, the less chance it would be forgotten by all.

Though I wasn't sure, I started seeing a pattern of when black beads got strung. This discovery started when I finally got strong enough to raise so high I could see all the beads on my body back to the black one. Actually to every one's black one which started at a black wall.

I could also see all the beads on my closest friend. Just as I noticed his light was a bit dim and he had no gray beads on his string at all, a black bead jumped up and over his tip. In a moment, he and his string of beads was pulled back. The last I saw of him was that black bead popping through the black wall. There wasn't even time for good-bye.

I was shocked and terribly sad, not to mention frightened.

I started observing the behavior of black beads and the golden threads with lots of gray beads. There was a pattern. Once a golden thread had lots of gray beads, it became less mobile, less bright and much more often was being chosen, than choosing. Due to this weakened condition, the thread would start collecting more and more gray beads. Grays not converted to Ah Ha's seemed to weigh the poor golden thread down, and you could almost predict a black bead was in its near future.

But then, the more I studied, I could see no absolute conditions to predict a black bead was in the near future.

My friend had no grays, partly because he avoided them with a passion. Others had so many grays they were weighted down. Both types seemed to attract black beads.

Then I saw what they had in common. Both were experiencing very few Ah Ha's!

I realized that attracting a black bead had more to do with the absence of Ah Ha's than the color or number of beads. Continuing to learn and brighten my light all of a sudden became a better idea than ever before. Now I could finally see why the gray beads were also good, even though they were certainly not the most comfortable. If I only took on the beads that were comfortable and brought me pleasure, my string of beads may look beautiful but my inner light would be dim and I'd be less mobile.

I made a mental note of the new Ah Ha I discovered. If you choose only pleasure and comfort, eventually your light will diminish and you'll attract the opposite to you.

This all made sense. Ah Ha's would always brighten the light, gray beads would dim it a lot, and colored beads would dim it only slightly. The only way to brighten my light was to experience Ah Ha's! I said, "Ah Ha," as I experienced another one and of course my light brightened. This time I noticed it was even without going through a bead.

I started looking at others differently. Instead of noticing how many colorful beads they had accumulated in life and how few grays, I started looking for how bright their inner light was.

I decided to make it okay with myself to string some grays, but to keep converting them to Ah Ha's by learning lessons so I could boost my light and not get weighted down. And of course, if I could learn in between beads that was great as well. It seemed to be working because my light became extremely bright and powerful.

Even with all my discoveries and success with stringing and transforming many beautiful beads, something was missing. What's this all for? I would wonder. I can consciously choose beads to string, or not choose, and be chosen. I'll still be strung, but for what purpose?

I used to think life was about avoiding pain, seeking pleasure and alluding the black bead as long as possible. Yet I always felt there must be more.

I finally found out all there was to know, but it wasn't until I had a tremendously bright luminance from all my Ah Ha's. Before that, however, I reviewed some of my valuable lessons hoping that the answer was within one of them.

- *Failing to thread a desired bead is of no great loss unless you continue to look backwards.*
- *Looking backwards can distract you from making wise choices of the future beads.*
- *Thread beads near an abundance of others that teach and learn with you.*
- *It's either choose or be chosen.*
- *There are no bad beads.*
- *Sometimes good choices come with unexpected consequences that don't always seem good.*
- *Teach what you learn to others.*
- *You are not the beads or the thread, but the light within.*
- *We're all in this together.*

Not finding an answer to what life was about in what I already knew, I decided to continue searching. I stretched high above all beads as far as possible, yet I could only see back as far as the initial black beads of all the golden threads. I vigorously tried to go higher, yet there seemed to be an upper limit that my beads and thread could go.

If only my light wasn't restricted to inside the golden thread, I thought. I had already discovered the ability to travel back through my long body all the way to the black bead. If only I could exit some how.

I positioned my tip so that approaching beads were a long way off so that there would be no unexpected stringing of a bead to force me back to the tip. Then, I pressed as hard as I could against the tip, but nothing happened. I had hoped for more.

Almost by instinct I imagined and willed all the light in my entire thread to come to the tip. My tip glowed incredibly bright as all my light rushed to the tip. Almost as if it was too much for the tip, my light floated out of it.

I was floating higher than I'd ever been before. I could see the length of my entire string which included my own tip. Though my thread now only had a dim light remaining, there was a small beam of light which continued from the tip and followed me like a spotlight higher and higher.

I could see a black wall or curtain was blocking my view to whatever was on the other side of the initial black beads. However, I was gaining such height I could see a glow coming over the top of the wall.

The glow got brighter and brighter and all of the sudden, everything was revealed to me and I had the greatest Ah Ha of my life. It was a most beautiful celestial sight and for awhile, I knew all there was to know about everything.

Millions of golden threads strung with beautiful beads stretched for what looked like forever. Each thread seemed to extend from directly below me, to the black bead on this side of the wall, to another black bead on the other side, through another set of beads, to another black bead and on and on. It was like each golden thread had thousands of beautiful necklaces strung together end to end. Each necklace began and ended with a black bead, separated by a black wall just high enough to block vision.

I could see the process, too. When a black bead completed a string, the string was pulled back through the wall so that the string was on the other side. After awhile, a new black bead would appear on this side of the wall and it's golden thread would poke through, except now it was learning to string beads all over again. I observed one just learning to move and select beads like I had learned. I felt empathy and love for it thinking about all that was ahead for it to learn.

The length of each thread and string of beads was amazing. They all stretched far into the distance where I could see the other ends of the golden threads. All the threads came from one giant ball of thread and light that glowed so brightly I could hardly gaze in that direction.

The millions of strings of beads formed a surface of beautiful multicolored beads in every direction. Interwoven together, they formed a fabric or blanket stretching as far as I could see. A truly beautiful sight.

I realized everything was good. There was nothing at all to fear. A wonderful peace came upon me, and I knew that I knew all that there was to know. It was all perfect.

Just then, the spotlight from my tip flickered, and I found myself falling quickly back to the tip. My tip was just entering a gray bead and demanded my attention and awareness, however, I quickly understood the lesson and the bead changed to a beautiful orange.

I felt good that I had returned, yet something was lost. I could not remember everything I'd seen, yet I knew that everything was good and was going according to some wonderful great plan. It was just that I could no longer recall much of what I'd actually seen. I knew a whole lot more than I did before, and during that incredible experience, I knew that I had known everything there was to know.

It was an odd feeling to know that I had known everything but no longer remembered. I concluded that it was so infinite, it wouldn't all fit back into my finite little golden thread.

I realized I may never know everything again, and though I could not remember what life was all about, it was clear to me that it was not about competing for who had the larger number of beautiful beads, or merely seeking pleasure, avoiding pain and hiding from the black bead out of fear. In fact, I felt it had very little to do with beads at all—a fact quite surprising since beads seemed to demand so much attention so much of the time.

Somehow, I did know that all beads formed a beautiful fabric with threads containing the divine light of life. I intuitively knew that all the light in all the threads came from one source. From then on I continued to string beads, but now it was with great love for the divine light within all other threads. I had inner peace and I continued to de-light with each new Ah Ha!

~ ~ ~ ~ ~ ~ ~

Once he had heard the story from inside, Shawn opened his eyes and looked at his grandmother sitting in Grampa's chair. She smiled and said, "Why don't you just close your eyes again and see if you're nearer a decision about your career."

"But usually it takes the whole evening . . . "

She interrupted and softly suggested, "You may find a difference this time, Shawn."

He was a bit skeptical because this was the largest problem he had ever had. Also, he thought *Beads* was an interesting story, but it was a little more difficult to understand than the others . . . how could I possibly decide so fast. Then he realized something amazing. He could now recall the story word-for-word. While he sat in silent amazement reviewing some of the words, his grandparents just looked at him in anticipation.

Shawn was now seeing that this decision was being treated like all others. He was being encouraged to go within and use his own free will. Even Gramma wasn't going to offer advice. He closed his eyes and did a short prayer that he would be divinely guided. Then he felt inclined to review the story *Beads* in his mind. Since he now knew it word for word, he reviewed it quite rapidly. In only a few minutes, he opened his eyes smiling at his grandparents. They were smiling back realizing that he had resolution.

He looked at Grampa and then at Gramma and said, "It's so clear and so obvious now . . . " Shawn paused then spoke slowly as though more was coming to him, "There is no way I could possibly continue to work in my career and violate what I believe in so dearly. *Beads* showed how we are all in this together, we're all connected. As each of us learns and evolves, it helps out everyone. I cannot consciously do something that will hurt others no matter how much I can gain, or how much I might lose! The material things must take a back seat to following what I believe is ultimately best for family, friends and Mankind. I've got to be willing to let go. Even the story *Eagles* has told me to be willing to let go. I can't sell out, no matter what."

His grandparents applauded him.

"Also," he continued, "from *Turtles* I know that I must follow my joy and hold on to my dream. Dreams change. Mine has changed. I reached island five and it's now time to chose the next island five. This weekend I've discovered a tremendous joy in sharing the stories. I love that more than anything. I don't know how that could possibly support my family, but I want others to be able to benefit from the stories! Of course, it would be with your permission, but that's my new island five. I can even predict that the whirlpool in *Turtles* has something to do with being willing to let go of my career and assets, too. But I know from experience how to get through it."

Gramma smiled and said, "Shawn, you're amazing! I believe that if you hold on to your dream, it will come true."

Remembering Jake at the picnic, Shawn sat up straight and asked, "Jake said I passed some kind of test. What was that all about?"

Gramma said, "Jake did relay a message to us that you passed the test. I guess I should tell you about it."

"I'm getting kind of old, and though I'm healthy, it is vital that these wonderful stories go on. I know that now more than ever, and of course, Jake won't let us forget if we tried." She smiled and glanced at Grampa as though it was some kind of personal joke between them. She continued, "These stories, and those to follow are so special! I needed to see if deep inside, you were the one intimately connected enough for a special transfer."

Shawn scrunched his eyebrows showing some confusion.

"You detected the flaw that I purposely implanted in the story *Comets* years ago. Requesting Divine guidance would be the first step, not the last. You demonstrated your intuition, love, integrity and assertiveness by skipping that story until it could be reviewed more carefully. This was the final confirmation to me that you would be capable and appropriate to carry on." As she finished speaking, she rose slowly and walked over to Shawn and sat on the other side of him and asked, "Shawn, would you like the gift to have the stories come directly to you, not just the ones you've heard, but new ones too?"

"Of course!" he said. "I can't think of anything more wonderful than that." Realizing the magnitude of what Gramma was saying, he then began to tremble slightly. It was still so strange for him to be talking with Gramma this way. She was so confident and powerful in her speech and movements.

She said, "Well, Shawn, you've already shown yourself to be qualified, and you certainly have the love and desire . . . it's time we talk about something that must remain among the three of us. Someday, in the future, you can reveal it but only with Jake's permission. Don't go any further with this unless you can agree and swear to this on all that is sacred to you. Do you understand?"

"Yes . . . " he replied. Some nervousness was creeping up his legs not knowing what he was getting into.

"Do you agree?"

"Yes."

"Jake is not from here . . . he's from a planet near the Belt of Orion. I guess you could say that Jake's an angel." She paused.

Remembering the story *Angels,* Shawn asked, "Is Vince really Jake? . . . is that a true story?"

"Yes, well, remember it's an allegory. Things aren't exactly as described, but the truth is still embodied in the story. We humans have a difficult time understanding things of such an infinite nature, so the stories can kind of bridge the gap. That's probably why Jesus used so many parables. However, Jake is abiding by the Angel Code of Ethics very carefully, and he is definitely from a planet near the Belt of Orion doing angelic things for us . . . even though he doesn't look or even act very angelic, eh Art?"

Grampa smiled and nodded his head in agreement.

"But, doesn't the code say angels aren't suppose to reveal their identities?"

"You mean the part that says: 'Creating, vanishing, altering or moving objects on the physical plane, or, revealing the actual existence of an angel, are allowed only in extremely rare situations in order to save the A.C.E. from being violated, or, to assist large groups of individuals on accelerating their steps on spiritual paths.'"

"Yeah, that's it. You did that from memory?" Then Shawn realized that if Grampa can remember the stories word for word, obviously she can.

"Just like you now know the story *Beads* word for word too. It's a talent Jake has, and he passed it on, but just for the stories. Anyway, Jake could move an object such as hold your car down and reveal himself to you, because you are key to accelerating the spiritual paths of large groups of individuals,"

"How am I key? What do you mean?"

"You love the stories; you always have. This weekend what did you feel when you shared the stories with others?"

"I felt incredible joy and even bliss that others could enjoy and benefit from the stories too."

"Don't you find it an interesting coincidence that you met people to tell the stories to and discover your new joy, the very weekend that this major decision needed to be made?"

Shawn nodded yes.

"In the story *Angels* it talked about *freeze-frames* and angels rushing around while every thing was stopped. Well, we've found that when Jake has a mind to it, he seems to be able to make amazing coincidences happen just like in that story. You know a lot of people think their prayers are answered by God, yet I've known for a long time they are indirectly implemented by angels and rationalized by many as coincidences."

"Are you saying that Jake set me up to meet Susie, Jack and Rich?"

Gramma just replied, "It wouldn't surprise me a bit. From now on, if you'll watch for coincidences, you may save Jake, actually any angel, lots of work . . . huh honey?" She glanced at Grampa for a response.

He motioned with his right hand a thumbs up gesture while he nodded yes.

Shawn thought back to the coincidence surrounding Susie and said, "You know when I was just about to read *Blade of Grass,* a hummingbird flew right up to Susie and hovered about two inches from her nose. Do you think that was some sort of angel hint or something?"

With a raised eyebrow Gramma asked, "Whenever those things happen, I always go inside and ask myself if it was, what does it mean?"

"Hmmmm . . . .Well, it seemed to be pointing to Susie, like pointing her out to me. With all that I know now, it feels like she somehow fits into what ever's happening with me."

"Time will tell," Gramma said.

Then he remembered about the books his grandfather had about the ancient pyramids and asked, "What about the pyramids? Were they built in alignment with Orion?"

Gramma said, "Oh you've been looking at the books your grandfather has. He's made quite a hobby out of investigating a connection. Yes, not only are they lined up with the Belt of Orion, but there are other pyramids nearby that match other stars of the Orion constellation, like the right shoulder and the left foot. Jake told us a bit about the pyramids, but we've had trouble getting much information from him. He's so cautious about A.C.E. Sometimes I think he over does it."

Grampa shook his head and raised his eyes showing that he agreed.

She went on to say, "Grampa used to get so upset with Jake until we both just gave up on being able to expect or even get some of the simplest answers out of Jake. On the pyramids, your grandfather was so curious he just made it a little project. What he did learn from Jake was that the Egyptians and people of his planet were quite connected long before the year 2450 B.C. when the Great Pyramid was completed. Something happened, we're not sure what, but Jake is now inwardly compelled to bring the stories to our planet. He once called them 'make-up gifts'."

Forgetting for an instant that Grampa couldn't answer, Shawn looked him and asked, "What things could he be making up for?"

Shawn shifted his eyes to Gramma when she replied, "It may have something to do with violations of free will and spiritual growth. After all, the stories are beads of truth set in a way that accelerates spiritual growth. They also develop inner guidance while inspiring free will. They also help people from being controlled and manipulated by others by placing greater value on their own connection with God. It's like Jake is making good for some evil that was done by him or others on that planet near the Belt of Orion. If you want to know more, you'll have to ask Jake yourself. I think Art has given up asking for more information, yet I know he is still deeply curious."

"But Jake hardly talks to me." Shawn said with a concerned voice.

"I think you're going to have much more opportunity to talk to him than you might imagine. Especially now since *The Orion Angel,* as we call him, has great interest in you spreading the stories."

Shawn felt a chill when she said that.

She continued by saying, "One of the reasons we concluded that Jake brings us stories is due to A.C.E. Jake cannot give specific direction lest he might violate free will. There are those who would give up responsibility for decisions due to his very presence as an angel. Jake's unique way of helping our planet is through the stories, though his presence and influence must be kept just between the three of us."

"Oh, I see, since the stories make you decide on your own, your free will is still intact." He paused a moment to think and then said, "Teenagers reach a point where they won't let their parents control them any more. Are they just fighting to have their own free will?"

"If any one violates the free will part of A.C.E., even parents, except when children are too little to be responsible, tremendous friction will result until free will is again established. God granted this and no man, angel or government will permanently take it away. Parents have the tricky role of having to transfer control to their children a little at a time instead of all at once when they leave home."

"Whew . . . Where's Jake now, why isn't he here saying all this?"

Gramma said, "Oh, he's around. Close by I'm sure. He just makes very rare appearances because he must also be careful that we don't create a dependency on him. Review A.C.E. You'll see how closely he follows it. Basically, we've found that we must live our lives from how we choose, listen to our inner voice, and not to depend or expect anything from Jake. When something does happen in our favor, we consider it a gift or a treat. About all you can depend on are the stories. You can spread those that you have however your inner guidance tells you, and you can almost be assured that Jake will give you others."

"One more thing," she added, "Jake had to search a long time for someone who could receive the stories. He found me, but my calling wasn't to spread them, neither was it your grandfather's calling to try telling them to large groups. You have the right genetic make-up to become a receiver of the stories directly from Jake, and I believe you also have the calling to spread them to the public. This should make Jake very happy and allow us to relax. Are you now ready to become a receiver?"

"Yes, more than ever!"

Gramma moved even closer to Shawn and looked more deeply and steadily into his eyes than ever in his life. She had never held eye contact with him this long, except for that brief time in the kitchen Friday night. He would have been extremely uncomfortable had he not felt so much love radiating from her entire face. Her kind eyes sparkled, and he felt as though no one else existed. He had an odd feeling that he and his Gramma were one. After a couple of moments, she placed her right hand over his heart and her left hand over his forehead and said with a very loud, firm voice, "God, make it so!"

Shawn tingled all over—like chills, except deeper . . . from his very bones. He opened his eyes and saw the incredible love in his Gramma's eyes. They hugged and Grampa joined in. Nobody seemed to notice Jake peeking in the door from the sundeck with a big smile.

Just then, Grampa Art cleared his throat real loud and coughed. Then he attempted to talk and said, "Hmmmm . . . My throat . . . my voice is back."

Gramma quickly said, "Now, Art, don't you strain it."

"No, no . . . its all right. There's no pain at all. It's back to normal."

Then Shawn's grandparents looked at each other and said at the same time, "Jake!"

Grampa went on to say, "By golly, he pulled another one over on us didn't he!"

Gramma nodded her head and said, "He sure did. I thought it was very strange for you to get laryngitis. Ol' Jake knew it would take something like this to finally get us to tell Shawn about you and me and the stories."

"But wouldn't causing you to have laryngitis violate A.C.E.?" Shawn asked.

Grampa said, "Naw, that guy is much more clever than he appears.

He probably used that clause that says memories can be brought to the forefront. I noticed that I was remembering a lot about the time I had laryngitis really bad in high school. Your own powerful thoughts can create symptoms you know. I'm sure that's what happened to me."

There was a noise at the door. As they all turned toward the sundeck, there was Jake knocking on the glass.

Gramma opened the door and Jake said, "Sure is nippy out here. Thanks fer lettin me in . . . I see things have been movin along some."

"Thanks to your little tricks." Grampa said with a bit of a laugh.

"Wal, to make it up to ya, Art, whut if'n I tell ya some more 'bout what ya been so durn wonderin' 'bout?"

"The connection between Orion, the Pyramids and the stories?" Grampa asked with some definite excitement showing in his voice.

"Shur nuf. Exceptin, I'd like to see if Shawn is receivin . . . so Shawn, ya ready to try out sumpin' new?" Jake moved closer to Shawn.

Shawn was speechless. He was now in awe of Jake after learning so much more about him. Though Jake was rather short, he now felt like this old man was ten feet tall. Finally, he just nodded his head yes. Jake asked everyone to sit down with Shawn in Grampa's chair and the three of them on the couch.

"Now Shawn, jes use yer intuition, see the pictures and answer yer Grampa's questions." Jake smiled as he leaned back on the couch and looked at Grampa Art.

Grampa leaned forward appearing rather excited about this. He asked, "Well, let's see . . . is it true that the great pyramids near Giza were built in some sort of alignment with the Orion constellation?"

Shawn raised his eyebrows as though he didn't know, but then he noticed Jake nodding at him to answer. Shawn closed his eyes and immediately saw an image of light beaming down from the three major stars from the belt of the constellation Orion. The light illuminated the three great pyramids in Egypt. Shawn said out loud, "Yes."

His grandfather said, "Why are they?"

With Shawn's eyes still closed, he saw images of Egyptians bowing down worshipping the stars. Then he saw the King's chamber of the Great Pyramid being used over and over in a three-day ceremony. After seeing many images flash by, he suddenly opened his eyes and looked at his grandfather and said, "I think I understand now."

"What?" Grampa said impatiently.

"The pyramids served many purposes. They believed Gods came from the stars in Orion. As a sign of worship and dedication, the pyramids were placed to line up with the stars and honor the Gods from Orion. Some great power was given to those who went into a deep three-day process within the King's chamber. The secret of the pyramid is not what's inside, but what it does to what's inside. One of the purposes of the pyramid is to bring forth a mystical power within a person. However, those not ready for this advanced step were literally driven crazy in those three days. Those who were ready, obtained great knowledge and powers over physical reality."

"So is that how they were built?" Gramma asked, "Did they move those great stones with those powers?"

Shawn closed his eyes and immediately saw images of large rafts carrying huge stones floating down the Nile from the quarries . Then he saw how the pyramids were actually built. He opened his eyes and looked at his grandfather. "I now know the stones were not put in place by dragging them on logs, using cranes or large machines!"

Everyone had their full attention on Shawn. He was about to unravel one of the wonders of the world that scientists have pondered for centuries.

Shawn continued, "The Nile floods every summer which causes the water to surge closer to the pyramid sites, especially during that era when the Nile's shifting path was naturally nearer the sites. The Egyptians created a canal and series of locks similar to those in the Panama Canal. They would flood the locks to raise the rafts carrying the stones, and drain them to lower the stones. The site of the pyramid in construction was one large lock where the stones were actually floated into place and lowered gently as they drained the lock."

Grampa's eyes widened. "So that's why there were no scars on the stones from being dragged and . . ." He paused. ". . . that would take far less men and effort! But, did they have pumps for the water?"

"They were given knowledge of pumps and the key tool, the butterfly valve. Those on Jake's planet even conveyed methods to pump utilizing many men at the same time. However, there is something even more amazing than all this." Shawn was enjoying the suspense he was creating by giving out little teasers—not unlike advertising techniques.

"So, go ahead, tell us!" Grampa said rather impatiently.

"You won't believe this, but the pyramid itself is a water pump!"

"Your right! I can't believe that!" Grampa looked at Gramma and then at Jake. Jake just had a strange smile, but Gramma looked puzzled. Then Grampa said, "I thought they were suppose to be tombs for Egyptian kings and queens. Or, like you just said, for use to bring great knowledge and power to those who stayed three days inside!"

Shawn smiled and replied, "They were also used as large markers for desert surveys since they can be used to triangulate positions, and don't forget, they were also monuments in tribute to Orion. They had many uses, yet the Egyptians were also practical. The main use of the larger pyramids were to draw water from the Nile and pump the water to irrigate crops." He closed his eyes and then continued, "The strange shafts and chambers inside the Great Pyramid form the key parts to a working pump. The King's chamber actually provided a place for a fire to create a vacuum which in turn drew water up the precision built air-tight shaft, called the Grand Gallery, and thus start the pump."

"Well, if it's a water pump, why didn't they recognize it as such years ago?" Grampa still sounded unconvinced.

Shawn closed his eyes again and after a couple of minutes said, "What I'm getting is that none of the modern Egyptologists had training in hydraulics, so they didn't recognize the unusual components of a very complex hydraulic pump. And, who would suspect something in the middle of the desert, especially that large, was a water pump!"

Jake was smiling and looking more peaceful than usual. Before Shawn continued, Jake gave him one of his double winks. "After the pumps proved successful, vegetation flourished for miles. The additional ground cover helped create more low pressure, altered prevailing winds and the climate changes created rainfall patterns that supported additional green growth. After many years, the pyramids were no longer needed as pumps and were sealed to form large monuments."

"Was Jake involved back then?" Grampa asked.

Shawn now saw images of the Orion constellation appearing to rush closer to him as though he was space traveling to a point near the three stars in the belt. He saw a planet which had an ultra modern civilization. In one of the buildings that appeared to be levitating, he learned what was going on at the time. He opened his eyes and said to Jake, "Now I know why you're here."

"Don't keep it a secret, Shawn. Tell us!" Grampa's voice showed his deep interest in this subject from years of curiosity.

He said, "The people on the planet Nabel thought they would help Earth people by giving them advanced knowledge and the power. They conveyed specific steps, guidelines and even details about how to build a pyramid and how to use it as a pump and a tool for obtaining special powers.

Jake was no longer smiling. His head was down and for the first time looked either sad, guilty or both.

Shawn went on to reveal things Jake must have known were coming. "They also taught how to choose and prepare a person for the powers. The key-contact Egyptians took the information and only a very select set of individuals learned to use it. No hieroglyphics were produced concerning the pumps or the powers since those in control protected the sacred information obtained from the gods of Orion. However, they used it for their own self-serving interests to control others. The information was passed on with the highest of secrecy. Believing falsely that they were receiving all of this from the gods of Orion, they chose sites for the pyramids in alignment with the constellation as a special tribute. The few that had the power forced hundreds of thousands of people to build more pyramids. They violated free will, retarded spiritual growth and tortured and killed many . . . "

"So why is Jake here?" Grampa asked.

"Well, not only had they indirectly caused great violations of free will on another planet, they had misused powers and grossly violated these fundamental rights on Nabel. Eventually, through a chain reaction of complex events, their own planet was destroyed and the remnants still float in space and show up as part of the Horsehead nebula near the Belt of Orion. Through many eons of spiritual evolvement, Jake finally came to Earth to try and make up for some of the horror his people caused on Earth and Nabel. However, even though he is using stories to assist, he is being quite careful not to repeat the same mistakes of the past. Therefore, he takes A.C.E. very seriously."

Grampa leaned forward again and said, "So Jake is working off some karma, eh? Hmmmm...couldn't the Great Pyramid still be used to gain the power by a person today?"

Shawn again returned within and saw an image of a baby with a halo sitting in the cockpit of a very large and complex airplane. He opened his eyes and said, "Without being more advanced . . . I think spiritually, it would either not work or the person would crash or perish somehow—maybe go crazy. A person making the attempt would need to be very spiritually evolved. Jake probably isn't going to offer any guidance in this area and repeat old mistakes."

Jake shook his head *no* confirming the last remark.

Then Shawn continued, "One more thing. Technology is a way of gaining portions of the power without going through the steps of spiritual evolution. At this time, technology is greatly outpacing man's ability to use it from wisdom, spiritual love for all people and the feeling of oneness. If people on Earth continue to gain power without enough spiritual advancement, Earth too could become a nebula. Passing technology on, especially weapons, to third world countries is similar to what Nabel did by passing the powers in the pyramids on to the Egyptians. Jake can see a comparison with his own planet Nabel."

Things got quiet in the cabin. Everyone had blank stares as though they were imagining the worst.

"That's raht, boy! Say, ya done some good receivin'. But its gittin late and I gotta go." Before anyone could hardly blink, Jake was standing at the door saying, "Shawn, it's a good thing we're doin. Jes remember to smile more." Then out the door he went, and they all watched as the now familiar bluish ball faded into the night.

"Boy, when he decides to leave, he sure doesn't waste any time!" Shawn said with a surprised look.

Gramma said, "Oh you'll get used to that. He's here one minute and gone the next. Looks like you'll be able to receive the stories just fine, Shawn."

"I don't even know where all that was coming from. I seemed to just know it somehow. Does that violate . . . "

Grampa interrupted and said, "Nope. It doesn't. He can place images and thoughts in the forefront of consciousness as long as it doesn't circumvent your free will. Besides that, you even gave him permission!"

"Well, Art, I guess you can put away those pyramid books now that you have the answers." Gramma put her arm around Grampa and looked at him affectionately.

"I suppose so . . ." he paused and looked at Shawn, "By the way, there's something I've learned about telling those stories."

"What's that?"

"You now have the ability to not only receive the stories and thus appear to have created them, but you also have the ability to tell them word for word as I have done all these years. For me it was a blessing and a trap. I've learned a few things over the years. People have tried to give me a lot of credit and praise; and sometimes they even want to give away their ability to make their own choices. I've learned to pass it on. It's safer for me to give the credit to God since indirectly that's where it's from anyway. Otherwise, the ego can cause all kinds of havoc. Also, I make sure I don't do anything that causes or encourages people to give up their free will, or it usually comes back and bites me where I sit! Most of A.C.E. applies to humans too, it's just that most people don't know it."

"I can see that. Thanks for the tip. This is really an exciting new adventure. I just hope I can convince Mary that I haven't slipped off the deep end and gone looney tunes." Shawn realized that was about as close to giving advice he'd ever heard from his grandfather. However, even this, he thought to himself, was just him telling about his own experience.

Grampa said, "Oh, she might at first, but she's a pretty insightful lady. I think she'll go along with you."

The three of them discussed whether or not Grampa and Gramma's secret about their story telling should remain as it was, or be revealed to everyone that Gramma actually comes up with the stories. Finally they all came to the same conclusion to leave well enough alone. There would just be too many people to explain things to and, it would be too difficult to avoid how Jake fit into the picture without exposing him.

After more tea and visiting, Susie pulled up in the driveway about 10:30 p.m. She bounced up the steps and petted Trinket before knocking on the door. "Hi, Susie," Shawn greeted her with a hug. "You want to meet my grandparents?"

"Hey, do stars twinkle? Of course!"

After a short visit and a phone call to Mary saying they were leaving, Shawn and Susie said good-bye to Gramma and Grampa standing on the porch. Gramma said to drive carefully and Grampa just gave a little wave good-bye. Trinket was leaning up against Gramma's leg.

Driving down the dark winding dirt road and seeing the pine trees casting their shadows once again reminded Shawn of his trip up. He said to Susie who was purposely being silent for him to think, "It seems like a lifetime ago I was driving up here, yet the weekend went by in a flash. Odd, how time does that, huh!"

Susie downshifted and slowed around a tight turn as she replied, "Yeah, well you know time is an illusion from that story *Angels* anyway. Sure is strange though . . . Hey, Shawn, how's that decision coming? Did you get another story?"

"Yes, I actually did and with the other stories it was enough to make my decision. I feel very good about it. You still want to be involved with the stories? You can be if you are still interested."

"Hey, that's great. I sure am! Whatever I can do—I love those stories."

As they completed one fairly sharp curve, another curve approached with a sign indicating it was a hairpin reverse curve with a suggested speed of 15 m.p.h. "This is where my car went off the cliff," Shawn said excitedly.

"Really, let's stop and see if it's still there." Susie sat up higher in the seat and put the lights on bright as she turned off the road onto the dirt lookout area. Once stopped, she turned off the engine and lights, grabbed her long 4 battery flashlight, and they walked over to the edge to look down.

Susie shined the flashlight where Shawn was looking and sure enough there was a light colored car lying at the bottom of the canyon. He looked at Susie and said, "You know, it's truly amazing that the car paused long enough to let me out. I could be down there right now myself."

"But if you were, we would have never met, all those people wouldn't have heard the stories and millions of other people wouldn't have experienced them either! I mean assuming you're going to have them printed."

"That's true." Shawn said as he was amazed at how she seemed to understand what was going on. After all, he is not permitted to tell her about the big picture with Jake, or even that it was Jake who saved him.

"Yeah, maybe one of those angels was doing serious negotiations in the freeze-frame just before you got out of the car." They laughed and he looked at her now wondering if she knew how close to the truth she really was.

Before they got back in the car, Shawn glanced up at the Belt of Orion and smiled. It still gave him a warm feeling inside, and now he knew why. He thought, that's where my new friend Jake and the stories are from. Susie paused before starting the engine to listen to the night sounds. Just then all the crickets stopped and even the sound of the truck on the grade was no longer present. There was only silence, the darkness, and the hint of pine trees huddled around their car as they sat in suspense. A glowing ball of light floated just above the roof of the car unnoticed by either of them.

They arrived at Shawn's house a little after 2:00 a.m. Mary came to the door as they walked up. After a big hug, he introduced Susie and they hugged like old friends. With a little hot chocolate, Susie and Mary got acquainted with each other. Shawn had trouble getting a word in edgewise, due to their fast paced conversation.

Mary showed Susie the guest room while Shawn went out to get her suitcase. As she turned down the bedspread for Susie she said, "I'm glad you'll be staying a few days. I feel so comfortable with you . . . it's as though you're family and that I've always known you."

"I feel like I'm part of the family too, Mary. I can see why Shawn loves you so very much. I can't wait to meet your children—I wonder if I'll feel as connected with them?"

Mary cautioned her, "Ron takes awhile to get to know . . . Julie will talk your ears off. Oh, and if she starts to like you, don't be surprised if she pulls one of her practical jokes on you . . . I hope you won't be offended."

"Me? Hey, you should hear about some of the jokes I've pulled in my family . . . sugar in salt shakers, plastic wrap over the toilet seat and all . . . "

Mary raised an eyebrow as if wondering if she should have mentioned anything.

Shawn brought in the suitcase and commented that he had finally learned how to travel light. As Mary and Susie looked at him he said in a serious tone, "Just leave your baggage at the bottom of canyons." They laughed, and then everyone wished each other a good night.

After Susie had gone to bed in the guest room, Shawn took Mary outside by the pool. He brought her up to date with his revelations over the weekend and his desire to do something with the stories. Of course, he had to leave the parts out about Jake and the ball of light, yet his enthusiasm really showed and she said, "I can sense something is very right, Shawn. There is a renewed spark in you. It's good. The decision will cause many changes, but I feel strongly that you are doing the right thing. Go with whatever your heart is telling you to do. I love you and though it's a bit scary, I'm with you all the way."

Over Mary's shoulder, Shawn winked at the pal who has been following him since Gramma said, "God, make it so!"

Jake smiled and gave a double wink back from behind the palm tree. The Belt of Orion was shining brightly over his head. Mary must have sensed Shawn's attention on something and turned around quickly only to see a faint bluish afterglow near the tree. "What was that?" she asked.

Shawn now realized the continuing challenge his oath of silence will cause and knew he'd have to talk to Jake about including Mary. For now he just sheepishly replied, "Well, that's another story."

The End

Cliff Durfee resides just north of San Diego in Encinitas, California. He received a B.A. in Education from Arizona State University, and worked for over a decade in the area of complex computer software design. It was clear early on that his primary talent and joy was through creativity. He pursued this in a major way by founding *Live Love Laugh*. This company published his first two books and a gift product he developed, called *Sprinkles*, which sold to over 2700 stores over a period of seven years. He has used his creativity to develop very innovative websites for clients, including *My Referral Club* (www.myreferralclub.com), which assists many business clubs across the nation in networking and business referrals. For over thirty years, he has been devoted to personal and spiritual growth, developing intuition, and supporting people in aliveness, love, and laughter.

Cliff's first book was called *Feel Alive with Love, Have a Heart Talk* and was published in 1979. It assists friends, couples, and families in having harmonious and loving relationships. The seven-step *Heart Talk* went on to become a popular communication technique used in youth groups across the nation. In 2005, a chapter of the book *The Success Principles* was devoted to honoring this technique, which Jack Canfield used in many workshops over the years.

His second book was a curriculum for teachers. In addition to receiving a teaching credential in Arizona, Cliff's affinity for teaching and love for children provided a natural way to expand upon his first book by bringing it into the classroom. This curriculum, *More Teachable Moments*, contains experiential lessons that assist students in developing listening skills, expression of feelings, and mutual support for achieving goals. These materials were endorsed by the world famous psychologist and author, Dr. Carl R. Rogers.

During the last two decades, before publishing *Stories for the Inner Ear*, Cliff practiced listening within. Wonderful words flowed out in the form of allegorical stories. Though he knew it was something he wanted to share, life's little (and big) distractions kept having him put things on the shelf until 2011. Finally, it was then he declared it would be published that year. As in the story *Turtles,* it was like Willy shouting out, *"I'm going to island five no matter what!"*

All of Cliff's books were produced out of love, creativity, and the desire for everyone to have a greater experience of life, love, and laughter. When asked if this latest book is a spiritual book, he answered, *"If you feel your inner voice and intuition are matters of spirituality, then this book may be very spiritual to you. However, if you are not of that belief, then for you, this may be a book that primarily helps you access your inner guidance. People view this book from their own unique perspectives."*

To learn more about the author's first two books and related products, visit:

www.LiveLoveLaugh.com

To refer this book to others and learn of products related to this book, visit:

www.StoriesForTheInnerEar.com

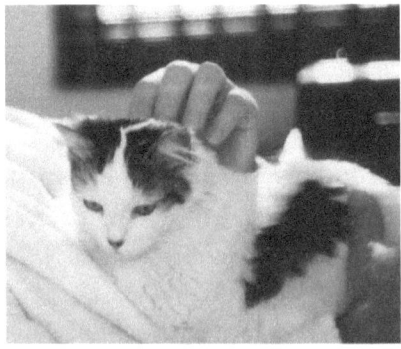

Blessings to my best friend
of twenty years,
Pooh-Cat